VAL TYLER

❧ THE GREENWICH CHRONICLES ❧

THE TIME WRECCAS

PUFFIN

PUFFIN BOOKS

Published by the Penguin Group
Penguin Books Ltd, 80 Strand, London WC2R ORL, England
Penguin Group (USA), Inc., 375 Hudson Street, New York, New York 10014, USA
Penguin Books Australia Ltd, 250 Camberwell Road, Camberwell, Victoria 3124, Australia
Penguin Books Canada Ltd, 10 Alcorn Avenue, Toronto, Ontario, Canada M4V 3B2
Penguin Books India (P) Ltd, 11 Community Centre, Panchsheel Park, New Delhi – 110 017, India
Penguin Group (NZ), cnr Airborne and Rosedale Roads, Albany, Auckland 1310, New Zealand
Penguin Books (South Africa) (Pty) Ltd, 24 Sturdee Avenue, Rosebank 2196, South Africa

Penguin Books Ltd, Registered Offices: 80 Strand, London WC2R ORL, England

www.penguin.com

First published 2005
1

Text copyright © Val Tyler, 2005
Illustrations copyright © David Wyatt, 2005

The moral right of the author and illustrator has been asserted

Set in Monotype Baskerville
Typeset by Rowland Phototypesetting Ltd, Bury St Edmunds, Suffolk
Made and printed in England by Clays Ltd, St Ives plc

British Library Cataloguing in Publication Data
A CIP catalogue record for this book is available from the British Library

ISBN 0–141–38156–6

To my wonderful children,
Chris, Edward, Henry and Bethia,
with love and thanks

I would like to thank Dr Nicholas Perkins at Girton College, Cambridge, for explaining to me the finer points of Old English, and also Jan Quinn for her help and patience.

Author's Note

The Old English in this book is as accurate as I can make it and still leave it readable.

The name, Wrecca, comes from the Old English 'wræcca' which means 'wretch, exile, outcast'. It is pronounced Wrecker.

Ruckus comes from the Middle English word 'ruck' (and is probably related to the Old Norse 'ruka') and means 'to fight'.

Tid is Old English (and also Norwegian) for 'time'.

'eagan ne shawiath' is Old English and literally means 'eyes do not see'.

'tide healdath, ealle brucath' is also Old English and means 'we guard/keep time; everyone uses/enjoys it'. The final 'e' in 'tide' would be pronounced but not stressed and so the pronunciation is verging on 'teeda haldath, alla brucath'.

Vremya, Wakaa, Zeit and Seegan all mean 'time' in the language of each Guardian.

Contents

1

The Beginning of the End

Old Killjoy was miserably sitting on top of the smelly pile of rags that he liked to think of as his throne, picking his nose.

'It's finished,' he grumbled.

'Yer, him's finished building it now,' Stink confirmed.

Old Killjoy threw him a threatening look and he immediately fell silent. A nervous hush fell on the Wreccas, who were huddled together in a gloomy underground chamber. No one knew what to say. They shifted and shuffled uncomfortably.

After an uneasy moment, Sniff ventured an opinion, hoping to make Old Killjoy feel better. 'Doubt it'll work.'

'Yer, doubt it,' echoed the other Wreccas, desperately trying to please their leader.

Old Killjoy sulked. 'It will work. Us hasn't even slowed him down!'

Each Wrecca tried to think of something useful to say, but Wreccas were not very good at thinking.

'Isn't there nothing us can do?' asked Stink.

No one answered.

'Us can't give up!' he added.

'Can't give up,' chorused the others.

The Wreccas were gathered together in the Underneath. Unless it has changed since this story happened, the Underneath is a series of dark, damp, dingy tunnels that smell very musty and are dimly lit by flaming torches. The Wreccas live here. They are nasty, dirty, stupid beings who are smaller than Humans and usually very skinny due to lack of proper food. They have stooping shoulders because they spend most of their time in low tunnels, their hair is matted because none of them understands what a brush is for and their fingernails are grimy because they seldom wash their hands. They have forgotten how to make things better and so they eat rotten food and dress in rags. Their only amusement is to pester and persecute others. If they are not causing trouble they easily become bored. Their leader is Old Killjoy. He is the nastiest of them all.

On this particular day everyone was feeling gloomy, everyone, that is, except Scratch. He was the second-in-command and was called Scratch because he liked scratching people with his long, carefully sharpened nails. He had a little more brain than the rest and could be relied upon to think of the most diabolical plan or the worst punishment. Old Killjoy depended on him because Old Killjoy, like the others, was not very clever. Scratch really should have been the leader but he was too scared to suggest it and knew he had to bide his time. One day, he hoped to get the better of Old Killjoy and take over, but until that day he would keep coming up with the ideas and Old Killjoy would keep passing them off as his own.

Scratch's gaze lingered on the dejected Wreccas, who were lounging in disorganized heaps on the bare earth floor. He had an idea. He enjoyed announcing good ideas because it demonstrated how clever he was. Standing up, he waited for all eyes to fix on him. When he finally spoke, he tried to sound very important.

'There is a way to stop it working.'

Everyone stared at him, wanting to hear more.

Scratch enjoyed the attention and paused dramatically before saying, 'Us can steal the Tick!'

No one knew if this was a good idea. Scratch had said it and so it probably was, but everyone was waiting to see what Old Killjoy thought. All, that is, except Sniff. He rubbed his long nose with a bony finger and asked, 'How can us steal it? Us doesn't know where it is. Us doesn't know how it works. Us doesn't know why it was maked and us doesn't . . .' He sniffed as he hesitated, trying to remember what else they did not know.

'Us doesn't know nothing!' said Snot triumphantly.

'Shut up, Snot!' Old Killjoy snapped. He had no time for silly girls. He was eager to know what despicable plan Scratch was coming up with this time.

Snot's smile faded on her lips. She was not very good at being a Wrecca. Although she tried hard to be nasty and unkind like the rest, it did not come naturally to her. Being only a child, she was often bullied and so she accepted Old Killjoy's rebuff without comment, as nothing more than her due. Wiping her nose on her sleeve, she listened to Scratch.

'If I know Old Father Tim, and I does,' Scratch was

saying, his deep-sunken eyes scanning the upturned faces of the Wreccas, 'him willn't be able to keep his big mouth shut. The Timepiece thing has taked ages to make. Him will've telled somebody that it's finished.'

'Who?' everyone asked together.

Scratch paused, basking in the limelight. Eventually, he said, 'Tid.'

'Oh, I hate him!' Snot exclaimed.

Nobody took any notice.

'So what if Tid knows?' Old Killjoy was asking. 'How will that help us?'

'Us can kidnap him,' ventured Sniff, 'and make him tell!'

Everyone liked this idea and they started shouting out thoughts of their own.

'Us'll pull his hair out!'

'Stamp on his toes!'

'Shout in his ears!'

'Tickle him to death,' said Snot, not too loudly, nervous in case the others did not agree.

Scratch clipped her around the head because she was saying too much.

She rubbed her head sulkily, but said no more.

'One of us . . .' Scratch paused for effect. The Wreccas leant closer so that they did not miss anything. 'One of us,' he repeated, '. . . can go Topside,' their eyes widened in horror, 'pretend to be nice and kind, make friends with young Tid and trick him into telling where the old fool's workshop is.'

There was an awed hush from the gathered throng

that was eventually broken by Sniff asking, 'What's "nice and kind"?'

Old Killjoy was beginning to understand and he nodded to himself. After a while he started to smirk, and so did Scratch. Although none of the others understood why they were both smiling, they began to smile too.

With a nod of his head towards Snot, Scratch silently suggested to Old Killjoy that she should be the one to go. He thought she would be able to make friends with Tid because they were roughly the same age. Old Killjoy liked this idea and also turned his cold gaze upon her. One by one the other Wreccas did the same.

Being noticed by everyone was terrifying for such a young and frightened Wrecca, but not half as terrifying as the thought of going Topside. As Snot slowly realized what was being suggested, she started backing away.

'Ner, not I,' she said, looking at Old Killjoy. 'I hate that Tid.' She had never seen the boy but she had heard the others talking about him.

Old Killjoy stood up and began walking towards her.

Snot tried to catch Scratch's eye, in the forlorn hope that he might rescue her. He had no intention of doing so.

'Tid's horrid,' Snot whined, 'such a goody-goody. Him's all clean and knows numbers and things!'

As she backed away, the other Wreccas drew closer. From deep in their throats there arose a low, menacing, monosyllabic, grunting chant that echoed throughout the tunnels.

'If you doesn't do it,' Scratch said, his threatening

voice rising above the chant, 'I'll scratch you,' and he lashed out at her with his long, vicious nails.

Snot ducked out of the way, just avoiding injury.

'If you doesn't do it,' said Spit, not clever enough to work out what Snot was going to do, but desperate to support his leader, 'I'll gob in your food.'

Snot started to tremble.

'Her will do it.' Old Killjoy's voice was so cruel and menacing that all the Wreccas shook with fear, even big ones like Sniff and Scratch who often went Topside. 'Her will do it,' Old Killjoy continued, 'because if her don't I'll deliver her up to the Ruckus!'

Snot felt her heart beating wildly and she pressed her hands against her chest so that the others might not hear it.

The Wreccas continued their chant but it was different now. Slowly and rhythmically it was changing from a grunting sound into, 'Ruckus, Ruckus, Ruckus . . .'

Snot looked from them to Old Killjoy. 'I's like to help,' she said in a small voice. 'I's really like to, but him willn't believe I. The Guardians doesn't trust Wreccas.'

'Him don't have to *know* you's a Wrecca,' said Scratch, stroking the nails on one hand with the fingers of the other.

'How will him not know?' Snot asked. 'I look like a Wrecca, I smell like a Wrecca. I *is* a Wrecca!'

'Us'll give you a bath,' Stink volunteered.

They all wrinkled up their noses in disgust.

'Us'll tidy your hair,' Sniff suggested.

This was also not considered a pleasant thing to do.

'And,' Scratch added, 'I'll steal you some clothes from the Topside.'

This time they all smiled and murmured their agreement. Stealing was considered fun.

'Then you willn't look like a Wrecca and you willn't smell like a Wrecca . . .'

'. . . But you will still think like one,' Old Killjoy interrupted. He leant right over her and she could feel the heat of his foul breath on her face.

Snot was more scared than she had ever been in her short life. She swallowed nervously before saying in a trembling voice, 'Yer, Old Killjoy. I'll do it.'

If you happen to be walking through Greenwich Park and feel a shiver of excitement, it may be that you are in the presence of one of the Guardians. We Humans cannot see them because it is not easy to see the unexpected. Our eyes can deceive us, but behind our eyes there is a reality that only some of us understand.

Old Father Tim is the Old Father of the Guardians. Each day he walks through Greenwich Park to his workshop. He is a majestic figure who some find rather frightening, but if they look deep into his eyes they can see the gentle side of his nature. He carries a heavy wooden staff and wears a full-length tunic under a long, dark blue outer coat with just a hint of sapphire and starlight. His hair and beard are more silver than white.

This was a special day and Tid Mossel felt the excitement as he ran along the path on his way home from school. His short tunic was awry, no longer held straight by the leather belt he wore around his waist.

Tid was not concerned about his appearance, being far too interested in what he hoped he was going to be allowed to see. 'Have you finished it?' he called excitedly as he skidded to a halt in front of his grandfather.

'Hello, young Tid,' said Old Father Tim.

In the Guardian world it is important to be polite. Tid sighed. Manners were very boring.

'Sorry, Grandfather. Hello,' he said, respectfully. Then he quickly added, 'Have you finished it?'

His grandfather chuckled and put out a hand to straighten Tid's tousled hair. 'Yes, Tid,' he said, signalling to his grandson that his tunic was askew. 'It is complete.'

'Can I see it?' Tid eagerly asked, looking down at his tunic and attempting to straighten it.

'Yes, you may.'

Together they walked towards a large and imposing tree. As you may know, there are many magnificent trees in Greenwich Park; inside one of them is Old Father Tim's workshop.

As they approached, Old Father Tim lifted his hand and said in a deep, powerful voice, 'Eagan ne shawiath.'

At the sound of these words a tremor passed through their bodies and in a whisper of a moment they had disappeared from view. They had not gone anywhere. Old Father Tim had spoken a Guardian charm that momentarily protected them from the prying eyes of those who can see their world.

As soon as they were out of sight, Old Father Tim moved the palm of his hand over a knot in the gnarled bark and a door sprang open. Then, Tid and his grandfather climbed down the deep, worn steps into the workshop.

It lay below ground but was not rough and gloomy like the Underneath. Light was provided by a warm glow that emanated from the walls, floor and even the large, oak workbench that took up most of the space. This was cluttered with pieces of shiny wire, nuts, bolts and tiny wheels that were parts of various mechanisms used by Old Father Tim in his work. The walls were lined with wooden shelves that were as tidy as the bench was disorderly. Measures, hand drills, screwdrivers, paper-thin sheets of gold, delicate cords and tins of stardust were neatly placed where they could be easily found.

Tid loved the workshop. He was not allowed to go there by himself but was sometimes permitted to sit and watch his grandfather work. There were some things he was allowed to touch, like the glass-domed paperweight set on a heavy triangular base. If the dome was lightly tapped, shafts of light swirled within. Tid liked to touch it every time he entered the workshop. However, it was the small components scattered across the workbench that he longed to finger. He imagined how difficult it might be to put them together. Sometimes Old Father Tim would allow him to help with the easier tasks. Tid was a quick learner and his grandfather was certain that one day his grandson would have skills to match his own.

'Wow!' Tid said as he gazed up at the new Timepiece that stood alone on a large wooden platform at one end of the workshop.

You and I would have recognized it as an ornate grandfather clock. Intricate patterns had been created with different coloured woods down the sides. At the top there were delicate snowflake shapes that flickered with a hint of sparkle. Stars surrounding the face of the clock seemed to be constantly moving, although they were, in fact, quite still. But it was the clock face itself that took Tid's breath away. It was as deep and mysterious as the night sky. As Tid looked up at it, he felt he was seeing far into time itself. The hands stood still, shimmering with distant starlight, waiting to blaze a trail into the new year.

There are similar clocks in the Human world that were named after the grandfathers who made the Timepieces. This is how we know some Humans can see into the Guardian world.

'It's amazing!' Tid said, in awe. 'How long did it take to make?'

'One hundred years.'

'Wow.'

'But it will give time for a thousand,' Old Father Tim explained.

'Who made the Timepiece we have now?' Tid was thinking of the old Timepiece that stood at the Guardian Meridian Line in Greenwich Park.

'That was made by my great-great-grandfather. It has served us well and now needs to be rested.'

'Who will make the next one?'

'I hope,' he looked down at Tid, 'that it will be made by your grandson.'

'Will you show him how?'

'No, not I. His grandfather will do that.'

'And who will show him?'

'You.'

'Me?'

'Yes, you. You will be his grandfather.'

Tid's eyebrows shot up his forehead in surprise at the thought of being anyone's grandfather. He looked around the workshop with its glowing shelves that groaned with neatly placed pieces of equipment. Much as Tid would have liked to pretend that he did, he actually had no idea what most of them were for. It seemed ridiculous to suggest that one day he would know enough to tell someone how to make anything as miraculous as a new Timepiece. 'I couldn't!' he exclaimed. 'I wouldn't know where to begin!'

Old Father Tim smiled. 'Many winters will pass before you are required to undertake such a task. By then you will know.'

'But, Grandfather . . .'

'Trust me,' Old Father Tim said gently, 'you *will* know.'

Tid did not really believe his grandfather, but he did trust him and was reassured.

The Guardians look after time for all peoples. Humans always rush around, claiming that they do not have enough time, but no one thinks of guarding it. The

Guardians do this and in every region of the world there is one who protects time for us all.

Old Father Tim started sorting through a collection of bolts and wheels on the workbench. Tid watched his aged fingers picking them up with the dexterity of a far younger man. His grandfather was totally engrossed in his work. Picking up a tiny silver wheel, Tid thought, 'If I'm quiet, he won't notice.'

Quickly he scanned the bench for another that might fit it. Spying a smaller wheel that sparkled with a glimmer of cosmic dust, he fitted the little cogs together and turned the small wheel. This made the bigger wheel also turn. He then searched through the clutter and picked up a couple of tiny golden rods. His idea was to fix these rods through the centre of the wheels so that they would turn easily.

'Tid.'

His name was spoken quietly but Tid knew what it meant.

'Sorry, Grandfather,' he said, hastily putting everything down, 'I was only . . .' But he did not finish. A glance at his grandfather's face told him that the old man knew exactly what he had been doing. Playing with precious pieces of equipment was definitely not allowed.

Tid stepped away from the workbench with a sigh. At home he spent hours inventing simple machines and building them, but the mechanisms that his grandfather used were far more interesting.

Tid turned his attention to the new Timepiece once more. 'I can't hear it ticking!' he exclaimed in panic as he clambered up on to the wooden platform where the Timepiece stood and put his ear against it. 'It's broken! It doesn't work!'

'It will not start until the first second of the new era.'

'The very first second?'

His grandfather nodded.

'What will happen if it doesn't?'

'It will.'

'But if it doesn't, what will happen?'

Old Father Tim knew that a new Timepiece had never failed. Such a thing was unthinkable, but he answered Tid's question with patience born out of many years of living, learning and understanding.

'If that should happen, young Tid, then time would stop for eternity.'

❋ 2 ❋

Snot Goes Topside

Tid ran through the park, anxiously darting a look over his shoulder. Had he been seen? Hot and breathless, he dashed past the Observatory and onwards to the place where the roads crossed. Which way?

Quickly changing direction, Tid rushed on, every now and then casting a worried look about him. At last he saw the cover he had been heading towards, a border of large bushes that were leafless at this time of year, but dense enough to hide a boy. Heedless of the twigs that scratched his face and clung to his hair, he dived into the middle of the largest. Had he been in time? Nervously he peeped out, trying to keep his breathing steady. He was pretty sure he was out of sight but was worried that his heavy breathing and pounding heart might give him away. Pushing his damp hair from his eyes, he settled down to wait.

Greenwich Park was full of people. Some were hurriedly going about their daily tasks while others were just having fun. Boys were noisily playing football on the grass, while others were sitting in groups, talking. Although Tid could see the Humans, he took no notice of them, certain in the knowledge that they could not see him. Occasionally, a Human walked straight through him, and when this happened it gave Tid an odd feeling. Just occasionally, a Human would stop for a moment, look confused and say to his companion, 'I've just had the strangest feeling.' It was so peculiar an experience that they could never quite describe it. Neither could Tid.

Tid's breathing was coming easier now. He wondered how long he would have to wait. His question was soon answered. Three sleek and nimble squirrels came into view. They were approaching at speed. Tid held his breath.

'He can't be far,' said Cob Bushytail, who was their leader.

The other two stopped and looked around.

'Walnut, you check those trees.'

Walnut took off at speed.

'Hazel, you search the bushes.'

Hazel scampered off.

Tid froze. Would he be seen?

Hazel ran agilely along the low fence behind the bushes, peering into them as she went. Tid shut his eyes.

'He's not here!' she called back to Cob, disappointed.

Walnut returned. 'He's not in the trees either.'

Hazel jumped down from the post she was sitting on and sighed. 'He's too good at this.'

Cob said nothing, but from his expression Walnut realized that he had seen something.

With a swift movement, Cob ran across the dark earth

that would be teeming with life and colour as soon as spring arrived. Tid opened his eyes and watched Cob scamper straight past. With a smile of satisfaction, he cast a look towards the others, who were standing on the grass, waiting for Cob to return. Suddenly there was movement in the bush. Tid's very own bush! Looking up, he saw Cob grinning down at him.

'You're good, Master Tid,' Cob said, 'but not good enough to outwit Cob Bushytail!'

'I thought I had you beaten this time!' Tid exclaimed as he tried to stand. It was not easy in the dense and prickly bush.

Hazel and Walnut came scampering over. Together they helped Tid out. He grimaced at the scratches he now noticed and he pulled bits of twig off his tunic.

Guardian People are not as big as Humans. Old Father Tim would not reach a Human man's shoulder. Thus, compared with Tid, Bushytails were not so very small. When Cob sat up on his haunches, his head reached Tid's knee. When he stood, his strong bushy tail reached the hem of Tid's tunic.

'You would have to get up early to beat Cob at a game of hide-and-seek,' Hazel said, casting a loving look towards her sweetheart.

'You're good,' Tid reluctantly agreed. He hated to be beaten. 'But I know I can find an even better place to hide. You'll just have to give me longer, that's all.'

'Cob!' Walnut's manner had altered. He now spoke as if he were a guard on sentry duty, reporting to his commanding officer. 'Humans approaching.'

Cob instantly spoke with military correctness. 'We must go.'

'But we're having fun!' Tid protested.

'Humans are not your problem,' Cob explained. 'They cannot see you, but they can see us.'

'And we have to pretend to be timid,' Hazel added.

'Why?' Tid asked, reluctant to allow his friends to leave.

'We are a link between the Guardian and Human worlds,' Cob explained. 'When Humans see us, we try to look cuddly. They even try to feed us, as if we needed their food! If they knew we could talk, they would never accept us sitting in the branches, listening to their conversations. Passing on important pieces of information to the Guardians is how we Bushytails can be of service.'

'But who will I play with?'

'Cob, we have to move.' Walnut's voice was tinged with anxiety. Tid looked across and saw a Human family approaching.

'I cannot help you, Master Tid,' Cob said quickly, and then he issued orders to his companions. 'Walnut! Across the grass! Hazel! Along the fence! Now!'

Both Bushytails ran off. Cob waited long enough to see them get away before making his own escape, but he was too late. He had been seen.

'Mum!' A small child was pointing towards Cob. 'A squirrel! Mum, look!'

The child's mother smiled. 'Isn't he sweet?'

Tid watched with interest at the bizarre behaviour

of his friend, who no longer looked as if he was the much-respected leader of the Bushytails. He now appeared to be a cute little squirrel, sitting on his haunches, passing a delicate paw over his nose. Then, acting like all the squirrels in the park, he flinched, as if seeing the boy for the first time. Placing all four paws upon the ground and keeping his body low, Cob cautiously approached the child, as if seeking food. The boy was thrilled and, with a cry of delight, ran towards the squirrel in order to get a closer look. This was the opportunity Cob had been waiting for. Pretending that the movement had startled him, he quickly ran away, bouncing lightly from one clod of earth to another.

'He's gone!' wailed the boy.

Tid sighed. He wished that Bushytails were invisible to Humans like he was. He kicked a stone and watched it skipping over the ground. It gave him an idea. Taking a piece of chalk from his pocket, he drew a hopscotch grid on the path.

Guardian hopscotch is similar to, but not the same as, Human hopscotch. The grid is bigger and the skipping more complicated. There is a good deal more hopping on one foot and then the other. Finally you have to jump backwards before moving up a level and throwing the stone again. Tid picked up the stone that he had kicked and began to play.

Snot watched from a distance. She felt most peculiar, standing Topside under the crisp winter sky. For the first time in her life, she was beyond the confines of the

Underneath. There was too much light, too much space and too many bright colours. Reaching out her hand, she pressed it against the trunk of the tree that she and Snatch were hiding behind. Somehow it helped to have something to hold on to.

Screwing up her face, she tried to filter out some of the sun that poured down from a clear blue sky. It made her eyes hurt. The sky was dazzling blue and the grass brilliant green. Even the clothes worn by passing Humans seemed to Snot to be unnaturally highly coloured. To her half-starved senses, everything was too vivid. Her hand started trembling and she gripped the tree to make it stop.

It was, however, the never-ending space that unnerved her the most. Never had her eyes had to focus on distant objects because there was no distance in the Underneath. She had often peered into the gloom of some of the longer tunnels, but that was nothing compared to the panoramic view of the park. Everything smelt and felt different. Snot longed to be back in the surroundings that she knew so well.

The job of cleaning her up had started that morning. For the first time in her life she had taken a bath. It had been cold – no one had thought to warm the water for her – and it had made her skin feel very odd. Scratch had put something into the water to make it smell as though she came from the Topside. He said that it was a horrid smell, just like roses. Snot wondered what roses were. Her hair, now clean, was unnaturally light. She could not resist slowly running her fingers through it.

Scratch had combed it with his long nails and, although he was none too gentle, it had been worth it.

The clothes that had been stolen for her were clean, and that was odd in itself. In the Underneath she wore the same ragged clothes as everyone else: trousers, shirt and jacket that were all various shades of dismal brown. Today she was wearing a tunic, much like Tid's but without a belt. It was the same colour as the sky, Scratch called it blue, and it was covered in little white flowers. She wore it over trousers and for the first time in her life Snot was wearing socks. She tried to wriggle her toes but the socks were too small and squashed them. It was very uncomfortable. The shoes were too big. Scratch had had considerable trouble stealing them. She squirmed inside her new outfit.

In short, Snot was not looking, smelling nor behaving like a Wrecca. But she was thinking like one.

She knew what she had to do. Her task was to make Tid believe that she was his friend. Propelled by a sharp push from Scratch, Snot began skipping through the park. She attempted a smile in order to look friendly, but was too scared to look relaxed.

Snot had been watching Tid's game carefully and knew the exact time to reach him. Just as he was skipping backwards, she darted behind him and they collided. Instantly, she fell to the ground and, grabbing hold of her knee, rolled around as she had seen the boys doing in the football game just down the hill.

'Are you all right?' Tid asked, bending down.

Snot had done a good job, her knee hurt beneath her

trousers and there was some mud on her tunic. She began to cry softly, genuinely distressed, not because of the pain, this was a minor injury for her; it was the dirt on her tunic that she found upsetting. She brushed at it with her hand, but did not have time to wonder why it should bother her.

'No need to worry about I,' she said. 'It wasn't *really* your fault.' She spoke in a way that implied that it had been.

'My fault?' asked Tid. 'Was it my fault? I'm so sorry. I was concentrating on the game. I wasn't looking where I was going. Are you hurt?'

'It's nothing,' said Snot, dragging up her trouser leg and squeezing a drop of blood from her knee.

'But it's bleeding,' said Tid. He took a clean white handkerchief out of his pocket. 'Let me wrap this around it.'

As he bent down to her, Snot suddenly felt nervous of what he might do and quickly shuffled backwards. Never having known kindness, she thought he was about to play a trick on her.

'Keep still,' he said gently, reaching to tie the handkerchief around her knee.

She watched him carefully, just in case he hurt her, but he did not.

With a satisfied smile he sat back and said, 'That's better.'

Snot looked at the clean bandage around her knee. It was as white as the lone cloud in the sky. This was the first time in her young life that she had been treated kindly, and it made her feel peculiar. She looked at Tid, wondering why he was being so considerate. There had to be a reason. No one could be this thoughtful without an ulterior motive. He was returning her stare with a guileless smile. Was he for real? If so, then this Tid was nicer than she had imagined. She began to doubt herself.

Unsure how to continue, she looked about her and saw Scratch in the distance, peeping out from behind the tree. He was too far away for her to see the expression on his face, but Snot knew him well enough to realize that if she did not keep going, she would be in serious trouble.

Tid helped her to her feet.

'Does you want to play?' she asked hurriedly, failing to sound casual.

'My grandfather says I'm not to play with people I don't know.'

'Why not?' Snot asked, trying to look innocent.

'They might be Wreccas.'

Snot took a deep breath. Her heart was beating wildly. She had practised hard for this moment. She had to do it right.

'Does I look like a Wrecca?' she asked, with a nervous smile.

Tid looked at her carefully and slowly shook his head. 'No, you don't.'

Relieved, and with a little more confidence she asked, 'And does I smell like one?'

Tid stepped towards her and sniffed. She smelt like a rose. He knew Wreccas smelt, but not of roses.

'No, you don't smell like a Wrecca.'

'And is I all dirty like one?' Snot asked, now fully confident that her disguise had worked. 'Except for my tunic where I falled over.'

'No, you're very clean and your hair's neatly brushed. I've never heard of a Wrecca with neatly brushed hair. But you do talk differently. Where do you come from?'

Snot was surprised by Tid's question. It had never occurred to her that the Wrecca way of speaking was different. Scratch had not mentioned it when he was preparing her to come Topside.

Fear of failure spurred her to think quickly. She had no time to ponder the best answer. Her reaction had to be instantaneous, and she reacted in the usual Wrecca manner: when attacked, attack back straight away. 'You's the one who talks odd. I doesn't!'

Tid thought that he had offended her and was genuinely sorry. He tried to soothe her by saying, 'I didn't mean to be rude. It's just that I haven't seen you in the park before and I thought that you might come from the other side of the river.'

'What does they speak like?'

'I don't know,' Tid confessed. 'I've never been there.'

Snot found this very encouraging. Although she had never heard of a river, she thought she could safely agree that this was where she came from. 'I *is* one of the Guardian people and I *does* come from the other side of the river.' She paused. Tid seemed to accept her answer, so she carried on. 'Is you going to play?'

Tid thought about it for a moment. 'All right,' he said, still not totally convinced. 'My name's Tid, what's yours?'

Snot relaxed and smiled. 'Sn . . .'

✿₀✿❄ 3 ❀₀✿❀✿

Secret Places

Everything was going well and Snot was feeling so confident that she had nearly given the game away and told Tid her real name. Coughing a little to hide her mistake, she tried to remember what Scratch had told her.

'Sofi,' she said, making an effort to look as if it were true. 'I's called Sofi.'

'Nice to meet you, Sofi,' said Tid, remembering his manners and holding out his hand like his grandfather did when meeting someone. Tid expected her to shake it.

Snot looked at his extended hand. She felt there was something she was meant to do with it, but she did not know what. To cover her awkwardness, she put her hand down to her knee, as if it still hurt. This distracted Tid, who seemed to forget that they had not shaken hands. Danger of discovery had passed.

Neither Snot nor Tid spotted Scratch running back to the Underneath to tell Old Killjoy that their plan was working.

'What'll us play?' Snot asked.

'I was playing hopscotch.'

Snot did not know any games. 'I's not sure how to play that,' she said rather uncertainly.

'Not know hopscotch!' Tid exclaimed. 'Everyone knows how to play hopscotch. Everyone, that is, except a Wre–'

'Oh, hopscotch!' Snot interrupted, trying to recover the situation. 'I thinked you sayed ... er ... hoppity-scotch.'

'Hoppity-scotch?' Tid was puzzled. 'I've never heard of that. How do you play it?'

Snot knew she could not make up a credible game on the spot. 'Oh, it's a very silly game. Much like your hopstitch.'

'Hopscotch,' Tid corrected her. There was something not quite right about this girl.

'Yes, that too. I hate it. It's a boring game. Let's run.'

Tid liked the idea of running. He was a good runner. So, pushing all doubts about Snot to the back of his mind, he said, 'OK, I'll race you to the park railings.'

'All right.'

'Ready, steady ...' but before Tid could say 'Go!' Snot had taken off, running as fast as she could without any thought of her injured knee.

'Hey! I wasn't ready!' Tid called out indignantly. But it was too late; she was disappearing. If Tid was to stand any chance of catching her, he would have to follow without delay.

After the race, which Snot won, they played chase

for a while, but Snot was unused to such wide open spaces. Soon she found that running made her chest hurt and breathing difficult. She stopped to catch her breath, and she shut her eyes in an attempt to blot out a strange, dizzy feeling. It was not long before Tid made her laugh again.

To her surprise, Snot found that she was enjoying herself. The Topside was fast becoming less intimidating. There was so much to see. Humans fascinated her. She was thrilled to discover that they could not see her, although she was careful not to let Tid see that she had not known this before. 'Don't it feel odd!' she said as she ran straight through an old lady.

However, dogs were different. A little white one had seen Snot and Tid and pulled on his lead, eager to play with them.

'Oscar,' the owner said, jerking him away, 'what are you doing?'

Oscar pulled harder in an attempt to move closer to the children. He started whining.

Tid backed off. 'Grandfather says it's best not to go near them when they behave like this,' he said, and so they ran away, leaving a disappointed Oscar behind.

The Bushytails, however, were a different matter. Like most things Topside, they terrified Snot. Her initial reaction was to run away from them, but she could not. Tid seemed to be their friend. If Snot showed her fear, she would give herself away, so she had to hide it as best she could. After a while, she found she got used to them, and she discovered they were not the frightening creatures she had first taken them to be. In fact, some of them were quite nice.

Eventually Tid and Snot found a bench and sat down. She was tired but she knew that she could not put off indefinitely what she had come Topside to do. Scratch would be somewhere, watching and waiting.

'What will us do now?' she asked.

'Can you whistle?'

'What does you mean?'

'You know, whistle!' And Tid pursed his lips and let out a high-pitched note. This was something he had only just learnt to do and he enjoyed demonstrating his new skill.

Snot watched him closely. She had never seen anyone whistle before. She doubted that she could do it and did not want to make a fool of herself trying. 'Ner, I can't.'

'Girls aren't very good at that sort of thing,' Tid said, knowledgeably.

This statement annoyed Snot. Why should a girl not be able to whistle? It did not look all that difficult. Feeling a little disgruntled, she resolved to get on with what she had come Topside to do. 'Let's explore.'

'What's there to explore?' asked Tid. 'I have always lived in the Park. I know every inch of it.'

'So does I,' lied Snot. Then she pretended that she had an idea. 'Does you know of a secret place?'

Tid looked at her curiously. Of course he knew of a secret place, but he was not going to tell her about it. He remained silent.

'I know one,' she said mysteriously.

Tid was intrigued because he thought he knew everywhere in the park. 'Is it a really secret place?' he asked.

'Really, really secret,' said Snot.

'Is it in the Wilderness, where the deer live?'

Snot did not have the slightest idea where he was talking about. 'Ner, somewhere else,' she said, and then repeated, 'Does you know one?'

'Well, yes,' Tid said uncertainly.

'If you show I your secret place, I'll show you mine,' said Snot with a friendly smile.

'I can't show you mine,' said Tid, 'because it's not my secret. It's my grandfather's and I can't tell you his secret.'

Reference to his grandfather encouraged Snot. A delicious feeling of optimism surged within her. She was pushing him in the right direction.

'My place is a really, really secret place and it's not my secret either,' said Snot, lying with ease. 'It's my grandmother's really, really, really secret place.'

'Where is it?' asked Tid, 'I bet I know it. I know everywhere.'

'Not this, you doesn't.'

'Tell me where it is.' Tid was very interested now.

'I'll show you when you's showed I.'

Tid hesitated. He really wanted to know where Sofi's special place was, and yet he knew he should not show anyone his grandfather's workshop. Perhaps if he pretended that he was going to show her, maybe he could discover hers without having to tell her anything. It

was not a very honourable thought, but it was how Tid
justified what he did next.

'You mustn't tell anyone,' he said.

Snot nodded enthusiastically.

'Not anyone in all the wide World and especially not
a Wrecca.'

'I promise.' Snot was used to lying.

'All right, then. I'll show you.'

Tid took Snot to a row of magnificent trees, just down
from the Guardian Line. He hesitated. 'Why don't you
show me yours first?' he asked hopefully.

She shook her head.

He looked at the tree. Now he was there, he knew
he would have to reveal it to her, and that made him
feel uncomfortable. But he reasoned that there could be
no harm in showing her just the tree. Knowing about
it could not hurt. He was not going to show her how to
get inside.

He did not give himself time to think it through
carefully because the idea of finding a new secret place
was just too tempting. He hoped that Cob did not know
about it either. How he longed to win in a game of
hide-and-seek. His mind was made up.

'You must promise not to tell anyone.'

'Of course not.' Snot's mouth went dry. She was
certain he was going to show her the workshop, and the
anticipation was making her nervous.

'Well, it's here.'

'Where?' asked Snot, looking around, very confused.
She could see nothing that looked like a workshop.

'This tree,' said Tid.

'How can a tree be secret?' It was hard for her not to show her disappointment. 'It's only a tree. Anyone can see it.'

'Yes,' said Tid, lowering his voice to a whisper. 'They know about the tree, but they don't know what's inside.'

The hair at the back of Snot's neck stood up as she realized that this was it! This was the workshop and she, Snot, one of the most despised and ridiculed Wreccas in the Underneath, was going to find it! Even Old Killjoy would have to acknowledge that this was a job well done.

'How does you get in?' she asked, failing to hide her excitement.

'I can't tell you that.'

'That's not fair,' she said irritably. 'I's not going to show my place if you doesn't show yours.'

'But I can't,' said Tid.

'Then I can't neither,' and she turned away, pouting.

Tid thought for a moment. It had been difficult at first to convince himself that there was nothing wrong in telling her about the tree. It was now relatively easy to go one step further and show her how to get into it.

'Oh, all right, then.'

Quickly, he lifted his hand and moved it sideways over the secret knot in the gnarled trunk. At once, the door sprang open.

Snot sucked in her breath in surprise as she peered inside. She could see steep steps disappearing down into the ground. Instinctively, she moved towards them, but Tid barred her way. The door shut with a soft clunk.

'I wants to go inside.'

'We can't.'

'Then I's not going to show you mine!' She pretended to sulk. Her job was done. She had located the workshop. How pleased Scratch would be! There was no reason for her to stay any longer, and this was the perfect opportunity to go. Without another word, she ran off, leaving a startled Tid behind.

His initial reaction was to chase her in order to make her show him the secret place she had been boasting about, but he did not move. Instead, he stood watching her disappear. He had a strange feeling inside. Something was not right. He had told her the most secret thing that he knew, and now he was beginning to wonder if he had done the right thing.

'That wasn't very nice of her,' he said to himself, finding it easier to cope with the guilt if he blamed her. Thrusting his hands deep into his pockets, he thought he would go home. He wanted reassurance, and he always got that with a hot drink and one of his grandfather's stories.

Down in the Underneath there was much merriment. Snot had expected everyone to be pleased with her, but somehow, in all the high spirits, she had been overlooked. They had forgotten that she had been the one who had found the workshop. Old Killjoy was basking in the glory of all their congratulations. Everyone told him how clever and wise he had been, and he accepted their praise as if it was rightfully his.

Although Scratch joined in the congratulations, he resented it. This had been *his* idea. *He* had prepared Snot for her task, stealing the clothes, tidying her hair and teaching her what to do. All the praise should have been his. Running his sharp nails lightly over his chin, he glared at his leader.

Snot was feeling very sorry for herself. She had carried out the task exactly as Scratch had told her. She had been scared, and yet she had pushed that fear to one side and succeeded. Now she was being ignored.

Miserably, she turned away and leant against the damp wall. It occurred to her that she could never do anything to please anybody. Whatever happened, however hard she tried, she was still regarded as worthless.

Enjoying the admiration of the others, it did not occur to Old Killjoy that Scratch deserved any glory. When he thought of Snot, it was not because he was grateful. 'Snot!' he bellowed, looking around the chamber.

She looked up. Was she going to be thanked?

'Is you sure you can find your way back there?'

'Yer,' she said, eager to demonstrate that she had done a good job.

'You's better be right about this, snotty-Snot, cos if you's lying . . .'

'I's not. I does know, really I does. Him opened the door and everything.'

Old Killjoy turned to Scratch. 'If it's so easy to see, why has no one ever spotted him going in?' He was not sure he trusted Snot – after all, she was only a girl.

'Magic,' Scratch assured him. 'There'll be some kind of magic password to make him invisible.'

Old Killjoy nodded to himself, as if he had known all along. He turned once more towards Snot and grabbed her by the throat. Lifting her up so that only her toes were in contact with the ground, he snarled, 'If you's lying to I . . .' His voice tailed off threateningly.

'I's not . . . I's not . . .' Snot croaked back, finding it difficult to breathe.

Old Killjoy let go and she stumbled to the ground.

'Scratch, you go and get the Tick when it's dark and empty,' he ordered. 'Take Sniff and Spit.' He turned away, 'Oh and,' he grabbed Snot by the arm, 'you's better sort Miss Topside out before her gets a liking for blue tunics.'

'I willn't. I hate being clean,' Snot lied.

Scratch threw her rags back at her and waited until she had returned her Topside clothes. She was very sorry to be replacing her clean outfit with the old, smelly one, although she was careful not to show it.

Snot had taken care to keep Tid's handkerchief hidden. As soon as she was able, she crept away to her secret hiding place. This was a deep hole in the wall of one of the darker tunnels. She had found it by accident some months before and, although she could not be certain, she thought she was the only person who knew about it. Her hideout was the one place where she felt relatively safe. Sitting inside, she pressed the handkerchief to her nose. It still smelt of the Topside. Carefully, she tucked it inside her sleeve for safekeeping.

Late that night, four shadowy figures crept through Greenwich Park, led by the smallest. The others followed closely. Silently, they tiptoed up the Wide Way until they came to where the roads crossed. Then they turned left and walked straight to the tree that hid the workshop. For a moment, they stood around it, looking confused.

'Well, where is it?' Scratch asked.

'Here.'

Scratch, Spit and Sniff all started looking around for something that could possibly be a workshop.

'If you's lying, Snot scumbag,' Spit breathed venomously, grabbing her hair and spitting into her face as he spoke, 'I'll remove every hair from your head.'

Snot stood as still as she could. His grip was too tight and he was hurting her a great deal. 'I's not lying, honestly I's not. It's here in this tree.'

Spit released her and she backed off a few paces, rubbing her sore head.

The other three looked at the tree. Then Scratch began to sneer. 'In a tree? Mr Wonderful-I-is-the-leader-of-the-ghastly-Guardians hides his workshop in a tree?'

'A little'un hides things better!' Sniff scoffed. 'A tree! What a fool!'

Not to be outdone, Spit added, 'Calls himself the Old Father, but him has the brain of a dung beetle! Easy to find and easy to get in!'

All three of them stood looking at the tree, not

knowing how to proceed. Suddenly Scratch felt foolish, standing there doing nothing, and, to cover this, he clipped Snot around the head. 'Come on, Snot, us hasn't got all night!'

'All right,' she mumbled, and walked around the tree, looking at every twist in the knotty bark. She had watched Tid very carefully but she was finding it difficult to locate the exact place in the dark. She selected what she hoped was the correct area and moved her hand sideways across it. Immediately, the door swung open and light flooded out, bathing them in its warmth.

Snot looked at the others, hoping for a word of praise, but none was forthcoming. They were wallowing in the comforting sensation of the workshop's light and seemed to have forgotten everything else.

Suddenly, Scratch pulled himself together. In order to hide how he was feeling, he clipped Snot around the head once more. 'Get out of my way, Snot-face!'

Snot tottered aside.

'Spit, you stay here and keep your eyes open!'

Spit looked about him nervously. He was scared of staying outside in the dark with only Snot for company and he forlornly watched Sniff and Scratch disappearing down the steps. He wiped his dribbly chin on his sleeve nervously and tried to convince himself that they would not be long. He paced up and down, pretending to be on guard duty, but all the while apprehensively glancing about to make sure that he was safe.

After a very short time he asked, 'What's taking them so long? Something's wrong. I know it. Scratch has fallen down and breaked his neck! There'll be blood and guts all over!' He looked up and his eyes fell on Snot. Bullying her might be a way to help him through this frightening ordeal. His long skinny finger poked her shoulder. 'It's all your fault, snotty-Snot!' he said, jabbing her. 'All you needed to do was trick that idiot Tid. It's only pestering. Easy-peasy!' Then Spit suddenly slapped his forehead with the palm of his hand as a new idea struck him. 'It's a trap! That pinhead, Tid, seed you coming! Him taked you for a proper nut-head!' Then terror filled his mind. 'They's waiting down there. And now they's coming up here . . .' his voice trailed away in panic, '. . . for I!'

It was at this precise moment that Scratch appeared in the doorway. He was walking backwards, with Sniff walking forwards after him. Between them they were carrying what looked like a cumbersome, but not heavy, cube-shaped box. Sniff's dirty jacket had been thrown over it to try and hide its light, but, even so, a warming glow filtered through the grimy folds.

'Out of my way!' Scratch said, kicking Spit.

Too relieved to object, Spit jumped out of the way and watched as they set off, taking the Tick back to the Underneath. 'You got it!' he exclaimed.

'Keep your voice down!'

'Us is so clever,' Spit whispered and, turning to Snot, added, 'I sayed so, didn't I?'

Snot made no answer. She was watching as the door of the workshop softly clunked shut. A strange sensation crept over her, although she did not recognize it. Something did not feel right. Could it be that Tid had trusted her as a friend and now she had betrayed that trust?

'Us can do anything!' Spit was still wallowing in the joy of success. 'Us is the best! Old Killjoy will be dead happy. I'll tell him I led the whole operation. Very likely give I a medal!' Spit was standing in what he considered to be a noble attitude. He held his hand over his heart and he was wearing an expression that implied modest acceptance of the fact that he was a genius. He looked around him to see if the others were impressed – and suddenly realized that they had gone without him.

'Scratch!' he bleated. 'Sniff!' He looked desperately for them. 'Where is you?' He saw two figures stealing noiselessly through the park. 'Wait for I!' With a pathetic whine, he dashed after them.

None of them noticed that Snot had not followed. She stood alone by the tree, thinking about Tid and the trouble he would be in when his grandfather discovered the Tick was missing. She wanted not to care, but she could not help wondering what kind of terrible punishment awaited him. She shuddered as she thought what Old Killjoy would have done to her if she had been tricked into disclosing a Wrecca secret. But Tid was one of the Guardian People! He was the enemy! He might be fun to play with and he might have been kind to her, but she knew he was a baddie, just like Old Father Tim and all the rest of them.

She sniffed and wiped her nose on her sleeve.

Something fell to the ground. It was Tid's handkerchief. Picking it up, she pressed it to her nose. It no longer smelt of the Topside. Having been up her sleeve for a while, it now smelt like the rest of her.

She sighed. She was like this handkerchief. Briefly, she might have been all clean and fragrant in pretty blue clothes but, in reality, she was Snot, grimy and smelly, just like everyone else in the Underneath. That was the way it was. A Guardian was a Guardian and a Wrecca was a Wrecca, and no amount of wishing could make it different.

4

The Great Gathering

Old Father Tim stood in front of the new Timepiece with his hands to his forehead and a look of disbelief on his face.

'I could have sworn I put it in,' he muttered to himself.

He had been searching for the Tick all morning. First, he had looked in the places where it should have been, but he had not found it. Then he had looked in the places where it might have been, but it was not in any of those. Last, he had looked in all the places it could never have been, but it was still nowhere to be seen.

The Tick was definitely missing. It was too big to have been misplaced on a shelf or in a drawer. No, it had gone.

Tid clambered down the workshop steps. 'Grandfather, have you seen my football?'

Old Father Tim did not seem to notice Tid.

'What's the matter?' Tid asked.

'It's gone,' his grandfather mumbled, more to himself than to his grandson.

'I know. I can't find it anywhere.'

Old Father Tim was not listening. He just kept looking

at the new Timepiece and scratching his head through his silvery hair.

Slowly Tid realized that his grandfather was not concerned about his missing ball. 'You're not talking about my football, are you?'

Still no answer.

'Grandfather!' he said loudly. 'What's wrong?'

Old Father Tim spoke slowly because he did not really believe what he was saying. 'The Tick is missing.'

'No,' Tid said, 'I saw you do that bit. You put it . . .' He looked at the place in the new Timepiece where the Tick should have been. 'It's not there!' he exclaimed. 'The Tick's gone!'

Tid's grandfather scratched his head once more. 'I don't understand. It is just as if someone has removed it. Look.' He stepped up on to the platform and climbed a well-worn, oak stepladder that was leaning up against the Timepiece. Reaching up, he pointed to some bare wires. 'Look at this! It is just as if someone has pulled the Tick out.'

'That's not possible! No one would do that, and besides, nobody knows where your workshop . . .' Tid's eyes suddenly opened wide in alarm as it dawned upon him that someone knew exactly where the workshop was. Too ashamed of himself to admit what he had done, Tid looked about him, desperate for a sign that the blame lay elsewhere. 'Has the door been broken?'

'No,' his grandfather said, climbing back down again. 'That is what is so strange. No one has broken in, everything else is as it should be.'

Both grandfather and grandson stood in silence for a while before Tid asked in a very small voice, 'What are we going to do?'

This was a good question. Old Father Tim knew the answer but dreaded it. 'The Guardians must be told.' He could not imagine how he was going to face them. 'I must summon the Great Gathering.'

Tid was full of awe. 'The Great Gathering of the Guardians! I've learnt about those in history lessons at school.' He looked up at his grandfather, and suddenly all excitement left him and he became afraid because he saw something in that old, wrinkled face that he had never seen before. Normally, his grandfather was calm and capable. There was never a question that Tid could ask, nor a fear that he could voice, that Old Father Tim could not answer. If anyone in Tid's world was totally dependable, it was his grandfather. He was the solid part of Tid's life, the one aspect that never failed – and yet now, looking at him, Tid realized that his grandfather was deeply troubled.

'A Gathering is seldom summoned,' Old Father Tim said, stepping down from the platform. Then he absentmindedly added, 'but I think we need one now.'

'They can't come now,' Tid said, 'not before the Mashias.'

The Mashias was the ceremony that heralded the new year. Tid had never been to one; Old Father Tim said he was too young.

'We will celebrate it here.'

'But then there will only be one.' Usually, every region

across the world held a Mashias to help the old year smoothly run into the new one.

'One Mashias in Greenwich has as much power as hundreds of small ones all over the world.'

'I thought that something bad happened if they weren't done right.'

'It will be done right.'

Reassured, Tid's mind moved back to the problem at hand. 'When they are here, will the Guardians settle on another Tick?' he asked.

Old Father Tim looked down at his grandson and slowly shook his head. 'There is no other Tick to be settled upon. Only one Tick is created for each new Timepiece. It was my fault it has gone. I should have guarded it more carefully.'

Tid was appalled. 'But there must be another one somewhere!'

Old Father Tim shook his head sadly.

'But you made it, why can't you can make another?'

'It takes time,' Old Father Tim explained. 'The Tick is a crucial part of the Timepiece. There can be no mistakes. Deep magic is bound into every aspect of its construction. Such magic is not available at a snap of the fingers.' He clicked his fingers.

Tid looked at them, hoping that the snap would bring about sparks or lightning or any sign that there was deep magic in the air. Nothing happened.

'No, young Tid, there is no other Tick to be had. The one we have must be found.'

Tid's stomach began to twist uncomfortably.

'They won't blame you, will they?' he asked in a small, frightened voice.

'Who else is to be blamed?'

The Great Gathering was summoned, and soon Guardians from all over the world were arriving in Greenwich. After the sun had sunk in the sky, they assembled in the park at the Guardian Meridian Line.

Tid watched the procession of Guardians as they approached. No light was needed to illuminate their way because Guardians generate their own radiance, infusing the surrounding area with a warm glow.

Each Guardian carried a heavy wooden staff and was dressed in a similar way to Old Father Tim. Some had decorations on their coats and Tid tried to work out which part of the world each Guardian came from. Seegan had a very ornate and brightly coloured dragon on his coat. Tid guessed that he came from China.

'Guangdong,' his grandfather told him.

'Oh,' said Tid, disappointed that he had got it wrong.

'Guangdong is in China,' Old Father Tim explained.

Tid's grandfather had said he should be present at the Gathering. 'It is fitting that you attend, just as I did when I was a young one.'

Tid was filled with dread. If his conscience had been clear, he would have been excited, but it was not. He had shown a stranger where the workshop was, and now the Tick was missing. He knew there had to be a connection.

Tid watched as the Guardians took their places in a great Circle at the Line. When all had gathered,

Old Father Tim walked into the centre. Tid kept close by his side, trying to hide himself in the folds of his grandfather's long coat. He was careful to keep his face hidden, overawed by the thought of so many noble Guardians. Standing in silence, he waited for his grandfather to speak.

The seconds turned into minutes and still Old Father Tim said nothing. Tid knew that his grandfather never hurried and he was used to long pauses, but this one was going on forever.

The old man meant to speak, he even tried to, but looking around at the faces of his fellow Guardians his voice failed him. For many years he had been their leader, travelling to all parts of the world as the need arose. Only in recent times had he remained in the Park so that he could provide Tid with a home. These days, Guardians visited *him*. Old Father Tim's wisdom was legendary. He guided them in their decisions and redirected their thoughts when confused. Now he had to speak words that would horrify them all. Old Father Tim felt the weight of his failure keenly.

The Guardians became restless. A Gathering had been called, so they knew something very important was about to be announced, but why was the Old Father taking so long?

Finally, Old Father Tim took a deep breath and spoke.

'I stand before you, kinsmen, with my head hung low in shame.' Having found his voice, it was strong and commanding. No one listening could have realized how bad he was feeling. 'Whilst in my care, the Tick has gone missing from the new Timepiece.'

There was a gasp of horror. Tid peeped out from the safety of his grandfather's coat. Each Guardian had understood the enormity of this announcement, and this frightened him. He slipped his hand into his grandfather's for comfort.

'I am to blame,' Old Father Tim continued, 'for it was in my keeping.'

'Where was it when it went missing?' asked Wakaa, a very stern-looking Guardian from the Great Rift Valley in Kenya.

'In my workshop.'

'Who knew of its location?' asked Vremya, a gentle, elderly Guardian from the Ural Mountains of Russia. His voice was not loud and some Guardians failed to hear him. In order that everyone should understand, Old Father Tim phrased his answer carefully. 'Only I knew of its location.'

Tid knew that this was not exactly true and he pulled at his grandfather's hand. Old Father Tim ignored him.

Seegan spoke. 'Was the entrance forced?'

'No. It must have been opened with the secret device. Nothing was broken.'

Tid tugged again at his grandfather's sleeve and whispered, 'Grandfather!'

Seegan continued. 'Is it your belief that the Tick was taken by someone who knew about the workshop?'

'It may look like that, but no one except myself knows of it.'

'Grandfather,' Tid whispered again, 'I know.'

Old Father Tim looked down at his grandson. 'You may not speak at a Gathering,' he said severely.

'But I know about the workshop.'

'That is of no interest to us.'

'It may be,' Wakaa said, as he stood up slowly. 'Did I hear correctly? Does the Old Father Grandson know the location of the workshop?'

'He does,' Old Father Tim agreed, 'but that is of no importance to the Gathering.'

'Did the Old Father Grandson tell anyone about the workshop?'

'He did not.'

Tid was desperate to tell his grandfather. Yanking on his sleeve he whispered loudly, 'Grandfather!'

'Tid! You must not speak!'

Wakaa looked down at the partly hidden boy and wondered what he was so anxious to say. 'Let the Old Father Grandson speak!'

Old Father Tim inclined his head very slowly towards Wakaa in agreement. As a Guardian had called for Tid to speak, he must be allowed to do so. Old Father Tim let go of Tid's hand and, stepping away, left him alone in the centre.

Tid suddenly felt very small and scared. He wished he had not opened his mouth. His throat had gone dry and the palms of his hands were wet.

'Speak, Tid,' said Old Father Tim, giving him an encouraging smile. 'You have been called upon to speak.'

Tid looked towards Wakaa, who sat down, and then to his grandfather. He twisted his fingers nervously and said in a small voice, 'I know about the workshop.'

'What does he say?' called Vremya, cupping his hand to his ear.

Old Father Tim repeated Tid's words.

'Did you tell anyone?' asked Zeit, a severe-looking Guardian who came from Niedersachsen in Germany.

Tid shook his head. His grandfather smiled to himself. He knew that his grandson would not have done such a terrible thing.

Tid was beside himself. He did not want to say what he knew he must. Although terrified, he took a deep breath and spoke as loudly as his failing courage would allow. 'But I did show somebody.'

There was sudden intake of breath from those Guardians who had heard. A hum of voices echoed around the circle as these Guardians passed the information to the others.

Old Father Tim stared at Tid in disbelief.

Large tears started to roll down Tid's cheeks as words tumbled out. 'Her name was Sofi. At first I said that I shouldn't play with her. You always tell me to be careful, Grandfather, and I was. She spoke a bit funny but she didn't look like a Wrecca, she didn't dress like a Wrecca and she didn't smell like a Wrecca. So she couldn't have been one, could she?'

'Where does she live?' Old Father Tim asked.

'On the other side of the river.'

'Who are her grandparents?'

'I didn't ask.'

'Why was she in the park?'

'She didn't say.'

Old Father Tim paused for just a moment before asking the most important question of all.

'Did you show her my workshop?'

'It was a game! She said she knew a really secret place, somewhere I didn't know. If I hadn't shown her, I would never have found out where it was.'

'Where was her secret place?' Old Father Tim asked.

Tid hung his head. 'She didn't show me.'

'But you showed her the workshop?' Wakaa asked.

'Yes.'

Everyone fell silent. No one spoke. Each Guardian was evaluating the facts. Tid wanted to look up to see what was happening, but he did not dare. He kept staring at his shoes.

After waiting what seemed like a very long time, his grandfather spoke. His voice was deep, calm and steady. 'My grandson broke the Covenant. He told an outsider. He told a girl called Sofi. He is my grandson and I share in his shame. I ask that we should be disgraced together.'

The Guardians turned to each other and spoke in hushed voices. Some of them were shaking their heads, others were resting their foreheads in their hands. Several seemed to be wiping tears from their eyes. Tid realized they were reluctant to agree. At length, 'Aye' echoed mournfully around the Gathering.

Wakaa stood once more.

'It is with regret that we accept your disgrace.'

Old Father Tim bowed very low and placed his staff on the floor. Slowly he straightened up.

Tid looked at the Guardians. Some of them shuffled uncomfortably in their seats whilst others stared at the floor. Many more looked totally distraught at the decision they had just taken. Vremya gave Tid an encouraging smile, but Tid could not return it. It had all happened so fast. Tid was finding it hard to accept his grandfather's fate. He had been disgraced and it was all Tid's fault!

With a heavy heart, Tid unhappily followed Old Father Tim away from the Gathering, and together they walked home. It was a long time before either of them spoke.

'When I get home I shall go straight to bed,' Tid said miserably.

'We shall share our hot chocolate together first, as usual.'

'I thought you wouldn't want to talk to me tonight.'

'Tid.' Old Father Tim stopped and looked down at his grandson. 'I will always want to see you, no matter what you have done,' and he held out his large hand so that Tid could slip his smaller one into it. Tid found this simple gesture reassuring.

They continued their slow journey along the tree-lined paths of Greenwich Park. Neither spoke.

Eventually, Tid asked, 'Will the Guardians be able to find the Tick?'

'We must hope so.'

'But they must!' Tid cried, desperate for things to be made right. 'We can help.'

'I fail to see how.'

Tid's mind was racing. There had to be an answer, if only he could think of it. 'There must be something we can do,' he said.

'It is no longer our concern.'

Tid looked up at his grandfather in dismay. He seemed to be giving up. This was worse than losing the Tick. Tid rounded on him, shouting, 'Time will stop forever if we don't find it! That will be the end of everything!'

'Tid,' Old Father Tim said soothingly, trying to calm his grandson down, 'my mind has been searching for an answer. I have been thinking of nothing else.'

'Yes?' Tid asked hopefully. His grandfather always knew what to do.

'But I cannot find one.'

Tid could not believe what he was hearing. This was appalling! His grandfather knew everything – but now, because of something Tid had done, he was helpless.

Old Father Tim looked down at his frightened young grandson. 'Our task now is to leave everything to those who have the authority,' he said gently. 'The Guardians have guarded time for thousands of years. They will find an answer. They will make everything right. We must believe that and we must allow them to do their job. They will not leave the Gathering without deciding what course of action has to be followed.'

'Has a Tick ever gone missing before?'

Old Father Tim knew that it had not, but no good would come of telling Tid this. Instead he said, 'We have to be sensible. We shall go home and let those who understand such matters do the thinking.'

'But . . .'

'No buts.' Old Father Tim squeezed Tid's hand reassuringly. 'It is not our concern.'

Tid wanted to say more. There had to be an answer. His brow furrowed. They continued walking.

'Why did you leave your staff at the Gathering?'

'Only a Guardian may carry a staff.'

'But you are a Guardian!' Tid cried. 'You're the Old Father Guardian!'

'Not any more. I am now one of the Guardian People like many others.'

Tears welled up in Tid's eyes. 'Oh, Grandfather, I *am* sorry.'

'Are you really?'

Tid nodded and wiped away a tear with the back of his hand.

'Are you so sorry that you will be more careful in the future?'

'Yes.'

'That is how we gain in wisdom,' his grandfather said gravely. 'Each of us makes mistakes, but if we learn from those mistakes then we become wise.'

Tid wanted this to be true, but feared that it was not. He did not believe that anything good could come from anything so calamitous. His grandfather was ruined and it was all Tid's fault. Time would end for eternity and that too was Tid's fault. If his grandfather knew of no solution, then there was no solution to be had.

5

A Stranger in the Dark

Tid could not sleep. After tossing and turning he tried closing his eyes and counting to one hundred, but still he lay awake. Guilt weighed heavily upon him. He knew that his reckless behaviour had lost the Tick and deeply injured his grandfather.

In the early hours of the morning, Tid left his warm bed and crept outside. Carefully, he shut the door behind him. Deeply ashamed of himself, he hoped that a long walk in the dark would help him shake off some of his misery.

The night air was crisp and cold, but he did not feel it. Neither did he notice the direction in which he was walking. With hands deeply thrust into his pockets and eyes fixed on the ground inches in front of his feet, he never altered his pace. He saw and heard nothing. All he could think about as he trudged along was the Tick, the Guardians and his grandfather.

He had no notion how long or far he had been walking when he heard a sound. It was not loud but he was certain he had heard something. The black night prevented him from seeing far and he paused,

inclining his head to one side so as to hear better.

Who or what would be out at this time of night? Like the Guardian People, Humans usually slept at this hour. Perhaps it was an animal: cats roamed about late and so did foxes.

There it was again. Suddenly, a new thought occurred to him.

'Oh no!' Tid murmured, as he took a few steps backwards. The sound was approaching. He could hear someone panting, someone running. Fear twisted his stomach. He knew that Wreccas came above ground at night.

Tid panicked. Still blinded by the blackness of the night, he turned and ran. Why had he gone out alone? Why had he put himself in such danger? How often had his grandfather warned him?

In his terror, Tid was not cautious. He could see nothing ahead of him and yet he blundered on at top speed into the blackness of the night.

Suddenly, a sharp pain stung his shin. It took a fraction of a second for him to work out that he had run slap into something. With a loud cry, he flew over the object and tumbled to the ground.

He lay in a crumpled heap, wanting to cry out in pain but not daring to. He was still aware that someone was following him. He gripped his shin and listened. Someone was near. He could hear breathing. Tid's heart pounded loudly and he held his breath hoping that the 'someone' would go away.

Then the 'someone' spoke.

'Is you all right?'

The stranger sounded concerned. Tid thought he must be a friend and whispered a warning. 'There's a Wrecca.'

'Where?' The stranger's voice quavered in fear.

'Over there, where I came from.' Tid could not be more precise, for the fall had disorientated him and he could not be certain which direction that was. 'It followed me. I heard it panting.'

The stranger chuckled.

Tid was indignant. 'I heard it,' he repeated. 'He sounded big.'

'Did it pant like this?' The stranger did a fair impression of the sound.

'Yes,' said Tid, puzzled. This stranger must have heard it too.

'That's no Wrecca,' the stranger declared. 'It followed I too. It's a dog!'

Tid was certain it could not have been just a dog. 'Are you sure?'

'Of course I's sure. Us played. Him's big with a wet nose and a lollopy tongue. Him licked my face.'

Tid felt an idiot. What a fool to have been frightened by a dog! He sat up and held his leg. It was stinging badly.

'You falled over my leg. I was stretching out. Is you hurt?'

Tid squinted and through the darkness he saw a dirty, scruffy boy rubbing his own leg.

'No, I'm fine,' he said, trying to be brave. He rolled up his trouser leg to look at his injured shin.

'You's bleeding,' said the boy, kneeling down to get a better look. A small strip of skin had been grazed from Tid's shin, and blood was oozing through. No wonder it hurt so much.

From his filthy sleeve, the boy took a clean white handkerchief and tied it round Tid's leg. 'That'll make it better.'

'Thank you,' said Tid, looking first at the white handkerchief and then at the boy. There was something familiar about him but he could not work out what it was. Was it the way he spoke? Then a damp, stuffy smell drifted through the air to Tid's nostrils. In the gloom he saw the dirty clothes, the scruffy hair – and there was no mistaking that smell! He had often been warned about it.

'You're a Wrecca!' he exclaimed, jumping up and preparing to run.

'Don't go!'

'I don't talk to Wreccas,' said Tid, backing away.

'But I's scared of being alone in the dark!'

'Then go back to the Underneath where you belong!' Tid shouted unkindly.

'I doesn't belong there,' said the boy. He sounded as if he was trying to stifle a sob. 'I's runned away.'

Tid could just make him out in the gloom, wiping his face on a grimy sleeve. He knew he should go quickly and leave the boy alone, even if he was crying, but curiosity got the better of him.

'Why have you run away?'

'I doesn't know.'

'That's stupid. No one runs away for nothing.'

The boy did not explain himself, he just shrugged his shoulders and sniffed before asking, 'Why's you here?'

'I'm not telling you.'

'Cos you doesn't know either,' declared the boy, triumphantly. 'You's no better than I is.'

Tid was incensed. Everyone knew that a Guardian boy had to be better than a Wrecca boy. 'Yes I am, and I haven't run away!'

'Why's you here then?'

Tid had to say something or else look an even bigger fool. 'Because,' he began reluctantly, 'I broke the Covenant.'

There was a slight pause before the Wrecca boy asked, 'What's "the Covenant"?'

Tid had not expected the boy to ask a question. He had always been told that Wreccas were not clever. It was well known that they never asked sensible questions. 'Do you really want to know?' Tid asked, intrigued.

'Yer.'

Tid had had so many of his own questions answered by his grandfather, by teachers at school and other grown-ups that he answered the boy in the same thoughtful manner.

'It's a sort of a promise. I broke it and the Guardians are very cross with me.'

'I's frightened of Guardians.'

This admission made Tid feel a little better because, if he was honest, so was he. Not that he would admit that to this boy – and anyway, he wasn't frightened in the same way. Tid was more in awe of them.

'You don't have to be,' he said, trying to sound very grown-up and brave. 'They are wise and good and look after time for all peoples.'

'I's still frightened of them.'

Tid felt that the boy deserved some honesty in return. 'Well, I'm frightened of Wreccas,' but then he added more brightly, 'but I don't think I'm frightened of you.'

'And I's not frightened of you.'

It was a good feeling. There they were, in the dark, enemies, and yet neither one was afraid of the other.

'Well, it's been nice talking to you and I hope that you get your problems sorted out,' Tid said politely, 'but I'd better go because I'm not allowed to talk to Wreccas.' The last thing he wanted was for his grandfather to discover that he had been breaking rules again.

'I's not allowed to talk to you either,' the boy admitted. 'Us doesn't have to say anything. Just stay 'til it's light.'

Tid rather liked the thought that he was protecting a fearsome Wrecca. He reasoned that his grandfather would not mind him staying as long as they did not talk.

Together, Tid and the boy found a grassy slope and there they sat without either saying a word.

If he had been sitting with his grandfather, Tid would have had no trouble sitting in silence, but it felt awkward not talking to a stranger. He was relieved when the boy finally spoke.

'I like being Topside.'

'What's Topside?'

'This. Here. Us is Topside.'

'Oh, we call this the World,' Tid explained.

The boy muttered the word to himself as if he was trying to remember it.

They fell quiet again. Tid was bursting with questions. To be sitting with a real live Wrecca and not to ask him anything was too difficult for Tid's enquiring mind. If he kept the conversation away from Guardian topics, he reasoned it could do no harm.

'What do you call the Underneath?'

'The Underneath,' the boy replied.

They both laughed, and that felt good too.

'What's it like down there?'

The boy thought for a moment. 'It's dark, cold and damp, really wet in places, and it don't smell nice.'

'What does it smell like?

'Well, sort of dirty.'

'Like you?'

The boy did not like being told that he smelt badly, but he nodded. 'But that's not the worst of it.'

'What is?'

An unhappy look crossed the boy's face. 'I's always scared.'

'What of?'

'Everything. They's nasty.'

'Who are?'

'The other Wreccas. They like to bully.'

'Do they bully you?'

The boy nodded.

Tid was not surprised. He knew that Wreccas were not nice. 'Why?'

'Ner reason 'cept I's useless at everything and I's small. They's mostly older and know I can't get them back, so they does what they like. I hate it.'

Tid had always known how horrid Wreccas were, but he thought they must choose to live that way. It had never occurred to him that some of them might not like it.

'Are all Wreccas unhappy?'

'Ner, just I. At least, I think it is.' The boy thought for a moment. 'There's a little'un I wonder about sometimes . . . but it's probably just I. That's why I runned away. I like it Topside. I like the blue sky and being clean.'

'Were you ever clean?'

'Just once.'

The glow of first light on the horizon made it possible for Tid to see a smile tugging at the corners of the boy's mouth.

'It was lovely. I weared a blue tunic covered in little white shapes. I think they's called flowers, and my hair was light and bouncy.'

'Little white flowers? I thought you were a boy!'

The Wrecca laughed. 'Ner, I's a girl.'

Tid liked her laugh. 'What's your name?'

'Snot.'

Tid's brow furrowed and his nose wrinkled up in disgust. 'How horrid!' he said without thinking. Then he quickly added, 'I'm sorry, I didn't mean to be rude.'

'That's all right. It is a horrid name,' she agreed. 'When I was Topside I was called . . .' she hesitated.

'Called what?'

She had known all along to whom she had been speaking, but now she was nervous of revealing her own identity.

Tid waited. Why would she not want to tell him?

When she spoke it was in a tiny voice.

'Sofi.'

Tid's eyes opened wide in horror. Of course! He knew he recognized her way of speaking. He jumped to his feet and started shouting. 'It's you! The handkerchief! I knew I recognized it. It's you! You stole the Tick! It's because of you that Grandfather is disgraced. It's all your fault!'

Snot started crying.

'You said you weren't a Wrecca. You lied to me! You tricked me! You made me look stupid and I had to stand in the middle and tell the Guardians what a fool I'd been! I had to tell them all! And they looked at me and I felt so . . . so . . .' Tid was running out of words. 'It's all your fault!'

This last accusation made Snot cry louder. Tid stood looking at her, a little out of breath. His outburst had released much of his anger and now all he wanted was for her to stop crying.

He stood looking at her with her head buried in her hands and her shoulders shaking. Bending down, he took the handkerchief from his knee and gave it to her to blow her nose, but Snot was a Wrecca and did not know how. Wreccas sniff or wipe their noses on their sleeves. Tid, seeing her perplexed expression, explained what she should do. Then she blew her nose loudly into the handkerchief and felt a little better.

When she was quiet Tid asked, 'It *was* you who stole the Tick, wasn't it?'

Snot nodded. 'I's very sorry. I wish I hadn't.'

'A bit late for that now,' Tid said harshly.

Snot hung her head.

'You must have had help,' Tid continued. 'It would have been too big for you to carry.'

'Some of the others comed too.'

'When did you do it?'

'In the dead of night.'

Tid became silent. Neither spoke. Tid shuffled his feet and studied the ground, before finally sitting down beside her. He stared ahead for a while before asking, 'Did you really know of a secret place?'

Snot shook her head.

'I thought not.' It was strangely depressing to discover that there was no new place in the park for him to explore. The sun began to rise.

Tid was thinking. He had been careful to open the workshop door for her very quickly and was certain she could not have seen how. Now, he was just a little impressed that she had not only seen but had remembered it well enough to open it in the dark. Perhaps she was not as stupid as the average Wrecca and, if not, she might be able to help them get the Tick back. After all, she had said that she was sorry. Tid knew that Wreccas could not be trusted, but he felt she was telling the truth. Anyway, it had to be worth a try. He looked at her for a moment and then asked, 'Will you come and tell my grandfather what you did?'

She shook her head. 'I'll never talk to a Guardian and 'specially not the Old Father,' she said.

'How do you know who my grandfather is?'

'Us knows all about you.'

This made Tid feel very strange. It had never occurred to him that anyone in the Underneath could be interested in him. But he dwelt on this for no more than a moment before saying, 'But Grandfather isn't a Guardian any more.' Then he added unkindly, 'Not since you stole the Tick.'

Snot said nothing.

'He's just my grandfather now. Please come and speak to him.'

Snot stubbornly did not answer.

'I think that you should.'

She shook her head.

'He's suffering more than either of us, and yet none of this was his fault.'

Snot looked sulkily into her lap.

'Do you know what's going to happen if we don't get the Tick back?'

She shrugged her shoulders.

'Time will stop forever. Do you understand what that means?'

Snot maintained her silence.

'It means the end of everything. Time will just stop. That will be it. The end. Nothing.'

Snot had never heard of such an extraordinary thing. Genuine interest broke her silence. 'How?' she asked.

Tid had never really thought how this might come

about, but he was not going to admit that. 'Everything will just stop,' he told her. 'You won't be able to move, breathe, hear or see anything.'

'Will it hurt?'

'Probably,' Tid embellished, trying to make it sound as dramatic as possible.

Snot had no more questions and so she repeated, 'I's sorry.'

'So you'll come?'

'Ner.'

Tid looked about him, as if seeking a solution to his problem.

'Will you see Grandfather if I bring him here?'

Snot looked doubtful.

'You owe me that.'

A pang of guilt sparked in Snot's heart. This was an emotion she was unused to feeling. Looking at Tid, she could see in his eyes how much this meant to him. It was all very odd but she had an overwhelming desire to do the right thing.

'I suppose so.'

Tid's relief was clearly visible. 'Wait here and I'll go and get him.'

Feeling more positive now, he stood up, ready to leave. He felt sure his grandfather would know what to do. 'You won't mind being left alone, will you?' he asked. 'The sun's almost up.'

There was nothing about this situation that Snot did not mind, but she nodded her agreement.

'It may take a little while to fetch him,' Tid warned.

'Grandfather is old and doesn't have his staff any more.'

Snot was staring at the ground. She did not look as if she was happy about him going. He wondered if he could trust her but decided he did not have a choice.

'You'll feel better if you wash your face,' he said, thinking it a good idea to give her something to do. 'There's a clean puddle over there.' From his pocket he pulled a comb and handed it to her. 'You could use this.'

Snot looked at it. She had never seen a comb before. Tid understood at once and, lifting the comb to his head, pulled it through his own shaggy hair and quickly made it tidy.

Snot was grateful that he had shown her how to use it without making her feel foolish. When he held it out to her again, she put out her hand to take it, but Tid did not release it immediately. He wanted to make absolutely sure that she would not leave before he returned. 'You will wait, won't you?'

Snot nodded.

'Promise?'

'Why does you ask a Wrecca to promise?' Snot pouted. 'Everyone knows a Wrecca never tells the truth.'

Tid could tell that he had hurt her feelings. 'But I think you will,' he said gently.

Snot felt a warm glow in her stomach. No one had ever trusted her before. She smiled. 'All right.' And then she added, 'I promise.'

6

Doubts and Fears

Tid ran home. He and his grandfather lived in a cottage with two bedrooms upstairs and a cosy kitchen down-stairs. The roof was thickly thatched and the garden well tended. Tid pulled open the front door and ran up the stairs before bursting into his grandfather's bedroom. He could only see the top of the old man's head peeping out from under the blankets.

'Grandfather! I've found her!' He ran to the bed. 'Sofi! She's on Blackheath.'

Old Father Tim opened one eye. 'What is all this noise?'

'I've found her. Sofi. I've found her!'

His grandfather opened the other eye. 'Who is Sofi?'

Tid tried to be patient. 'She's the girl, the one I told you about. You know . . .' he hesitated, not wanting to mention his previous wrongdoing, '. . . about your workshop.'

Old Father Tim lifted himself up a little and leant his weight on one elbow. 'The girl?'

'Yes, she's on Blackheath.'

'Who is she?'

Tid took a deep breath and hoped he was not showing the frustration he was feeling. 'I told you, she's the one I showed . . . you know . . .'

'Yes, Tid, I understand. But *who* is she?'

'Sofi!'

'Yes, but do we know where she comes from?'

Tid understood what his grandfather was asking and it made him feel uncomfortable. He had hoped he would get away without actually stating who Sofi was.

'Well,' he hesitated, 'she's a Wrecca,' and he quickly added, 'but she doesn't like being one and has run away.'

He had intended telling his grandfather more about Sofi's misery down below ground, but one look at the old man's face halted his words.

'A Wrecca?' Old Father Tim asked incredulously.

'Well, yes,' Tid admitted in a small voice.

Old Father Tim sat up. 'You have been talking to a Wrecca?'

'I . . . I know it sounds bad and I probably shouldn't have, but she *is* sorry, really sorry.'

'Have you learnt nothing?' Old Father Tim asked. 'Was it not talking to this Wrecca that got us into trouble in the first place?'

'But she didn't mean it, and now she's run away and she's sorry, really sorry. I thought she could help us. She took the Tick and so she must know where it is, but she never knew how dangerous it was taking it in the first place.' He paused to draw breath. 'Grandfather, please come and meet her. You can see into people's hearts, you will know if she means what she says, and if she does

67

then maybe she can help us. We could get the Tick back and everything will be all right!'

Tid stopped, a little out of breath, and waited, desperate for his grandfather to agree with him.

'You say she is sorry?'

'Yes, and I believe her.'

'Where is she?'

'On Blackheath, like I said.'

Old Father Tim gave his grandson a reproachful look. 'You were on Blackheath at this time of night?'

Tid knew he had done wrong yet again, but his shame was overshadowed by his desire for Grandfather to meet Sofi. 'I couldn't sleep. I am sorry and I deserve to be punished – but please do it after you've seen her. She's very scared and may not wait for us or they might find her.'

'They?'

'The Wreccas. She's run away because she doesn't like it down there. They're nasty to her. She's really unhappy.' Tid started pulling back the blankets. 'Please come, Grandfather. Please!'

Old Father Tim lowered his legs over the side of the bed but did not attempt to stand. 'Tid,' he said seriously, 'you realize this could be another trick.'

Tid looked solemnly at his grandfather. 'I trust her.'

The old man studied his grandson's face and understood that the boy did trust this girl, but Old Father Tim saw no reason why he should. He did, however, love Tid and for his sake he was prepared to talk with her, although he doubted she could help them find the Tick.

'You must promise me one thing first,' Old Father Tim said.

'Anything.'

'You must keep your eyes open. If you see any Wreccas, you are to run straight to Pa Brownal's house for help.'

'I honestly believe she's telling the truth.'

'Very well,' Old Father Tim agreed. 'But if you see anyone, you run as fast as you can and do not wait for me.'

'All right, Grandfather.'

Snot had carefully washed her hands and face in the puddle, and dried them on the handkerchief. To her dismay, it was now smeared and dirty. She pushed it back into her sleeve before combing her hair. This was not as difficult as it might have been if Scratch had not so recently used his nails for the same purpose. Then she waited.

When the sun was fully up, she felt that she was too much out in the open. If one of the Wreccas had noticed that she was missing, they would be looking for her. If they found her, Snot knew that she could expect nothing less than being delivered up to the Ruckus. She shuddered with fear and, leaving the grassy knoll, went searching for a hidden spot where she could wait in safety. When she had found it, she sat on the ground, hugging her knees.

It was hard to believe that she was waiting for Old Father Tim. His was a name that she had known all her life. The Wreccas often spoke of him and, although their comments were always rude or mocking, deep down she knew they were very frightened of him.

Thinking of the Wreccas brought back the familiar feeling of misery that she had always known. She dreaded the thought of being forced to return to the dark, damp tunnels where she was so despised and ridiculed. Down there, fear gnawed at her day and night. She was always on edge, always expecting the worst.

Tid was nice, at least he seemed to be. With a flicker of happiness she remembered his merry eyes and cheerful laugh. Then a grey shadow clouded her thoughts as it occurred to her that this could be a trick. Perhaps Tid was fetching more than one Guardian and she was about to be captured.

Snot buried her face on her knees and put her hands over her head. Even the fear of being held captive by the Guardians was not as terrifying as the thought of coming face to face with Old Killjoy and admitting that she had left the Underneath and talked to Tid without permission. She wondered if anyone had discovered her disappearance. They never noticed when she was around, so why would they realize she had gone?

Carefully, she thought through her options. If she left now, she might be able to slip past the guards at the Topside door without being spotted. Then, as long as her absence had not been noticed, she could go on living in the Underneath as she had before.

It was then that she realized something very important. She did not want to return. There could be nothing

Topside that was half so bad as life below ground. Never again did she want to face the cold misery that awaited her down there. No, she would not return. She would either live Topside or die trying. If Tid was kind, then maybe he would let her see him from time to time. She remembered the glow of pride she had felt when he had told her that she was a good runner, and the delight they had shared while laughing together. But happy thoughts did not stay with her for long. Once again, clouds of fear drifted back. She wondered how Tid had been punished because she had tricked him. She knew she should explain to Old Father Tim that it had not been his fault but doubted she would have the courage.

Time dragged by.

Snot saw Tid and his grandfather a long time before they saw her. She stayed hidden as Tid called her name. Nervously, she looked about her before stepping into the open.

Old Father Tim, who was wearing a long coat over his nightshirt, was leaning on Tid's shoulder. Slowly they approached. The closer they came, the stronger Snot's fear grew and the more she wanted to run away. But where could she go?

'This is Sofi,' Tid said, when they were still a few paces off.

She did not move, but kept staring at the ground.

Old Father Tim waited until he was close up to her before speaking in a very deep and serious voice. 'Sofi.'

She lifted her newly washed face and quite suddenly blurted out what had been worrying her the most. 'It wasn't Tid's fault! Him didn't know I was a Wrecca. I was all clean and smelling of roses."

Old Father Tim rubbed his chin through his thick, white beard. 'And so, young Sofi, your first thought is for Tid. I can see that you have a good heart.'

An uneasy smile nearly reached Snot's lips.

'And what are you now?' Old Father Tim asked.

Snot's smile faded before it had appeared. She had not quite understood the question, and in a mumbling fashion said so.

'Well,' Old Father Tim said seriously, ' you said you *were* a Wrecca. Are you telling me that you are no longer?' Old Father Tim asked.

Snot thought for a moment before saying, 'I was born a Wrecca and never thought it possible to change.'

Old Father Tim shook his head. 'To be a Wrecca is a state of mind and condition of the heart. Tid tells me that you are truly sorry for what you have done.'

She nodded.

'If you are truly sorry, then you have to change. You must cast off your Wrecca clothes, thoughts, words and actions.'

'I's happy to throw the clothes away,' said Snot, eagerly. 'I hate them. They smell of the Underneath. But,' she was trying to work this out carefully, 'I's sure I haven't thought like a Wrecca for ages. I have to try very hard to be mean. And so,' she wrinkled up her face, concentrating on saying exactly what she was thinking, 'if my thoughts is good then maybe what I does will be good too?'

Old Father Tim smiled appreciatively. 'Well spoken, young Sofi. You are certainly casting off the mantle of a Wrecca. But there is one more difficult thing you must do.'

Snot's brow furrowed as she concentrated on the old man's words. She found that she liked him and wondered why she had thought he would be frightening.

'You must tell us all you know about the missing Tick.'

'That's easy!'

'But in doing so,' Old Father Tim persisted, 'you will be betraying those you have lived with, who have fed and housed you all your life. This is no easy thing I ask of you.'

Snot looked at Old Father Tim with his kind, old eyes. Then she looked at Tid. His eyes were full of anxiety. She guessed that he was desperately hoping that she would say yes. She thought about her life in the Underneath, and suddenly she knew with absolute certainty that she wanted to change.

'Is it wrong to hate what's horrid, nasty and cruel?'

Old Father Tim nodded, impressed with her answer. Then he said, 'No, my child. It is not wrong.' He thought for a moment and then held out his hand towards her.

Snot had never held anyone's hand before, and she looked at it, unsure what to do. Seeing this, Tid took hold of his grandfather's other hand and smiled encouragingly at her. Snot understood that this was a grandfatherly gesture of kindness. Shyly, she slipped her hand into Old Father Tim's.

He smiled. 'Come home with us, Sofi.'

❋ 7 ❋

A New Beginning

Back at Old Father Tim's cottage, Tid ran Sofi a bath and then poured something into it that made the water smell wonderful. He explained that it was a herbal mix that someone called Enderell had prepared.

When left alone, Sofi sank into the hot water. Closing her eyes, she luxuriated in the sweet-smelling, steamy water. This was so much better than the cold bath she had taken in the Underneath. Afterwards, she dried herself and dressed in some of Tid's clothes that he had put out for her to wear. Although she would have preferred a blue tunic with white flowers, she was so happy to be clean that she did not mind that the clothes were plain.

Old Father Tim was downstairs in the kitchen, preparing food. He realized that the Guardians needed to know all that Sofi could tell them as soon as possible, but he was wise enough to understand that she could not be rushed. First she would need a little time and a lot of kindness.

He had decided that he could trust her. Looking deep into her heart, he could see the goodness there. It had been hard to see at first, but Old Father Tim was skilled in such matters. Although Sofi had buried this goodness all her life, it was there.

After dressing, Sofi crept downstairs. For a moment, she waited outside the kitchen door, feeling nervous. As she stood there, a delicious smell drifted through the crack under the door. She had never smelt anything like it from the galley chamber in the Underneath. The smell down there had always been rather unpleasant, as many different flavours bubbled together in a huge, greasy pot. This was completely different; it made her mouth water. Cautiously, she opened the door.

'There you are!' Tid said brightly. 'Come in.'

She shyly joined them in the kitchen. Tid was laying the table.

It was a cosy room, with brightly coloured curtains at the window and a cheerful rag rug on the tiled floor. Old Father Tim was whipping a saucepan of potatoes with a large wooden spoon. His backside rocked rhythmically from side to side as he put all his effort into making the mash smooth and creamy.

A check cloth covered the table, and knives and forks had been laid for three people. Tid was putting out glasses. Sofi had never seen such things before and she stared at them with interest. They were so clean she could see Tid's hand right through them.

When Old Father Tim was satisfied with the mashed potatoes, he began to bring the food to the table. Tid showed Sofi where to sit.

Never had Sofi seen such food. To her, it was the most magnificent spread, totally beyond anything she could ever have imagined. She was stunned when Tid apologized because it was only pie.

Old Father Tim piled her plate high with crispy pie, mashed potatoes, green peas and tiny orange carrots, all covered in steaming gravy.

Sofi found knives and forks rather awkward to use. She tried to eat politely like Tid and his grandfather, but it was very difficult when the food was so delicious and she was expected to use utensils that were strange to her. No one mentioned her lack of manners. They understood that she was doing her best.

Finally, Sofi finished everything on her plate, and her stomach felt pleasantly full for the first time in her life. She wanted to lick her plate, anxious not to waste one drop of the delicious gravy. Looking across the table, she noticed that Tid and his grandfather had rested their knives and forks on their plates and were patiently waiting for her to finish. Carefully, she put her knife and fork down as they had done and waited to see what she should do next.

Old Father Tim said they would leave the washing-up until later. Normally, this would have surprised Tid. His grandfather usually said, 'Never put off until later what you can possibly do now,' but today was different. His grandfather looked up at the sky through the window by the sink. Tid knew he was calculating the time. Although he was the maker of the new Timepiece and was perfectly capable of telling the time that way, Old Father Tim preferred to rely on the sky. He was accurate to the moment. It was a skill Tid longed to have.

When the dirty dishes were neatly stacked beside the sink, Old Father Tim settled himself in a large armchair that was piled high with many cushions. Tid offered Sofi the only other comfortable chair, in front of the fire; but, never having sat in such comfort, she preferred the floor and sat on the rug at Old Father Tim's feet. He sipped tea from a large cup.

'What will the Wreccas do with the Tick now that they have it?' he asked.

'I doesn't know,' she answered, 'and I's not sure they does.'

'But time will end forever if they don't give it back,' Tid said.

'I doesn't think they know that.'

'I never suspected that Wreccas understood the consequences of their actions,' Old Father Tim said grimly. 'Perhaps if we explained it to them.'

'What?' Sofi was alarmed. 'Does you mean, go and talk to them?'

'I do.'

'They'll never believe you. They'll think it a trick and if . . .' She felt uncomfortable saying this; Tid and his grandfather seemed so genuinely kind and good that she thought it might shock them. '. . . if they catched you, they'll do terrible things to you.' She gave a little shudder and Old Father Tim, who knew something of Wrecca ways, understood.

'They couldn't capture Grandfather, he's too powerful!' Tid said, indignant at the thought.

'They always sayed,' Sofi explained, sorry to have

offended, 'that if they got a Guardian in the Underneath, him'll be weak as a baby.'

'Grandfather would never be weak compared to them!' Tid exclaimed, even more annoyed.

Old Father Tim held up his hand in a gesture that Tid knew well, and he fell silent. 'Young Sofi is quite right,' the old man said, quietly. 'It would be difficult below ground.'

Tid did not like being wrong, especially in front of Sofi. He sat back, disgruntled.

Old Father Tim took no notice. 'I suppose they have never considered the fact that the Tick was here for a purpose?' he questioned. 'That there is an important reason for us building a new Timepiece?'

'I doesn't think so.'

Old Father Tim shook his head. 'Foolish creatures.'

For a while they sat in silence. Old Father Tim was gauging whether this was the right time to start asking the questions that were most important. Finally, he asked, 'Do you feel you can tell us all you know about how the Tick was stolen?'

Sofi did not mind saying. It was not difficult to explain who took the Tick, which entrance they had used and where it was being stored.

Old Father Tim listened in silence. When she finished, he said, 'This is important information. The Guardians need to know.'

'You will have to summon the Gathering,' Tid said, forgetting to be annoyed because he was happy to be able to demonstrate to Sofi just how much authority his grandfather had.

Old Father Tim shook his head. 'Alas, no longer being a Guardian, I cannot do that.'

'How are we going to get the Tick back if we can't ask the Guardians for help?' Tid asked.

'We can ask for their help. Everyone has the right to ask for help. It will just take a little longer, that is all.'

'How long do we have?'

'Time enough.'

'What do we do?'

'We live in Greenwich and so we must ask our own Guardian for help.'

'Will you go when you've finished your drink?' Sofi asked.

Old Father Tim looked down at her and then across at Tid. 'It is a long walk and I am too old.'

'Use magic,' Tid said.

'That would be difficult, even if I still had my staff.'

Tid understood what his grandfather was saying. It took Sofi a little longer.

'You mean Tid must go?' she asked.

'Tid does not have the information that you have,' Old Father Tim said, gently laying his hand upon her shining hair. 'You must be the one to talk to the Greenwich Guardian.'

Sofi's mouth dropped open and her eyes became misty with tears. She did not want to let Old Father Tim down, but she knew she would never talk to a Guardian.

'You must be the one to go,' she insisted. 'Us'll help. You's old and famous. They'll listen to you. Us is just children. Ner Great Guardian will take ner notice of us.'

Old Father Tim shook his head sadly. 'My child, you must change your thinking. It is only in the Under-neath that children are not appreciated. In the World, a Guardian will listen to a child and value her words.'

Sofi was not sure she believed him.

'It has to be you,' Old Father Tim continued.

Sofi was frightened, but Tid was ready. 'I'll run over to Pa Brownal's now,' he said, jumping up. Bryn Brownal was an old friend of his grandfather's and an Elder of Greenwich Park. 'He'll take her.'

Old Father Tim shook his head. 'That is not pos-sible. Bryn and the others are at the annual meeting of the regional Elders. Afterwards they will join everyone at the great picnic. They will not return until late.'

Tid had forgotten about the picnic. He had been looking forward to it for ages. 'Has everyone gone?'

'I believe so,' Old Father Tim confirmed. 'I had intended waiting until they returned, but now I think not. The Greenwich Guardian should hear what Sofi can tell us now.'

'Willn't the Greenwich Guardian be at the picnic too?' Sofi asked, not sure what a picnic was.

'She should be,' the old man replied, 'but, like us, she will not have gone this year.'

Old Father Tim had referred to the Greenwich Guardian as 'she'. Sofi was very much surprised. Living in a world of men, as she had been, it never occurred to her that an important person could be female.

Tid was ready for the challenge. 'Very well, I'll take her. Where shall we go?'

Old Father Tim smiled. He was very proud of his young grandson. 'You will leave the park,' he explained, acting as if Sofi had already agreed, 'and travel across Greenwich to the Hither House.'

'What's the Hither House?' asked Sofi, more misgivings filling her heart.

'It is the building where the Great Greenwich Guardian talks over important matters,' Tid explained. 'It's called the Hither House because any of the Guardian People may go there if they are in need.'

Sofi looked at Tid's eager face and wished she could be as keen as he.

'Tell the Greenwich Guardian all you have told me,' Old Father Tim said.

'Willn't she overpower I?' she asked.

'Did I overpower you?'

Sofi shook her head.

'Then neither shall the Greenwich Guardian. When you have told her all you have told me, she will know what to do.'

Tid looked into his grandfather's eyes. He wanted to be fearless, but this was the biggest thing he had ever been asked to do. 'I'm scared, Grandfather,' he quietly admitted. 'I don't think I'm brave enough. I've never been across Greenwich before, not even with you, and I don't know the way.'

Old Father Tim smiled reassuringly. 'You will leave

the park by the gates at the foot of the hill and make your way to the Great Ship.'

Tid nodded. He had often seen the Great Ship's masts towering over the rooftops.

'When you arrive there, stop and be still. You will know the way.'

'How?'

'If you are Mindful of me, I shall be Mindful of you.'

'I've never been Mindful before,' Tid said, 'I'm not sure that I can.'

'Of course you can. You just have to think very hard about me and I will think very hard about you. Then you will know the way because I know the way.'

'Will it work right across Greenwich?'

'No, that is too far. I can guide you most of the way, but when you can no longer feel me, you will have to call on the Greenwich Guardian for help.'

Tid nodded.

'It is most important that you remember to do that.'

'I'll remember,' Tid assured him. He was determined not to let his grandfather down.

'You have to be courageous and trust your feelings,' Old Father Tim explained.

His grandson tried to push the fear to the back of his mind.

'You had the courage to tell the Gathering of your disgrace,' his grandfather encouraged him, 'and so you will have the courage to complete this journey.'

Tid very much hoped this was true.

'And you, my dear,' Old Father Tim turned to

Sofi, 'had the courage to come out from the Underneath and tell us who you are and what you had done. Thus, I believe you will also have the courage to make this journey and speak with the Greenwich Guardian.'

Tid and Sofi looked at each other. Each hoped that Old Father Tim was right.

It was growing dark as Old Father Tim walked Tid and Sofi through the park to the place where the path sloped steeply down towards the gates. He could not take them to the gates since returning up the incline alone, without his staff, would have been too great an effort.

Tid put his arms around Old Father Tim's waist and hugged him. He wished with all his heart that his grandfather was going too. A small but very real pain gripped Tid's stomach. It made him feel sick. Old Father Tim leant over and kissed the top of his head. Tid found such a familiar show of affection comforting, but it did nothing to dispel his fear.

Sofi waited patiently. She wished that the old man would lean over and kiss her head too, but he did not. Instead, he touched her cheek with his finger. 'You will succeed,' he said. 'I believe it with all my heart.'

Sofi was grateful for the words and she wished she believed them.

Tid took her hand. He thought he did so to give her confidence, but in reality he was the one who needed the comfort.

Together they walked down the hill and began their journey.

❀°✿✸ 8 ✸°✿❀

Journey Beyond the Gates

Tid and Sofi left Greenwich Park through the Guardian door that was set in the imposing black iron gates which marked the boundary of Tid's world. Sofi clung tightly to his hand.

There were many people rushing along the festively lit streets. On a different occasion Sofi might have found this an adventure, but today it was daunting. Street lights, headlights, Christmas lights. It was all very confusing for a girl who had been brought up in the gloom of the Underneath.

Tid held Sofi's hand firmly in his and together they hurried towards the Great Ship. It was easy to find. They looked up at the black masts towering high above them. It made them feel even smaller than they were. Tid shut his eyes and tried to be Mindful of his grandfather. He knew that grown-up Guardian People were often Mindful of each other. He had learnt the theory of how to do it at school but had never actually tried it himself. He waited. Nothing happened. He thought very hard about his grandfather, trying to envisage his kindly old eyes and comforting smile.

Sofi was still looking up at the tall masts. A breeze caught the rigging, making it sway, and she found herself swaying too. Her chest was tight and she was finding it difficult to breathe. Then a sharp tug on her hand brought her back to reality, and they were setting off again.

Tid was not quite sure why he had suddenly lurched in that direction, it just felt right, and he hoped that being Mindful was working. Together they hurried along the side of the river. Tid was concentrating so hard on his grandfather that he paid attention to nothing else. He failed to notice Sofi dragging behind him, her hand still tightly clasped in his.

Every time he became uncertain of the way, he stopped for a moment and closed his eyes, before walking on. Each time he had to pull Sofi to make her follow. Occasionally he felt he had gone in the wrong direction. When this happened, he would return and try again.

Sometimes they walked on pavements, sometimes on grass and sometimes on cobbles. These were uncomfortable under their feet, but Tid never slackened his pace. He knew that time was short and the growing distance between himself and his grandfather was making being Mindful more difficult. Each time he stopped now, it took longer before he instinctively felt which way they should go.

It had started to drizzle. There were fewer people out now and Tid realized that it was getting late. He shut his eyes and concentrated on his grandfather. He got only a mild feeling of the direction in which they should go, and this worried him. His feelings had been getting fainter and fainter. He hoped he was doing it right.

Off he set off once more, tugging at Sofi. But this time she did not follow.

'Come on,' he said irritably. She was doing nothing to help. 'You can't hang about, sightseeing,' he said sharply, thinking that she was enjoying the excitement of new surroundings; but when he looked into her face, he realized he was mistaken. Her eyes had a faraway, distant look.

'Come on,' he said, more gently.

But she did not move.

He yanked at her hand, and this time it came very easily. Her balance was gone. Eyes rolling in her head, she slowly tumbled over and down on to the ground. There she lay in a crumpled heap.

Tid stared at her, not really believing what had happened. 'Sofi?'

She lay perfectly still on the ground.

He knelt down and called her name louder. Her eyes were shut. Tid looked about him for help. Several Humans were hurrying by. Someone walked right through them. Still she did not stir.

Tid brushed the hair away from her eyes. What was wrong with her? Why did she lie so still? He tried shaking her and calling her name yet again, but Sofi lay motionless.

His heart was wildly beating. What should he do? He ran his hand through his own damp hair and desperately tried to think. Sofi was ill, this much was obvious. If he was Mindful, would he be able to communicate this to his grandfather, and if so, would his grandfather be able to tell him what to do?

Tid sat crossed-legged next to Sofi, shut his eyes and thought hard. Nothing happened. He tried again. Still nothing. After failing one more time, he reluctantly accepted that this was not working. He was obviously too young to communicate such complicated messages. He was alone and would have to cope by himself.

He did not know what to do. He could not think clearly. His heart was pumping fast and he was breathing heavily. Looking up to the heavy sky, he allowed the drizzling rain to cool his face. Breathing deeply, he tried to calm down.

Two facts were uppermost in Tid's mind. He had to go on, and there was no one to help him. This being the situation, what should he do about Sofi? He could either take her or leave her. If he took her, he would have to carry her. He did not know how long he could do that. She would slow him down, but did he have a choice? It was very dark now and it was quite possible that the Wreccas were out searching. He could not risk them finding her. He decided to take her to the Greenwich Guardian. She would know what to do. Perhaps she would ask Enderell to give her some herbs that would wake her up.

Tapping her cheek in a last desperate attempt to wake her, Tid called her name once more. She lay as before, unmoving, on the wet ground. He would have to carry her.

Quickly working out the best way of doing this, he knelt on one knee beside her. Lifting her into a sitting position, he put his shoulder down and tried to pull her on to it. If only he could stand up, he thought he could carry her this way. He staggered a little as he got to his feet, desperately trying to find his balance, but it was no use. Slowly, he toppled over backwards. Sofi tumbled to the ground.

Tid crawled to her side. There was fresh blood on her cheek where the rough pavement had grazed it. He looked for a handkerchief in his pocket but did not have one. Pulling his sleeve over his hand, he tried to wipe the blood away with his cuff.

'Sofi,' he said forlornly, 'I cannot take you.'

He had to leave her, this much was certain, but where? He did not want to leave her where Humans would walk straight through her. He looked about him. She would be safer by one of the trees that had been planted along the edge of the pavement. Humans could see trees and tended to avoid them.

Dragging her across the pavement, he propped her against one of them. The drizzle had stopped. At least she would not get any wetter. He tried to make her comfortable but, slumped against the tree with her head lolling on her chest, she looked anything but comfortable.

'I'll be back as quick as I can.'

With one last look, he ran off.

Being Mindful was even more difficult, now that his thoughts were preoccupied with Sofi. Several times he went in the wrong direction and had to retrace his steps.

Eventually he stopped altogether. He had no thoughts about where he should go next.

'Oh, Grandfather!' he cried out loud. 'What shall I do?'

Then he remembered. When he stopped feeling his grandfather, he was supposed to call upon the Greenwich Guardian. He quickly imagined her face and was surprised to discover that he knew where to go. He realized that he must be close for the thought waves to be so powerful. He ran down the street and around two corners before coming to a halt once more.

It had started raining again. The street lights reflected on the shiny pavements. It took him a moment to realize that he had arrived. He turned a full circle, trying to see which tall building could possibly be the Hither House. There were all sorts of human dwellings but nothing that he felt could be of importance to a Guardian. Again he turned around and peered into the dark shadows, but he saw nothing that resembled a Guardian structure.

'Greenwich Guardian, please help me!'

Within seconds, it was as though a mist had evaporated before him. Nestled among the human dwellings, a house materialized. It had crooked walls, sleepy windows and steps that were worn and misshapen. The cracked old door was swinging open.

Tid dashed across the road, up the rambling steps and in through the front door.

The hallway was so surprising that he stopped still, wide-eyed, and stared at it. It appeared to be twice the size of the entire house. Large, marble pillars held up the high ceiling. To one side was a roaring fire, in front of which was a table laden with good things to eat. The warmth made Tid realize how very cold and wet he was. Seeing the food reminded him that his grandfather's pie had been eaten a long time before and he was hungry. But there was a more pressing problem.

'Greenwich Guardian,' he said to the walls.

As if from nowhere, someone approached. But it was not the Greenwich Guardian.

'Enderell,' Tid said, relieved to have found someone he knew.

Enderell was a tall, elegant woman with shining dark hair. She wore the long robes of the Guardian People, but on her they looked different. They draped stylishly over her gently curving body and swished attractively as she walked. From her waist a tiny gold timepiece swayed at the end of a long, delicate chain. Her dark eyes revealed the calm serenity that was her nature, and her full lips looked as if a smile was never far from them. Tid liked Enderell better than any other grown-up, except for his grandfather.

'We know where it is at least Sofi does but she's ill and I had to leave her but I can find her again but we should go now and get her and I think we should hurry as it is raining and she will be cold and I did try to carry her but I couldn't but I think she is all right as I put her by . . .'

Enderell held up her hand and Tid gasped. He had forgotten to breathe.

'Of what are you speaking?' she asked, surprised by the urgency in Tid's voice.

'Sofi!' he explained. 'I need to see the Greenwich Guardian. It's very important.' And then he added so as to make his mission sound more official, 'Grandfather sent me!'

'The Greenwich Guardian is in a meeting,' Enderell told him, 'a very important meeting, and she cannot be disturbed. Sit by the fire. You look cold. I have prepared supper for you.'

'How did you know I was coming?'

Her lips parted in a tranquil smile. 'Someone always comes.'

Tid would have liked to do as he was bidden. The fire was warm and he was hungry, but he knew he did not have the time to sit and eat. 'I have to talk with her.'

'These are desperate times.' Enderell spoke calmly. 'Each of us has to wait our turn.'

'But it is about the desperate times that I'm here. We know where the Tick is!'

As soon as he had spoken, Tid saw Enderell glance beyond him. Wheeling round, he saw that she was looking at a dark, handsome young man who was standing near the wall. Tid had not noticed him before. Nodding in response to Enderell, this young man quickly moved towards some large double doors that were situated at the end of the hall. Quietly, he opened one and went though.

'Who's that?' Tid asked.

'Joss,' Enderell explained.

Tid watched him go and then he drew breath to ask

where he was going, but immediately stopped because Joss had returned.

'You many go in,' Joss said, holding open the door for Tid.

Feeling strangely nervous, Tid entered the large room, where the Greenwich Guardian stood holding her staff. She was a striking woman in her middle years, with long, red, curling hair that fell to her waist.

Without wasting time on the usual Guardian greeting, Tid immediately blurted out, 'We know where the Tick is. At least, Sofi knows but I had to leave her and I think we had better go and fetch her, she must be frozen.'

The Greenwich Guardian held up her hand to halt him just as Enderell had done. 'One thing at a time,' she said. 'You know where the Tick is?'

Tid nodded. 'In the Underneath.'

She did not look impressed. 'We reasoned it would be.'

'No,' Tid said. 'Sofi knows exactly where.'

'And who is Sofi?'

'That's what I've been trying to tell you. I had to leave her because she fainted or something. We have to go and fetch her.' Tid took a shuddering breath. He was beginning to feel desperate. No one seemed to understand.

The Greenwich Guardian nodded to Enderell, who was standing by the door, and then she knelt down in front of Tid. Placing her staff on the floor, she gently rested her hands on his shoulders. 'Slowly, Tid.' She spoke calmly. 'Tell me slowly, but first, drink this. It will warm you.'

Enderell was standing by his side with a wooden cup. She held it out to Tid, who took it and swallowed the golden liquid. It was like nothing that Tid had ever tasted before. The delicious drink was sweet and thick and utterly mouth-watering. He ran his tongue over his lips to catch any lingering drops. A warm glow filled his stomach; it then spread up and down his body until he was warm and revitalized. He handed the cup back and then began again, this time at the beginning.

Carefully, he explained about Sofi and the Tick. The Greenwich Guardian listened patiently.

When he had finished, Tid waited in silence. He could see she was thinking and felt he should not interrupt her. When she spoke, it was to Enderell.

'You and Joss will go with Tid and find Sofi. Bring her back here.'

It was a much happier Tid who returned to the streets of Greenwich. Restored by the golden drink, he led Joss and Enderell back to the tree where he had left Sofi.

This was not as difficult as he had feared. With Enderell at his side and Joss walking behind, he felt safe and he quickly found the street where he had left her.

'I leant her against one of the trees,' he said, starting to run. Joss ran with him. Enderell did not. She continued walking gracefully but somehow still kept pace with them.

Tid found the tree – at least, he thought he had – but Sofi was not there. Confused, he looked up and down the street. He stepped back and counted the trees. 'I'm sure I left her here.'

Joss and Enderell exchanged glances.

'Did you get the name of the road?' Joss asked.

Tid shook his head. He had not thought to do that.

'Roads around here all look the same,' Joss said, kindly. 'Let's go and see if we took a wrong turning somewhere.' He stretched out his hand, but Tid did not take it. He was determined to look more confident than he felt.

After searching roads, lanes and alleyways for a considerable time, Enderell finally stopped. 'Tid,' she said, 'you have to accept that she is not here.'

'But she must be!' Tid was fighting back tears. He could not believe that she had disappeared.

'Perhaps she recovered,' Joss suggested, 'and is now looking for you.'

'Then she is lost.' Tears brimmed over Tid's lashes. He knew that Sofi would never find her way around Greenwich alone. Impatiently, he brushed the tears aside and breathed deeply in an attempt to stop them.

'And she will be found,' Enderell said comfortingly. 'The Greenwich Guardian will send out more people. We shall not give up, but we must take you back now. You are exhausted and need to rest.'

But Tid could not rest. He could not bear to think just how frightened Sofi must be if she was wandering the lonely streets of Greenwich – and yet, however appalling this thought was, he desperately clung to it, hopeful that it might be the truth. The other possibility was too terrible to contemplate.

Steadfastly, he tried not to imagine what might be happening to Sofi if she was back in the hands of the Wreccas.

9

Sheldon Croe

The smell was instantly recognizable. As the musty, damp aroma invaded Sofi's nostrils, her eyes flickered open. Flaming torches that had been thrust into the rough earthen walls cast a gloomy light in the chamber. It was all terrifyingly familiar. She peered into the shadows, dreading whom she might see. Her brow furrowed. Her mouth was dry. She was alone.

Metal springs sighed and screeched beneath her as she moved, and Sofi realized that she was lying on a bed. She had heard about beds, although this was her first time on one. Her eyes swept the chamber. There was much that was disturbingly recognizable, and yet there was much that was not.

Anxious to discover exactly where she was, Sofi started scrambling off the bed, but her efforts were quickly halted by something gripping her ankle. She peered at it. There was a metal cuff attached to a heavy chain, which in turn was fastened to the foot of the bed.

She was a prisoner, but where? Initially, she had thought herself to be in the Underneath, but she had never seen a bed like this down there, nor had she ever seen such a large, clean, comfortable chamber. Perhaps she was in one of Old Killjoy's private chambers, but she could not believe that. Prisoners were always thrown into one of the dungeons, not given the luxury of beds.

She was thirsty and her chest hurt when she breathed in, but otherwise she felt all right. Desperately, she tried to remember how she had come to be there. Her last recollections were of Greenwich and being dragged along by Tid.

Tid! Where was he?

Suddenly, she was frantic to escape. Perhaps Tid was being held captive in another chamber. He would need her help. She had to get out.

Sofi clawed at the band on her ankle, but it was solid. She turned to the foot of the bed and pulled at it, but the chain was firmly attached. She was stuck fast.

Just as she was trying to work out if she could possibly move the bed in order to investigate the door, she heard someone coming. Quickly she lay back down, closed her eyes and pretended to be asleep.

The door was pushed open.

'Sofi?'

The voice was cold and hard, but he had called her Sofi. No Wrecca would have done that. She opened her eyes.

Slouching in the gloom at the end of the bed was a tall, angular youth with beady, bird-like eyes. He was dressed in a similar way to Tid. This implied that he was one of the Guardian People, but something about him was wrong; it looked as if he had deliberately made himself scruffy. His hair was unkempt and his tunic was smeared with mud.

'Who's you?' Sofi asked.

The youth shifted his weight. With a curl of the lip that suggested he had been practising in front of a mirror, he said, 'Snarl.'

Sofi was tempted to laugh out loud. This was no Wrecca; he was just pretending. She looked steadily at him, unsure whether she should join in the joke. But he was not laughing.

Years of deception in the Underneath made it easy for her to keep her face expressionless. 'Where's Tid?' she demanded.

'What are you asking about him for? He left you to die. He couldn't care less about you. Tid's no good.'

So, this boy did not like Tid. Sofi's stomach twisted with fear as she wondered if he had hurt her friend; but she would not betray any emotion until she knew exactly what she was up against. She shrugged her shoulders. 'What's this place?'

'Somewhere safe,' he said, relishing his power.

'Is I a prisoner?' she asked, lifting her foot to show the chain.

He snarled once more. 'Of course.'

'So what's you going to do with I?'

'That's for me to know and you to find out.' He was very much enjoying himself.

Sofi was not going to give him the satisfaction of seeing that she was scared.

'Can't give a rat's tail!' she said, turning over and

closing her eyes. She was pretty certain he had expected her to cry and beg to be set free. She hoped that her indifference had annoyed him. She waited, pretending once more to be asleep. Then she heard him give a discontented grunt and stomp out, clanging the door shut behind him.

When she opened her eyes, she was alone.

Late into the night, Joss walked Tid back to Old Father Tim's house. His grandfather listened as Tid recounted how he had lost Sofi. He was distraught. He was convinced the Wreccas had captured her, and he blamed himself. His grandfather could say nothing to comfort him.

'She's ill, Grandfather, and I left her for the Wreccas to find!'

Old Father Tim suddenly appeared not to be listening. Something had just occurred to him. 'Of course!' he muttered, holding his hand to his mouth. He had remembered something vital, but he had remembered too late. 'Stupid of me,' Old Father Tim rebuked himself. 'Why did I not think of this before?'

'Think of what?'

Old Father Tim rubbed his chin thoughtfully before speaking. 'Sofi is newly out from the Underneath, where the air is stale and there is not much oxygen.' He was trying to explain in such a way that Tid would understand. 'Sofi's lungs would have been accustomed to extracting every last particle of oxygen from the air in order to breathe. In the World there is more than enough oxygen. She was taking in too much of it, that is all.' He ran his fingers through his beard. 'I suppose you were running?'

Tid nodded, remembering how he had dragged Sofi, at speed, across Greenwich.

'She would have been breathing heavily and gasping in more and more air until she just overloaded,' Old Father Tim explained.

'Will she be all right?'

'Oh yes.' Old Father Tim rested his hand on his grandson's head. 'No real damage done.'

'And if she's in the Underneath again, breathing the sort of air she's used to, she will be recovered by now?'

'I would think so.'

Somehow, this did not make Tid feel any better.

While Old Father Tim made certain that Tid had told the Greenwich Guardian all that Sofi had told them, Joss prepared a hot drink for them. At long last, Old Father Tim took Tid up to bed. 'Try to sleep,' he said, kissing him on his forehead.

Joss and Old Father Tim then sat before the fire and talked the matter through. There was more than the Tick to consider now. It was not long before there came a knock at the door, and then another. Talk of the missing Tick had dominated the day. One by one, as the Guardian People returned from the picnic, the Elders came to Old Father Tim to discuss the situation, just as they had always done in times of trouble or joy.

There were more people than chairs, even though the ones from the kitchen table had been put in front of the fire. Some of the Elders leant against the chimney breast and others crouched on the floor.

'It is good that the lad told Grenya everything,' Bryn said, calling the Greenwich Guardian by her given name; she was his sister. 'Young Tid did well to make it across Greenwich.' He was impressed that Tid had succeeded in being Mindful at so young an age.

There was, however, a little awkwardness. News of Old Father Tim's disgrace had also reached them. Many of the Guardian People could not remember a time when Tim Mossel had not been the Old Father. It was very unsettling not to have him as their leader now when things were so troubled. However, at this moment there was a more pressing problem. What should they call him? Clearly they could not use his old title, and yet to call him Tim, as many had done before, seemed disrespectful. Eventually, Bryn settled the matter. 'This is a mighty bad business, Pa Mossel, and no mistake.' Everyone nodded their agreement, and from that moment Old Father Tim was called Pa Mossel.

Upstairs in his bed, Tid could hear faint murmurings from downstairs. He did not try to catch what they were saying as he usually did. Tonight, all he could think about was Sofi.

Sheldon Croe had never been a popular boy. From his earliest days he had bullied and sneered at others. This was the way he treated his grandmother at home and he knew no other way of behaving.

When he had first started school, he had tried playing

with the other children, but they did not take kindly to the rough treatment he gave them if the game did not go his way. Quickly, children started avoiding him and eventually ignoring him altogether. As time went by, Sheldon tried to make friends with younger children, but his way of playing was to dominate and threaten, and soon even they kept out of his way. Finally, Sheldon found himself alone. As the years passed, he grew used to his own company. He never liked it, although he told his grandmother that he did.

Sheldon detested Tid. In reality, he was jealous of him, but Sheldon could not admit that to himself, and so he decided that Tid was a creep and thus it was all right to hate him.

Late in the afternoon, Sheldon had been hanging around by the park gates. He was surprised to see Tid leaving the park and was intrigued by the girl who was clinging on to his hand. Sheldon had never seen her before.

It was not difficult to follow them without being noticed. The girl seemed distracted and Tid was behaving very oddly. Sheldon tracked them through the streets of Greenwich, watching them carefully.

After a while, Sheldon decided that Tid was playing at being Mindful. All the moves were there, but exaggerated. Tid would stop, shut his eyes and screw up his face, as if he was concentrating very hard. Then he would rush off again.

Sheldon noted that Tid was not paying proper attention to the girl. She seemed to be less and less willing to follow him each time he started off at speed. Eventually, she appeared to collapse. This was when Sheldon learnt her name. Tid used it several times.

It was obvious that Tid was distressed. Sheldon watched with satisfaction, as Tid clearly did not know what to do. It amused Sheldon very much when Tid dropped her. It would have been so easy for him to offer help, but he would not help Tid under any circumstances. In fact, he found the whole episode thoroughly enjoyable.

It was after Tid had run off that Sheldon got the idea. His mean little eyes glinted as the plan formed in his head. This was the opportunity he had been waiting for.

Being much bigger than Tid, it was easy for him to hoist Sofi over his shoulder. He moved quickly so as to be out of sight before Tid returned. Very happy with his evening's work, Sheldon swaggered off with his prize.

The door of her prison opened once more. Sofi expected it to be her captor, but it was not.

'I thought you might like a drink, dearie,' an old woman said as she put a tray next to the bed, 'and a bite to eat.'

'Who's you?' Sofi asked suspiciously. In the Underneath, Sofi had only ever encountered men and children. She could not remember ever having spoken to a woman.

'I'm Ma Croe, Sheldon's grandmother.'

'Who's Sheldon?'

The old woman smiled. 'Of course, dearie, I'm sorry.

I didn't mean to spoil your game.' She held out a plate of sandwiches. 'I mean Snarl.'

Sofi had never seen sandwiches before. They looked tasty, so she sat up and took one. Although she did not trust this woman, she was hungry. The old woman sat on the bed and watched her eat.

'You've hurt yourself,' Ma Croe said, taking a handkerchief from her pocket. Sofi noticed that it was not as white as Tid's had been. Ma Croe leant towards Sofi in an attempt to wipe away the blood that was on her cheek. Sofi ducked her head out of the way.

'You've grazed yourself,' Ma Croe said, spitting on her handkerchief and approaching Sofi's cheek once more.

'T's all right,' Sofi said, not liking the idea of Ma Croe wiping her spit across her face.

The old woman hesitated before changing her mind. She blew her nose on the handkerchief and put it back in her pocket.

Sofi helped herself to a drink.

'I am so glad Sheldon has a friend. I know he likes to be alone, but I don't think it's good for him all the time.' Ma Croe flicked away a crumb that had fallen from Sofi's sandwich. 'I haven't seen you around here before. What's your name?'

'Sofi,' she replied, taking another sandwich. If it would help, she was happy to go along with the idea that she and Sheldon were playing a game. It did strike Sofi as odd that his grandmother expected a boy of his age to be playing with a young girl.

'Has Tid gone home?' Sofi asked innocently.

Ma Croe looked surprised. 'Tid? I didn't know there were lots of you playing.' The idea seemed to please her. 'You're the only one here.'

Sofi did not know whether this was a good thing or not. At least Tid was not a captive, but what had Sheldon done with him? She needed to escape as quickly as possible, and Ma Croe might just be able to help.

'Where's Sheldon?'

'He's gone out. Perhaps he's gone to join your friends.'

Sofi gave her sweetest smile. 'I's enjoyed playing with Sheldon, him's really nice, but,' she appeared to look worried, 'it's later than I thinked and my grand-mother will want I home.'

The old lady looked confused, 'But Shel– I mean Snarl, said you were staying the night.'

'Him's got it wrong,' Sofi said convincingly. 'My grandmother will boil over if I doesn't get back soon. I must go. Those sandwich things is nice, but can you undo this?' and she indicated the band on her ankle. 'I can't hang about no longer.'

The old woman looked perplexed. 'But Sheldon said . . .'

'It's not his fault, I forgetted.' Sofi lied with ease. 'Us has friends coming round.'

'I'm sure your grandmother wouldn't mind.' The old woman poured Sofi another drink. 'Who is she?'

Sofi thought quickly. She only knew the name of two Guardians and she did not think she could get away with being Old Father Tim's granddaughter. 'The Greenwich Guardian.'

Sheldon's grandmother looked impressed. 'Oh,' she said, and then she looked puzzled. 'I had no idea that the Greenwich Guardian had a granddaughter.' She seemed to be mulling this over in her mind before finally sucking in her breath and giving a knowing smile, as though she suddenly understood. 'Oh, it's all part of the game, isn't it? Like the way you're speaking.' She stood up and started to clear away the tray. 'You're doing it very well.'

'Ner,' Sofi said anxiously, 'it's not a game. Grandmother will be wild if I doesn't get home.'

Ma Croe picked up the tray and left. 'Of course she will, dearie,' she said, winking as she closed the door.

10

A Knock at the Door

The Guardians stood at the Line in groups of five or six. Their heads were inclined towards one another as they carefully discussed the proposal the Greenwich Guardian had placed before the Gathering. Eventually Wakaa held up his hand. This was the signal that called them to order, and the hum of talking died as they once more took their seats.

'Are we ready to make a settlement?' Wakaa asked.

Zeit stood up. 'Can we trust this Sheldon Croe?'

Wakaa stood back to allow the Greenwich Guardian to stand in the centre of the Guardian circle.

'I do not trust him,' she said. 'He has never been a popular boy and is not altogether what I would call normal. But it is rumoured that he constantly watches the Wreccas, so he might have seen or heard something that could help us. The more we know about their recent movements, the better. Even a small piece of information could be important. I think it would be prudent to talk to him at the very least.'

'Are you thinking of sending him into the Underneath to recover the Tick?' Seegan asked.

'You know that sending one of the Guardian People into the Underneath is a grave risk. We would only consider it if there was no alternative, but,' and she paused just for a moment, 'it is a possibility.'

'No!' Zeit was on his feet once more. 'The Middlers must be recalled. It is the only way.'

A buzz reverberated around the circle. This was a highly controversial suggestion.

It was Vremya who voiced the fears of many. He tried to stand but, being very old and frail, he found it difficult. Wakaa gestured to him to stay seated, and he gratefully accepted. Everyone leant forward so as not to miss anything the old Guardian said.

'The Middlers must not be summoned,' he said quietly in his rich, Russian accent. 'Such a thing has never happened. It may be catastrophic if they are disrupted.'

'It may be more catastrophic if they are not!' Zeit snapped in a less than gracious manner.

Vremya shook his head sadly. 'I cannot vote for their premature return. There must be another way.' He did not add what he was thinking, which was that if Old Father Tim was still the Old Father, he would have found the other way.

Wakaa was the Old Father now. He walked into the centre. 'It is time to put this matter to the vote. Do we summon the Middlers?'

A lone voice forcibly proclaimed, 'Aye!' It was Zeit. He stood, glaring at the other Guardians, silently cajoling them to vote yes. Gradually some of them did, but less enthusiastically.

Wakaa could see that the Gathering was split. 'I shall make preparations for the Middlers' journey, in case we need to call upon them,' he said. 'In the meantime they will remain undisturbed.'

'If we do that,' Zeit was on his feet once more, 'there will not be enough time. The Middlers must come without delay and attack the Underneath.'

'Preparations will begin,' Wakaa said. 'Everything will be made ready and they will be brought home at speed if no other plan can be decided upon.'

Zeit shook his head. 'Think how little time there is!'

'I understand that,' Wakaa said, a tinge of irritation in his voice. 'I am well aware of the magic that is required to return the Middlers at speed. It shall be prepared, and then we shall wait to see if it is needed.' He spoke with authority and Zeit knew that he should not push the new Old Father any further. The other Guardians nodded their approval.

'As Sheldon Croe is a member of the Greenwich Guardian's parish,' Wakaa continued, 'she and I will visit him together, this night.' Everyone agreed. 'And so, if there is nothing more to discuss, I suggest we return at sunset tomorrow.' He looked around to see if anyone had anything to add. Vremya lifted his hand to show that he had. With a nod of his head, Wakaa indicated that he should speak. This time the old Guardian did not try to stand.

'Old Father Wakaa,' he began. It sounded strange to give Wakaa this title, but Vremya would not deny him the respect his high office demanded. 'What of the little girl, the Wrecca called Sofi?'

Once more Wakaa gave the centre to the Greenwich Guardian.

'We have to assume that the Wreccas have taken her back into the Underneath.'

'When we recover the Tick,' the softly spoken Vremya continued, 'do we intend to rescue the girl too?'

'She got us into this trouble!' Zeit interjected. 'I really feel we have no obligation to . . .' He paused. Wakaa had stepped forward and was holding up his hand. Zeit respectfully fell silent. Wakaa stepped back to allow the Greenwich Guardian to give Vremya his reply.

'I never spoke with the child, although young Tid Mossel is convinced of her good character.'

'He is but a boy, and one whose poor judgement caused this crisis.' Zeit realized that he was at odds with the rest of the Gathering and, although he regretted this, he felt it was his duty to speak his mind.

'I understand that Pa Mossel also talked with her,' the Greenwich Guardian said, raising her voice just a little, 'and saw goodness in her heart. I think we should discuss this with Pa Mossel first.'

The assembled Guardians, including Zeit, highly approved of this. There was a general murmur of agreement, especially from Vremya.

Sheldon Croe was pacing backwards and forwards, trying to pluck up the courage to knock on the door. This is something he had long wanted to do but never dared. For many months he had spied on the Wreccas. This had made it possible for him to discover the whereabouts of one of the Underneath doors. He spent many hours waiting for the door to open. If he was lucky, he sometimes managed to glimpse the tunnel behind it.

The Underneath, and its inhabitants, had become Sheldon's obsession. Unable to fit into his own world, he had taken a liking for another where honour, truth and wisdom were not prized. He had regularly observed the Wreccas but had never had the courage to talk to any of them. He had often wanted to, but he knew he must have a good reason if he were to approach such fearsome creatures. Tonight he had that reason.

Taking a deep breath, Sheldon rapped on the door. Then he stood back, his heart beating quickly. It was a solid door, but Sheldon could hear some activity on the other side. Clearly his knock had caused something of a commotion. He stood and waited.

After some considerable time had passed, he debated whether he should knock again. He was just about to do so when the door opened a crack. Sheldon's hands went clammy with anticipation and fear. He bowed low. He thought it would be respectful to bow.

Sniff stuck his long nose out of the door. He was surprised to see a Guardian youth standing alone in the night, and totally amazed to see him bow. He eyed the area suspiciously. 'Who's you?' he demanded.

'Sheldon Croe at your service, sir.'

Sniff narrowed his eyes and watched Sheldon carefully. This had to be some sort of trick. He wanted to retreat into the safety of the Underneath, but Scratch had told him to answer the knock and was now standing right behind him, waiting to find out what was going on. Sniff dared not thwart Scratch.

Sheldon stood up from his deep bow. He did not look as if he was being artful. Sniff was beginning to think that this might not be a trick. He opened the door a little wider and stepped out, still looking carefully about him. 'What does you want?'

'I want to be of service.'

Sniff sniffed in derision. 'How can a beanpole like you help us?'

Sheldon did not like being called a beanpole, but he did not complain. 'I have a girl, a little Guardian girl, that I can give you.'

Sniff eyed Sheldon carefully. If he was telling the truth, this was something special. He needed to talk to Scratch. 'Wait here!' he spat, disappearing inside.

'Who is it?' Scratch demanded as soon as Sniff reappeared.

'A Guardian boy.'

'What?' Scratch did not believe he was hearing correctly. No Guardian boy would knock on an Underneath door.

'Not a little'un so much as a big skinny one.'

'Oh!' Scratch said. 'Is him tall and clumsy with beady little eyes?'

'Yer, that's him.'

'Him's always hanging about. Send him away with a kick up his arse!' Scratch nodded, confirming to himself that this was the best course of action. 'Yer, kick him hard.' Feeling that he had dealt with the situation, he began to walk away.

Sniff liked the idea of kicking Sheldon, but this might not be the time to do it. 'The thing is ...' he said, following Scratch, who did not stop to listen but just kept walking. '... him says him has a little'un. Some Guardian girl that him wants to give us.'

Scratch stopped. Had he heard correctly? Slowly, he turned his deep-sunken eyes on Sniff.

'Him has what?'

Sniff told him again and added, 'Think it's a trick?'

Scratch knew that this was a possibility. As a rule, it was a not good idea to trust one of the Guardian People, but this particular youth was different. Scratch had often seen him hanging around and had noticed that over the last few months the boy's appearance had changed. Recently he had looked much better, as if he was breaking away from some of the Guardian traditions.

There was, however, another reason why Scratch wanted to believe him. For longer than he could remember, Old Killjoy had wanted to kidnap a Guardian child as a trophy. Such a child would raise Old Killjoy in the esteem of other regional Wrecca leaders. If this Guardian youth was going to give their leader his heart's desire, then Scratch wanted to be the one to bring him in.

'Where's him now?'

'I told him to wait.'

'You told him to wait?' Scratch scowled, swiping Sniff around the head before heading back to the door.

'You telled him to wait? Him will have gone, you dung beetle!'

Sniff followed, dabbing at the blood that was dripping from the gash caused by Scratch's nails. 'What if it's a trick?' he whimpered.

Scratch was too intrigued to stop now. He would be careful, take no risks, but he would follow this through. The offer was too good to pass up. No Wrecca had ever got his hands on a Guardian child before.

Guardians were aware that their children were at risk. Mentally, adult Guardian People were too strong to allow a Wrecca to overpower them, but their children were not. This being the case, all Guardian children were protected by a powerful charm that prevented them from being dominated by a Wrecca. Thus, a child could not be taken against his or her will. But this was different. A Guardian youth was willing to give a Guardian child into the Underneath. It might work.

Sheldon had taken Sniff at his word and had not moved a muscle. When Scratch opened the door, he was standing in exactly the same place. Sheldon recognized Old Killjoy's second-in-command and bowed. He thought of Scratch as a hero.

'You's got a girl?' Scratch demanded.

'Yes, sir.'

Scratch nodded and ran a long nail over his chin. 'Why's you giving her to us?'

'I want to serve Lord Killjoy,' Sheldon said, and then he added, 'and you too, Pa Scratch.'

Scratch was gratified that Sheldon knew his name. He

had long wanted recognition and he had a weakness for titles. Pa Scratch was an acceptable name, although not as impressive as he would have liked, but it would do for now.

'And,' Sheldon had not finished, 'I would like the honour of presenting her to Lord Killjoy myself.'

Sheldon ached to see more of the Underneath. He had heard stories about it and, from the odd glimpses he had managed to sneak, he had tried to re-create it in the cellar at home. He believed that giving Sofi to Old Killjoy could be the first step to being accepted down there.

Scratch had no intention of letting this scraggy youth into their Underneath, but he did want the girl and so he had to play along. He placed his hand on Sheldon's bony shoulder. 'Bring us the girl,' he said, attempting a friendly smile, 'and Lord Killjoy himself will thank you.'

Sheldon returned the smile, but rather nervously.

'Very likely give you a medal!' Scratch added encouragingly.

Sheldon puffed out his chest. A medal, he would like that.

'When can you bring her?'

'This very night.'

'Us'll be waiting.'

Sheldon bowed. 'Thank you, Pa Scratch, sir,' he said, bowing again. 'Thank you.'

Scratch was enjoying the deference Sheldon was showing him, but he did not want to waste time. He was aware that Sniff knew of this girl and he did not want him telling Old Killjoy about her first and getting all the glory. 'Get out of here!' he blasted.

Sheldon jumped at the sudden force of the command. Then he ran off in delighted haste across Blackheath. He was anxious to get back to Sofi as quickly as possible. He was elated. Excitedly, he imagined the reception that awaited him in the Underneath. In his mind he saw Old Killjoy pinning a medal on his chest and everyone cheering. Wreccas were patting him on the back and calling him clever. In his imagination he was receiving the recognition he had always craved.

The Greenwich Guardian and Wakaa walked up the path that led to the house Ma Croe shared with her grandson. The gate was hanging off its hinges and paint was peeling off the window frames. Clearly Sheldon did not do the chores around the house that were traditionally the task of the grandson.

Ma Croe was sitting by the fire, cleaning Sheldon's boots. She was muttering to herself, wondering how he got them so muddy, when there came a sharp knock at the door. She was so surprised, she dropped a boot. No one came visiting these days. Carefully putting down the brush, she crept to the window beside the front door. It was dark outside but the moon was bright. It cast enough light for Ma Croe to make out the form of the Greenwich Guardian and one other. Horrified at the sight of them, she jumped backwards, tripped over a stool and crashed to the ground. She lay there like a statue in frozen silence, eyes wide open, hoping that she had not been heard.

'Did you hear that?' the Greenwich Guardian asked Wakaa.

He shook his head.

'I am certain I heard something.'

Wakaa stepped forward and knocked again, and this time both listened very carefully.

Ma Croe lay perfectly still.

'Maybe they are out,' the Greenwich Guardian said.

Wakaa nodded. 'We shall return after we have spoken with Pa Mossel.'

11

The Chase

Ma Croe lay on the floor for some time, not daring to move. Why had she not listened to Sofi? Had the poor girl not begged to be allowed to go home? She really had thought Sofi was playing a game, but who would believe that? And now the Greenwich Guardian had come to claim her granddaughter. Ma Croe wondered what sort of trouble she was in. She could be accused of kidnapping! At the very least she was guilty of keeping a child against her will.

Crawling to the window, she cautiously peered out, and struggled to her feet only after satisfying herself that the Guardians had gone. Wiping her brow with the back of her hand, she took a key off the hook and went downstairs.

Sofi's eyes were red. Ma Croe knew she had been crying.

'Don't take on so, dearie,' she said, crossing to the bed. Looking down, she immediately understood why Sofi's face was wet with tears. So desperate was her desire to escape that she had removed her shoe and tried to wriggle her foot out of the iron band. Ma Croe could only imagine how painful Sofi's repeated attempts at freedom must have been. The skin had been scraped off her heel, leaving it raw and bleeding.

'Oh, little one!' Ma Croe exclaimed, truly sorry to see her in such a plight. 'You shouldn't have done that.'

'I want to go home!' Sofi said defiantly.

'And so you shall,' Ma Croe comforted her.

'You's gonna let I go?' Sofi asked disbelievingly.

'I've got the key,' the old woman said, holding it up.

Sofi had never seen a key before.

Ma Croe sat down on the bed.

Sofi watched with nervous anticipation, ready to seize any chance of escape.

'We'll just take this off before sorting your poor little foot out,' Ma Croe smiled, 'and then I'll take you home.'

Sofi watched Ma Croe suspiciously, distrustful of every move.

The old woman hesitated, key poised, 'You will tell your grandmother that it was all a mistake, won't you? I thought you were playing a game. I didn't mean any harm.'

'Yer,' Sofi said. She would agree to anything if it would help her to get away.

The old woman slid the key into the lock.

Even in her state of anxiety Sofi found this interesting. Being old and rusty, it took a few moments before the key turned. The lock clicked. Ma Croe opened the band.

As soon as it fell from her ankle, Sofi ran. Grabbing her shoe, she jumped off the bed and bolted for the door.

Flinging it open, she dashed out of the cellar and up the steps.

'Oi!' shouted an angry voice.

Sofi had run, head first, into someone, her face buried in his midriff.

It was Sheldon.

'What's all this here?' he demanded.

Sofi tried to dodge around him, but the stairs were narrow. Grabbing her arm, he dragged her back inside the room.

'Sheldon!' his grandmother exclaimed in relief. 'Thank goodness you're here! You can take Sofi home.'

'Home?'

'The Greenwich Guardian came for her. She has to go home now!'

Neither Sofi nor Sheldon had expected this.

Sofi was elated. Tid had found the Hither House and people were out looking for her! She threw a triumphant look towards her captor.

Sheldon was as nervous as Sofi was delighted. If the Guardians had worked out what he was doing, he could be in serious trouble. If he did not want his plans to be ruined, he would have to get Sofi to the Underneath without delay.

'I'll take her home,' he lied to his grandmother.

'You're a good boy, Sheldon,' Ma Croe said lovingly. 'But she has hurt her poor little foot. Let me clean it up first. We don't want her grandmother seeing her like this.'

Sheldon looked down and smirked. The Wreccas

might be impressed if he presented her slightly damaged. It implied that he had treated her badly.

'Leave her be.'

'She can't go home like this,' Ma Croe tried to explain, bending down to Sofi's foot.

'I said, leave her be!' Sheldon snarled, roughly pushing his grandmother to the ground.

Ma Croe lay on the floor for the second time that evening, but this time it was not unexpected. 'Sorry, Sheldon dear,' she whimpered. 'I just thought ...' But Sofi did not have time to discover what she thought, for Sheldon dragged her up the steps, out through the door, into the night and away.

As he strode through the park, Sofi found it hard to keep up. 'Where's you taking I?' she asked. She did not believe they were going to the Greenwich Guardian.

Sheldon's only answer was to quicken his pace and tighten his grip.

'I's not going nerwhere 'til you say!' said Sofi, digging her heels firmly into the ground and trying to stop. This was difficult with only one shoe and a very painful foot. Sheldon, however, did not slow down. He just tightened his grip and pulled her harder.

'Let I go!' she shouted, trying to wrench her arm away.

With ease, Sheldon put his free arm around her waist and picked her up. Balancing her on his hip, horizontal to the ground, he continued walking without slackening his pace.

Sofi struggled to free herself. Wriggling this way and

that, she tried to loosen his hold. Wildly, she thrashed the air with her feet and clawed at Sheldon with her nails, lunging at his face, attempting to scratch his eyes, anything to force him to loosen his hold. His only reaction was to slap her hard. But Sofi was frantic now. With all her strength, she continued wrestling with him, using her knees to thump him on the back. Sheldon slapped her again but still Sofi did not stop. She tried to bite, fighting to find some part of him that she could sink her teeth into.

She was no match for Sheldon, but she was beginning to irritate him. He put his free hand in her hair and cruelly yanked at it. Sofi gasped in pain and immediately stopped struggling. Holding his large hand in her little ones, she tried to loosen his grip.

Realizing that struggling and demanding were getting her nowhere, Sofi tried a different tactic. 'Is us going to the Greenwich Guardian?' she asked sweetly.

'Shut up!'

'Tell where us is going and I'll walk proper.'

Sheldon said nothing and strode out of the park gates towards Blackheath. The Humans shut their gates at night, but the doors used by Wreccas and Guardians were never closed.

Sofi did not like leaving the comparative safety of the park. She liked even less the direction in which Sheldon was walking. It seemed to Sofi that he was making for one of the Underneath doors.

Her mind was working fast. She tried to gather the facts. The cellar had been constructed to look like the

Underneath. Sheldon was scruffy and dirty and liked to call himself Snarl. And now they were walking towards one of the Underneath doors. Sofi's stomach churned and her throat went dry.

It might have been that Sheldon was holding her too tightly round her waist, or it could have been the sickening realization that they were heading towards the place she feared most in all the world, but Sofi's stomach began to heave.

'Stop it!' Sheldon said, as Sofi's body went rigid with the effort of retching.

'I's going to be sick!' she moaned helplessly, before her stomach heaved and constricted and gave up the sandwiches and drink that Ma Croe had given her. Retching violently, Sofi vomited down Sheldon's leg and over one of his shoes. He jumped back in disgust, unexpectedly dropping her.

Sofi lay on the ground, limp from the effort of being sick.

'You revolting little brat!' Sheldon shouted, hopping on one foot, trying to shake off the vomit that clung to the other. 'You're gonna get it for this,' he fumed, distracted by his predicament.

Although Sofi's body ached from the retching, she did not hesitate. Scrambling to her feet, she darted back towards the park.

It was a few moments before Sheldon realized that she was making her escape. With a howl of rage, he set off after her. His long legs covered the ground at twice the speed of Sofi's and he gained on her with ease.

Sofi did not look back. She ran as quickly as her legs could carry her. If only she could make it to the park. There was cover there. She would be able to find somewhere to hide. Somewhere to rest. Her head was pounding. Her heart was thumping.

Sheldon knew he would catch her, and when he did he was going to give her such a wallop. He enjoyed being dirty like a Wrecca . . . but vomit! This was too much! He was enraged and disgusted. Just a couple more strides and he would have her.

Sofi did not look back. She guessed that he was gaining on her because she could hear his feet thudding on the ground close behind.

One more pace and he would catch her. She was within reach. He stretched out his hand.

Then suddenly, a tremendous noise assaulted their ears. It took both of them by surprise, but Sofi did not break her stride. She kept her feet speeding across the grass, heading for the gates.

A moment's hesitation caused Sheldon to miss as he lunged for her. His arms thrashed the air as he fought to regain his balance. He intended to continue the chase but then he quickly realized what the thundering sound was.

Heading straight for him was a very large black dog. There was a cruel ferocity about its thunderous bark. Strings of saliva flicked off the edges of its mouth. Its eyes were wild with the thrill of the hunt.

Sheldon's beady little eyes fixed on the dog. 'Nice dog,' he said, his long legs clumsily attempting to readjust to this new direction. He clutched at the side of his ribcage. He had a stitch. 'Good dog,' he murmured, trying to catch his breath, pressing his thumb into his side to try and lessen the pain. 'Good dog.'

The dog skidded to a halt, just short of Sheldon, and there it continued its barking onslaught. Tail erect, its body juddered every time a bark exploded from its slathering mouth.

Sheldon felt each bark vibrate through his entire body. He backed away, holding his other hand in front of him, trying to encourage the dog to keep its distance. 'Ssh! Good dog.'

The dog continued its noisy assault.

'What are you barking at, boy?' A middle-aged Human, out for a late-night walk, approached. His shirt buttons strained against the large stomach which bounced with each step. 'What did you see?'

The dog started snarling but, with its owner next to it, patting its muscular shoulder, its ferocity subsided.

The man looked straight through Sheldon. 'There's nothing there, Max. Stop being so daft. Come along.' Zipping up his coat, he began to walk away.

Sheldon stood still, holding his breath.

'Max!' the man called over his shoulder.

The dog fell silent and took a step towards Sheldon. A low growl reverberated in its throat.

'Max!' The man was getting angry now, and the dog knew it. With one last half-hearted bark in Sheldon's direction, it turned and followed its master.

*

Sofi made it through the gates and into the park but she did not stop and look for cover. The sound of the dog became fainter with every step and she knew someone else was the target of its fury. She hoped it was Sheldon. As long as she could hear the barking, she reasoned that he was being distracted. Thus, she could put as much distance as possible between herself and him. More than that, every step was bringing her closer to safety.

She did not know how much further Old Father Tim's house was. Nor did she notice the pain that stabbed the back of her leg each time her injured foot struck the hard path. Her heart was hammering. Her chest was hurting. Her head swam and her eyes were seeing only blurred images. Still she ran on. The barking was fading, or was it that something else was getting louder? The only sound she could hear now was her pulse throbbing in her ears. The only thought she had was Old Father Tim . . . Old Father Tim . . . Old Father . . .

Slowly her legs faltered. She was falling. Then everything went black.

Sheldon waited until the dog and his owner were at a safe distance before he set off once more towards the gates. He cursed the dog for the delay and Sofi for making her escape. He guessed she would make her way to Tid's house. He hoped that she had gone straight there. It would be easier to find her if she was not hiding. He knew he had lost time with the dog, but he was confident that he could still catch her before she reached the Mossel house.

His long legs quickly covered the ground and his vulture-like eyes scanned the area for his prey. Then he saw her. At first he was not sure who it was, so he slowed down just a little, to focus better.

Sofi had collapsed, her pale cheek pressed against the gravelled path. She was lying perfectly still.

With a cry of triumph, Sheldon quickened his step once more, only to stop suddenly and dive behind a tree. Someone was approaching. Sheldon peeped out, hoping that this intruder would not see Sofi.

Bryn Brownal was walking home. He and the other Elders had left Old Father Tim when the Greenwich Guardian and Wakaa had arrived. They could see there was important business to be discussed. Joss had stayed. He worked directly for the Greenwich Guardian and was allowed to sit in on such meetings. Bryn would like to have stayed too, but it was not his place. He would wait until the morning and then call on his sister to see if there was anything he could do to help. It was with a heavy step that he walked slowly home, deeply absorbed in the problem of the missing Tick.

His mind was not on his surroundings and he would have missed Sofi altogether, had he not nearly stepped on her. Stopping abruptly, he looked around but could see no one. Surely this young girl was not out so late on her own. He bent down. One of her shoes was missing and her foot was bleeding. He did not know who she was, but from her clothes he could tell that she was one of the Guardian People. Gently he pushed her hair from her face and saw dried blood on her cheek.

'Hello,' he said, hoping that she would respond to the sound of his voice.

She did not.

From behind the tree, Sheldon clenched his fists and ground his teeth in anger. What should he do? He squinted through the dark. He had recognized Bryn, or Pa Brownal as Guardian custom dictated that Sheldon should call him. Sheldon was forced to see him whenever he broke one of the park rules. He could not see the point of rules. What did it matter if he damaged a tree or hurt a squirrel? But Pa Brownal, like the others, thought these things were important, and when Sheldon was caught he was punished. However, Sheldon thought with satisfaction, he was getting quite good at not being caught these days.

As these thoughts passed through his mind, his dislike for Pa Brownal became overpowering. How good it would feel to knock him down. Sheldon thought that he could if he took him by surprise. Then he would grab Sofi and make good his escape. But Sheldon's hesitation had been fatal. By the time he had decided that this would be his best course of action, he heard another voice.

'Bryn?'

Two people were approaching. They too were returning from Old Father Tim's house. Usually they would have walked a different way home, but tonight they had taken the long way because they needed time to talk.

'What is it?'

'A young girl.'

The newcomers bent down to look at her.

Sheldon knew he was no match for three.

'Who is she?'

Bryn shook his head. 'I've never seen her before.'

'You don't think she's . . .'

Bryn finished the question, 'The girl Pa Mossel spoke of?' He nodded in answer, 'I think she may be.'

'Best take her back to the house.'

Helpless in his anger, Sheldon stood and watched the trio walking away with his prize.

12

Interview with the Enemy

'Where is her?' Old Killjoy demanded, his chin jutting out aggressively and his top lip twisting in a cruel sneer.

Scratch carefully stroked his nails on one hand with the fingertips on the other and looked nervously around at the other Wreccas, who were enjoying his discomfort.

'Him said him'll be here by now.'

'But him isn't!' Old Killjoy blasted.

'There must've been a setback,' Scratch explained, furious with himself for telling Old Killjoy about Sheldon before he had actually delivered the girl. Then he added in a whining voice, 'Very sorry about this, Killjoy. I'll send Sniff up to check it out.'

'You'll check it out yourself,' Old Killjoy said quietly, his words all the more menacing because this time he did not shout. He took a step towards Scratch. 'You'll go Topside and you'll find this Shendel Croe . . .'

'Sheldon,' Scratch corrected him and immediately regretted it. Old Killjoy was in no mood to be put right. Clenching his fist, he lashed out and hit Scratch full on the nose. Scratch stumbled backwards and fell against the rough wall.

'GET HIM NOW!' Old Killjoy roared.

For a fraction of a second everyone was silent. Then the chamber erupted with the sound of Wreccas making a quick exit. Every possible way out was crowded with bodies trying to remove themselves from the line of fire. A few moments later, Old Killjoy was alone, breathing heavily and feeling nothing but hatred for everyone and everything.

Scratch hid his bleeding nose as best he could from the gaze of the others and stomped along the tunnel, eager to be alone. His ego had been seriously dented. He silently vowed to be avenged for this humiliating treatment.

If Scratch had been thinking clearly, he would have realized that Old Killjoy had dealt with him leniently. The usual punishment for such a failure would have been the Ruckus. But Scratch was not thinking clearly. His mind was set on revenge, but Old Killjoy was too well protected as yet. For the moment, Scratch would have to content himself with punishing Sheldon Croe.

Old Father Tim held Sofi's cold, limp hand while the Greenwich Guardian tended her injured foot. As soon as Sofi had arrived, Joss had been sent to fetch Enderell, who would return with healing herbs.

Although unconscious, something of Old Father Tim's gentle words must have penetrated Sofi's fuddled brain. Sitting warm and comfortable in a chair and breathing quietly, Sofi began to recover. After a while her eyelids flickered.

'Sofi,' Old Father Tim said softly.

She opened her eyes. Of all the sights she could have beheld, Old Father Tim's kind old face was the most wonderful. She caught her breath in a shuddering sob and threw her arms around his neck. 'Grandfather!'

Old Father Tim took her in his arms and held her close. Sofi had never felt so safe.

Later that night, she was tucked up in the comfortable bed that had been made for her on the floor in Tid's room. They had been careful not to wake him. Sofi had asked if they could, not wanting Tid to worry about her a moment longer than he had to, but Old Father Tim said that he would not be worrying as he slept, and the first thing he would see when he awoke was Sofi. She accepted this and snuggled down. Her grazed cheek felt cool against the clean cotton pillowcase. A brightly coloured quilt covered her. She was warm. She was safe. But above all, she was happy.

Old Father Tim sat downstairs in front of the dying fire with the Greenwich Guardian and Wakaa and discussed all that Sofi had told them. Tightly gripping Old Father Tim's hand, she had explained how Sheldon had tried to take her to the Underneath. They had been horrified.

'Something must be done about that young man,' Wakaa was now saying.

'I shall take this matter up with the Elders,' the Greenwich Guardian assured him.

'Meanwhile,' Old Father Tim said, 'we still have the matter of the missing Tick.'

Amid the euphoria of Sofi's safe return, they had temporarily forgotten the more pressing subject.

'Sofi tells me that the Wreccas have no idea what will happen if the Tick is not restored in time for the ceremonies.'

'I never thought they did,' Wakaa said. Their lack of cleverness was well known.

'I was thinking that we should tell them.'

For all their wisdom, this simple solution was one that had never occurred to either Wakaa or the Greenwich Guardian, and it came as something of a revelation.

'Do you think they would listen?' Wakaa asked.

Old Father Tim ran his fingers through his short, thick beard. 'I have no notion, but we should try. What course of action have the Guardians settled upon?'

'It seems that the Middlers will have to be recalled.'

'No.' Old Father Tim spoke sharply. 'Forgive me, Old Father Wakaa,' he apologized, 'I realize it is no longer my place to say, but the Middlers must *not* be disturbed.'

'There is no other way,' the Greenwich Guardian said softly, laying her hand gently on Old Father Tim's arm. She had the utmost respect and affection for him.

'We should try telling the Wreccas,' Old Father Tim said stubbornly. 'Anything is better than recalling the Middlers. I shall go and speak to them myself.'

Wakaa nodded. Although he did not like the idea of confronting the Wreccas directly, every avenue had to be explored.

'Then I shall go as soon as we are finished.'

The Greenwich Guardian was deeply disturbed by

this, and worry lines were clearly visible on her forehead. 'It will not be safe.'

'It will be safe enough,' Old Father Tim assured her, confident that his magical powers would protect him.

'Do you think they will believe you?' Wakaa asked.

'We have to try.'

They all fell silent. Neither Wakaa nor the Greenwich Guardian knew what to say. It was Old Father Tim who finally broke the silence.

'What else has the Gathering decided upon?'

Wakaa and the Greenwich Guardian exchanged a brief look but said nothing. This worried Old Father Tim. Surely the Gathering had come up with something else.

'The Middlers are not the only solution that has been settled upon, are they?' he asked.

'We were going to talk to Sheldon,' the Greenwich Guardian said, trying to defend what looked like the ineffectiveness of the Gathering. 'But after all that Sofi has told us, there seems little chance that he will help.'

'There must be other plans,' Old Father Tim said. There had to be something they were not telling him. He looked questioningly at the Greenwich Guardian, and she gave her answer with a barely visible shake of her head.

'So,' Wakaa summed up, 'it is the Middlers or you. There is no other plan as yet, although Seegan did want to talk to me about something. I shall be meeting with him as soon as I leave here.'

A terrible feeling knotted deep in Old Father Tim's

stomach as he realized that the new leadership was not dealing effectively with this situation. The missing Tick was the most important issue in centuries. The Gathering should be humming with suggestions. The old man found himself regretting his offer to stand down as the Old Father. But he was a man who believed in rules. He was no longer the Old Father, and he would do nothing to change that without authorization from the Gathering.

'There may be another possibility,' he said quietly, his wise old eyes full of sorrow.

This was what the Greenwich Guardian and Wakaa had hoped to hear; it was the reason they had come. Recalling the Middlers and attacking the Underneath was not ideal. It could escalate into a terrifying war. It was well known that Wreccas fought like tigers.

Guardians were bred for thinking, not fighting. This is why they went away to become Middlers, so that they could learn the traditions of their people and become noble and wise.

When it was deemed necessary, there was the Harvest. This meant that many of the Guardian People who had reached a certain level of understanding would gather together and travel to a remote place. For many years they would live with the Sages. These were teachers who would lead the Middlers through an ancient course of learning. Whilst away, their children would live at home with their grandparents. After many years, the Middlers would return. With the wisdom they had gained, they would help in the task of protecting time for all peoples. By now, their own children would be grown up and married, with children of their own. It would now be the turn of the Middlers to become grandparents and bring up their grandchildren. This had been the practice for thousands of years. Never before had Middlers been disturbed before their time.

'What other way is there?' the Greenwich Guardian asked.

'We would need the strongest Guardian charms to bring the Middlers back in time,' Old Father Tim said, 'and even if they are recalled, how could we ask them to fight? Breaking their concentration. Bringing them back at speed. Asking them to betray their nature and fight. It is all too much. We would fail.'

The Greenwich Guardian and Wakaa believed he spoke the truth.

'And as for me talking to the Wreccas, well, we all know this is unlikely to succeed.' Old Father Tim paused and rubbed his chin. 'I think it may be necessary to have someone inside the Underneath.'

'Sheldon?' the Greenwich Guardian asked. 'I do not believe that the lad is committed to our cause.'

Old Father Tim was shaking his head. 'No. Not Sheldon. I was thinking of . . .' he paused, unwilling to say it. He desperately wished that there wam an alternative way, but he could think of none. He took a deep breath. 'I was thinking of Sofi.'

For a moment neither the Greenwich Guardian nor Wakaa spoke. Sofi? Both felt uneasy, but for different reasons. Wakaa was not sure he wanted to place so important a job in the hands of a Wrecca, however well intentioned she might be. The Greenwich Guardian, on the other hand, felt that Sofi was too young to undertake such a dangerous task.

'She knows where the Tick is and she understands how Wreccas think,' Old Father Tim explained. 'She, alone, could get into the Underneath undetected.'

Each thought of the options available to them. If only there was another way.

'I suppose we could ask her,' Wakaa said uncertainly. 'After all, we should try everything.'

Old Father Tim looked at the Greenwich Guardian. He knew what she was thinking. How could a man like Old Father Tim, who protected and cared for children, expect one so young to take on such a dreadful responsibility? Old Father Tim was wondering the same thing. He would have felt better if someone else had come up with the suggestion.

At first light, before the sun had risen, Old Father Tim stood, robes gently blowing in the breeze, by one of the Underneath doors. He was quietly muttering to himself, conjuring up powerful magic of protection. When he was ready, he stepped forward and rapped loudly on the door.

Scratch's pride hurt more than his nose. He cupped his hand over it to hide the damage from sniggering Wreccas. No one laughed in front of him – they would not have dared – but he knew that behind his back they were very much amused.

Quite by accident, Old Father Tim had chosen the door that Scratch was now approaching. He was on his way Topside to try and find Sheldon. There was nobody about. He looked around for the guard. Disorganized as Wreccas generally were, a Topside door was never left unguarded. When Scratch heard the knock he immediately lunged for the door and dragged it open, expecting to find Sheldon and the girl on the other side.

It was hard to tell who was the more surprised, Old Father Tim on the outside at the speed of the reply or Scratch on the inside, coming face to face with the person he feared most in all the world.

Scratch cowered in the doorway, too nervous to move. Old Father Tim stood majestically in front of him. A light wind gently moved his garments, giving a hint of a sparkle in the dim light.

'Good morning,' Old Father Tim said formally.

Scratch did not know what to do. His instinct was to run back inside and slam the door shut, but he was so shaken that he was powerless to move.

'I think you must be Scratch,' Old Father Tim said.

Scratch did not respond.

'And I believe you have something that belongs to us,' the old man continued.

Scratch assumed he was talking about the girl whom Sheldon Croe was bringing to them. He was very much relieved, thankful that Sheldon had not yet returned with her. All he had to do was tell the Old Father that they did not have her and he would go away.

'Ner.'

'I know that you do,' Old Father Tim said, as if talking to a naughty child. There was command in his voice and power in his eyes.

Scratch could not look him in the face. 'Us doesn't have nothing of yours!' he said, averting his eyes.

'I know that you do,' Old Father Tim repeated. 'And if it is not returned to us at once, it will be catastrophic for us all.'

Scratch did not know what 'catastrophic' meant.

'Not only disastrous for the Guardian People,' Old Father Tim continued, 'but also for you in the Underneath.'

Scratch knew a threat when he heard one. 'There's nothing you can do to hurt us down here,' he said, nervously looking down to make sure he had not stepped over the threshold and that he was still in the safety of the Underneath.

'If you do not return what is rightfully ours, it will be the end of everything, even for you in the Underneath.'

'Us doesn't have nothing!' Scratch shouted.

How he longed to lunge at the Old Father and drag him inside. How glorious it would be to get him into the Underneath, where he could be overpowered. On the Topside, things were difficult because the Old Father could use magic, but in the Underneath Scratch would have the upper hand. He stole a fearful look at Old Father Tim and it occurred to him that he might be able to trick the old man into entering the Underneath, but he would have to be sneaky. In a wheedling voice he tentatively suggested, 'You can step inside and talk it through.'

'Is this an admission?' Old Father Tim asked, hopeful that he was making a breakthrough.

'Us could talk about it in here,' Scratch whined, ignoring the long word.

'You know I shall come no further,' Old Father Tim said sternly. 'Do you take me for a fool?'

'Please yourself!' Scratch retorted and, stepping back, put his shoulder to the door and heaved it shut with a bang.

Old Father Tim was left standing alone in the half-light.

Scratch was shaking from head to toe. He had spoken to the enemy and got away with it. He leant against the door. Thoughts were buzzing through his mind. So, the Guardians had somehow found out what Sheldon was up to. He would not like to be in his shoes when they caught up with him.

Scratch played his nails across his cruel lips as he thought. He would not tell anyone about the interview. The fact that the Guardians had threatened them was interesting but it did not unduly worry Scratch. If the Wreccas stayed below ground, he knew they were safe.

Clearly, the Guardians had not yet found Sheldon Croe or they would know that the girl had not been delivered. They must be searching for him. Scratch would have to find him first. He would take Sniff with him to save time.

Scratch smiled an evil smile. Sheldon Croe was in trouble now.

13

Morning in the Park

Tid's feeling of guilt was so great that, before he was fully awake, this heavy burden filled his heart and mind. He could not forgive himself for leaving Sofi alone in Greenwich. He wondered how he could have slept when she must be so frightened.

With a deep sigh he opened his eyes. As they began to focus, so they grew bigger. Tid was staring in surprise at Sofi's bed. He shut his eyes for a moment and then reopened them, just to make sure. Without a doubt, there she was, peacefully sleeping in her made-up bed on the floor.

He wanted to wake her and find out how she had got there, but she was sleeping so peacefully, he did not think that he should. Treading lightly, Tid crept into his grandfather's bedroom.

Old Father Tim was scrunched down in a comfortable, threadbare armchair. His chin was resting on his chest and his breathing was slow and heavy. He too was asleep, but not for long. The movement of the door disturbed him and he opened his eyes as Tid entered.

'Sofi is asleep in my room!'

Old Father Tim put his finger to his lips and nodded. 'She was brought back to us last night,' he explained in a whisper.

Propping himself on the arm of Old Father Tim's enormous, old, comfy chair, Tid listened, wide-eyed, as Sofi's story was told.

It was not long before Sofi herself awoke to the sound of their whispering. Rubbing her sleepy eyes, she wandered in the direction of the voices. At Old Father Tim's invitation, she shyly sat on the other arm of the chair. However, she could not remain shy for long and was soon proudly showing Tid the bandage that the Greenwich Guardian had put around her injured foot.

'Was it that lack-of-oxygen thing that made her faint?' Tid asked.

'I suspect so.'

'Is she going to keep on doing it every time she runs?'

'No. Sofi's lungs will be adapting all the time. She will soon be like you and me.'

This comment pleased Sofi more than either Tid or his grandfather could possibly have imagined. The thought of being like one of the Guardian People filled her with delight.

In due course, a wonderful aroma drifted through the open door. Tid looked questioningly at his grandfather.

'That is Enderell,' Old Father Tim explained. 'She stayed with you two last night while I went out for a while.' He sniffed the air. 'And if I am not mistaken, there is bacon for breakfast.'

With a whoop of delight, Tid and Sofi tumbled down

the stairs. Sofi did not know what bacon tasted like, but the delicious smell and Tid's reaction were good enough recommendations.

Happily they sat around the table and eagerly swallowed bacon and pancakes topped with a delicious syrup that was Enderell's own invention. Old Father Tim joined them and poured himself and Enderell a cup of tea. Sofi positively glowed with happiness.

It was when the breakfast was nearly finished that Tid remembered something. His expression turned serious and he said, 'We still have the problem of the missing Tick, don't we, Grandfather?'

Old Father Tim nodded.

'Have the Guardians decided what they are going to do?' Sofi asked.

Old Father Tim looked at his tea before turning his eyes upon the eager young faces before him. 'They have.'

From his manner, Tid immediately understood that his grandfather had something difficult to say. Even Sofi realized that something was wrong.

'As you may imagine, there has been a great deal of talk,' Old Father Tim began, 'and many plans have been discussed and even tried, but,' he combed his fingers through his beard, 'the Guardians believe that the best way to restore the Tick is for someone to go into the Underneath and bring it back.'

Tid nodded. It seemed logical.

'No one'll get in without being finded out,' Sofi said.

'A Guardian could,' Tid corrected her. 'They can do anything.'

'Ner,' Sofi contradicted him. 'You see, they'll smell a Guardian.'

'Guardians don't smell!' Tid said, more than a little offended.

'They does to a Wrecca.'

Tid looked at her disbelievingly and she nodded to confirm that it was true.

Old Father Tim spoke again. 'Someone will have to go into the Underneath, locate the Tick and, hopefully, bring it out.'

'He would have to be very brave,' Tid said, 'whoever he is. If he can't sneak in, then he would have to fight and the Wreccas are good at that sort of thing.' He looked puzzled. 'Do we have a Guardian who could fight?'

Old Father Tim shook his head.

A flicker of fear stirred behind Sofi's eyes. 'Who'll go?'

Old Father Tim took her hand. 'Will you believe me when I tell you there is no one else?'

Sofi withdrew her hand.

Tid's mouth dropped open in astonishment. 'You don't mean Sofi!'

Old Father Tim said nothing, and Tid knew that he did.

'I can't,' she said uneasily. 'I's like to help,' her voice faltered, 'but I can't.'

Old Father Tim nodded. 'We understand.'

Sofi sat in silence. She had been in this position before, when Scratch had decided she should go Topside and put into motion the events that would eventually lead to the Tick being stolen. She had been reluctant at first, but she had gone all the same. She looked up at Old Father Tim. He was not bullying her. He was not threatening her. She was not frightened of him. Something in her heart told her that she was not being fair. After all, it was her fault the Tick had been stolen. Should she now refuse to put things right, just because Old Father Tim was decent, kind and honest?

Slowly, a chill gripped her heart as she began to accept the truth of what she was going to do. Her new-found conscience would not allow her a choice. She would return to the Underneath.

Sheldon had spent the night in deep thought. Now, he sat under a tree, staring into thin air. The grass where he was sitting was damp, but he did not notice, even though the moisture had soaked through his trousers. He was trying to work out the possibilities that were open to him. As he saw it, he had three options. He could go to the Underneath, explain that he had lost Sofi and promise to try to do better next time. However, he did not think that Old Killjoy would receive this news kindly.

The second option was to stay as he was, go home to his grandmother and wait. He did not know why Sofi had collapsed but he reasoned it had more to do with exhaustion than anything more serious. It was reasonable to assume that she had recovered by now and would have told the Guardians everything that had happened. It would not be long before they came looking for him.

Sheldon had been in trouble many times before.

When very young he had often been hauled in front of Bryn Brownal and lectured. After a time, it was deemed that he was too far out of control for Bryn and they would take him to see Old Father Tim instead. Sheldon hated these interviews. Old Father Tim had a way of making him feel terrible. It was not so much what he said as the way that he said it. Sheldon shuddered. No, he would not go through that again – and it suddenly dawned on him that what he had done to Sofi was far beyond local disapproval. Perhaps it would be Improvement School this time. He had no idea what that would be like, and he had no intention of finding out.

These thoughts made the third option seem the most attractive. He would leave Greenwich and start a new life somewhere else. This might have been easier if he could have gone home first and collected a few things, but it was not worth the risk.

He quite liked Greenwich and, now he had decided to leave, he was sorry. However, the world was a big place and he would look upon this as an adventure, something to tell his grandchildren.

Standing up, he thrust his hands deep into his pockets and started walking. Sheldon had never felt like one of the Guardian People. He remembered with shame the day the other children had watched their parents begin the journey that would take them across the world to become Middlers. Tears overflowed the eyes of the young, but their chests swelled with pride as they stood at the docks and waved goodbye. Sheldon would have done anything to be one of them, to be able to watch his own parents departing with the rest. But they had not been chosen for the Harvest.

Sheldon's father had never been one for book learning or school, preferring to doze in front of the fire. As the day of the Harvest approached, Sheldon remembered his father going to the door each morning to see if his Harvest registration papers had arrived. Day after day he would sit at breakfast and say, 'They'll be here tomorrow, you see if they're not!' Eventually, he slouched at the untidy table and grumpily demanded, 'Tea, woman!' No wonder Sheldon's mother had disappeared soon afterwards.

Mother. Sheldon felt that familiar, painful longing as he remembered her face. What had happened to her? Sheldon's father had never explained where she might have gone, and the boy knew better than to ask, having felt the back of his father's hand too many times before. He could not even remember if there had been an argument. The shouting and crying was an everyday event. It was normal to him. But one morning she had not been there and he had never seen her since.

He noticed the whisperings at school.

'Have you heard?' a freckly, pigtailed girl called Pippa asked her playmate. 'His mother ran away! She couldn't stand being with smelly Sheldon a minute longer!'

'Well, my cousin says his father bashed her on the head with a spade! Then buried her in the garden!' offered an excited boy.

Sheldon had never seen his father work in the garden, in fact he was sure they didn't even own a spade, but where was his mother and why hadn't she said goodbye?

He wondered what might have happened if she had stayed. Maybe everything would have turned out better. Maybe his father would have had a second chance at the Harvest.

Some people seemed to get over the shame of not being Harvested. Sheldon's grandmother had got over it and continued with her life, but his father had not. He had watched many of his generation leave on the ship and then decided that he too would go away.

'I'm off, boy,' he had said. 'I'm going to make my fortune and when I return I will build the grandest house anyone has ever seen and they will all realize how wrong they were about me. "Never amount to anything." That is what they say. Well, I'll show them!'

'Take me with you,' Sheldon pleaded, dreading the thought of staying alone with his humiliation.

His father gave him an appraising look and, for one glorious moment, Sheldon thought he was going to agree. But then he gave a derisory laugh and said, 'I don't want a dead weight around my neck.'

'But I could help you.'

The only answer Sheldon received was a clip around the ear. The next morning he had woken up to discover that his father had left during the night, without a proper word of farewell.

For many years Sheldon had dreamed of his father returning a rich and important man, but after years of waiting he had given up. Obviously his father was having too good a time to remember his son.

As he walked through the park, he swallowed the pain of rejection that had lingered, without decreasing, since his father had left. But he was used to burying it now.

With a little nod of decision, he worked out what he would do. He would seek his fortune, like his father, in some far-off land. There would be one difference, though. Sheldon would return. One day, when he was rich, he would come back to Greenwich and sneer at Tid and all the others. He would show them how foolish it was to go seeking wisdom when fortune and glory were far more important.

Feeling a little brighter, Sheldon quickened his step.

'Where's you going?'

The voice came out of nowhere, and he nervously looked around. Sniff was leaning against a tree, picking his nose.

'I-I was coming to the Underneath,' Sheldon lied.

'You's walking the wrong way.'

This was someone else speaking. Sheldon spun round and came face to face with Scratch.

'Oh, Pa Scratch,' he said, bowing, but not too low. He did not want to take his eyes off either of these two. 'I've been looking for you.'

'It seems you's looked in all the wrong places,' Scratch said, not bothering to hide his contempt.

'I-I-I've run into a little problem,' Sheldon stammered.

Scratch's mouth twisted into an evil smile. 'Really?'

'Yes.' Sheldon looked about him, wondering if it would be worth his while to try and run for it. Sniff seemed to understand his intentions and hovered menacingly.

Sheldon swallowed, 'I-I can't bring the girl to you at this exact moment.'

'Why?'

Sheldon's brain desperately tried to think of a reason, but none came to him. He finally blurted out, 'Because I've lost her!'

Scratch leant forward and grabbed Sheldon viciously by the ear. 'Lost her, has you?'

Sheldon tried to speak, but his mouth had gone dry and he could not utter a syllable. Instead he attempted a nod, but Scratch was holding him too tightly to allow his head to move without considerable pain.

If only Sheldon had paid attention at school or if he had been thinking clearly, he would have realized that all he had to do was take courage and remember the Guardian charm. Most boys of his age no longer needed the protection charm, but Sheldon was weak-minded and still did. Unfortunately, he was too alarmed to think logically. He offered no resistance as Sniff and Scratch frog-marched him away.

14

Preparing to Leave the Park

Much of the day was spent in discussion. The Greenwich Guardian and Wakaa came back to Old Father Tim's house to talk through Sofi's return to the Underneath. No one doubted that this was a dangerous course of action.

'You've been here for ages,' Tid said to her. 'Won't the Wreccas be angry with you?'

'I doesn't have no friends down there,' she said without a trace of self-pity. 'They pretty much ignore I. There's a good chance they'll never know I was gone.'

Her initial task would be to find the Tick. If she was correct and it was in the safe chamber, this would not be a problem. Once located, she would have to take it Topside. That would be the tricky part.

'Sofi will need someone to help her,' Old Father Tim said. 'She cannot carry it on her own. It is far too cumbersome.'

'I'll do it,' Tid offered loyally.

Sofi was grateful for the thought, but she had to refuse. 'The Wreccas'll smell you,' she told him.

'Not if I made myself all dirty,' Tid persevered.

'It wouldn't work,' the Greenwich Guardian said, 'any more than giving Sofi a bath works for long. After weeks of regular bathing, Sofi will smell like one of us, but until then she will have to have two baths a day.'

Sofi stared at the ground. It was embarrassing to be talked about like this, but she acknowledged the truth of it. They all fell silent once more as they tried to think of a solution.

'Perhaps this Sheldon Croe could help,' Wakaa suggested.

'I do not trust him,' the Greenwich Guardian replied, 'and anyway, he cannot be found. Bryn has been waiting at his house since early this morning. He has not returned.'

'Is there any other Wrecca who might assist you, Sofi?' Wakaa persisted. 'Someone who is as unhappy in the Underneath as you were?'

Sofi shook her head, 'I doesn't know. I think I was the only one who hated it.' Then she remembered. 'There was a boy, but ...' she hesitated, '... ner, I doesn't think him'll help. Even if him's unhappy, him'll be too scared.'

Just when they thought there was no solution, Tid drew in his breath sharply as an idea occurred to him. 'What about the Bushytails?'

'They're too small,' the Greenwich Guardian said.

'But they are strong, and they wouldn't smell like us.' Tid looked hopefully at his grandfather. 'Would they?'

'I do not think so,' Old Father Tim replied.

'But they are not big enough,' the Greenwich Guardian persisted.

'It might work,' Old Father Tim said. 'They have extraordinary tails. One of them might be able to balance one side of the Tick if Sofi was to hold the other.'

The Greenwich Guardian was not convinced. 'It will not be easy.'

'Nothing about this is easy,' Old Father Tim muttered. 'But it might just be possible.'

Thus it was that Cob Bushytail was found and told about their problem. Without hesitation, he volunteered to help and even demonstrated with pride just how strong his tail was and how much he could balance upon it. A box of the correct proportions was found, and he and Sofi walked up and down, practising the best way of manoeuvring it.

Enderell groped around at the bottom of the dustbin for Sofi's old clothes. Wrinkling up her nose in disgust, Sofi put them on. She tried to make her hair look scruffy by ruffling it with her hand but it did not look untidy enough. Enderell helped by putting some foul-smelling lotion on it that made it go all clumpy. Between them, they made it look a real mess. Sofi had not had a bath for a while and so her Wrecca aroma was returning. Reluctantly, she removed the bandage that the Greenwich Guardian had so gently bound around her foot. Such a wrapping would have given her away at once. The heel stung as the bandage was peeled off and Sofi had to bite her lip to prevent herself from crying out.

Late into the afternoon, she stood forlornly in front of the mirror. When Tid had first stood her in front of it the day before, it had been something of a revelation. Dressed as she was in her Guardian clothes, she had stared at her reflection with delight. Now she looked in dismay. Sofi was no longer visible. It was Snot who was staring back at her.

At dusk they walked in silence to the gates by Blackheath. No one spoke. Each had their own thoughts and their own doubts. Tid looked up at the worried adult faces. His grandfather looked older than usual.

When they drew near the park gates, Sofi's step faltered as her courage began to fail her. Old Father Tim noticed and tried to encourage her. 'This is a very brave thing you are doing, Sofi. We thank you.'

She wanted to tell him that she was not being brave. If she was brave, her heart would not be hammering and her hands would not be trembling. It was hard to understand why Old Father Tim was being so nice to her. This was all her fault! They should all be reproaching her for what she had done; she wondered, not for the first time, how strange these Guardian People were. They seemed to forgive when forgiving was not deserved and they thanked when they should blame.

Old Father Tim took both of Sofi's hands in his. Bending down, he knelt before her so that his loving eyes were looking straight into hers. 'Sofi,' he said. 'We, the Guardian People, shall be forever grateful for the courage of a young girl.'

Sofi could bear it no more and tears welled up in her

eyes. She ran a dirty sleeve across her face to prevent them from falling. 'But this is all my f-fault,' she stammered, 'If . . . if I hadn't lied to Tid . . .' but her sobs prevented her from finishing her confession.

'Sofi . . . Sofi . . .' said Old Father Tim soothingly. 'When you did those bad things you were someone else, you were a Wrecca. Now you are transformed. You are Sofi, and Sofi is a good friend of the Guardian People. You cannot be blamed for the things you did as a Wrecca, but you can be thanked for trying to put them right.'

He smiled a smile that was so full of love Sofi felt warmth running through her whole body. She stopped crying and put both her arms around his neck and gave him a hug. Old Father Tim could feel her trembling. He spoke softly into her ear so that only she could hear. 'What else troubles you, my dear?'

Sofi pulled back from him so that she could see his face. She did have one overwhelming fear and it was hard to put it into words. For a moment she said nothing, but Old Father Tim encouraged her with a smile.

'I's scared,' she began, 'that when I's in the Underneath, I'll be discovered.'

Old Father Tim knew she was not telling him her greatest fear. He put his hands on her shoulders and said, 'No, my dear. There is something more.'

'How does you know?'

'I may not be a Guardian any more, Sofi, but I can still see into your heart. What else frightens you?'

This time Sofi spoke so quietly that he had to lean

towards her to hear her words. 'I's frightened that I's not brave enough,' she said. 'That when I's back in the Underneath, I'll be too scared to bring the Tick out.' She drew in a shuddering breath. 'I'll be too scared to leave.' She paused. The next part was difficult to say but she felt it passionately. 'If I doesn't leave, I'll always be a Wrecca. I want to be one of the Guardian People. I want to be clean and happy. I want to go to school and be Tid's friend. But most of all I want to . . .' tears trickled down her face, '. . . I want to be loved.'

Old Father Tim smiled. His big heart was overflowing with compassion. 'You will have the courage to complete your task, young Sofi. I know this because I can see courage in your heart. But – and this is even more important – while you are away we shall be Mindful of you.'

'Like you and Tid when us goed to the Hither House?' she asked.

'Yes. We will hold you in our minds all the time you are away. When you are frightened or do not know what to do, you must be Mindful of us. That means you must hold us in your mind so that our strength and wisdom can flow into you.'

'Can it?' Sofi asked. 'Can it help, even though I doesn't belong here?'

'You do belong here, because we love you.'

Sofi's jaw dropped. Had she heard him correctly? Happiness welled within her that she dared not feel.

'And what is more,' Old Father Tim continued, 'you love us.'

'Does I?' asked Sofi hopefully. 'I's never loved before, I doesn't know how.'

'That is the wonderful thing about love. No one knows how.'

'You know how. You know everything!'

'I do not know everything,' Old Father Tim chuckled, 'and I do not know *how* to love. Loving is something we just do. I love Tid. He is the dearest grandson an old man could ever have. However,' he paused momentarily, 'I always wanted a granddaughter. Will you be my granddaughter, young Sofi? Will you have me as your old grandfather?'

To be part of a loving family was beyond Sofi's wildest dreams. All her fear and worry about the future dissolved in a moment as she allowed the ecstasy of belonging to flow through her. Slowly and very seriously she nodded her answer and, touching her fingers to her lips, she reached out and placed them on Old Father Tim's mouth.

The Greenwich Guardian was deeply moved as she watched this tender scene. She would like to have given them more time, but it was getting late.

'The Bushytails are coming.' Wakaa had seen them first.

Sofi stepped back and wiped her face once more on her dirty sleeve, smearing the grime on her cheek that she had so carefully put there such a short time before. 'I's ready,' she said with a sniff. She smiled at Tid.

'I wish I was coming with you,' he said.

'It's better this way,' she replied.

Tid wanted to tell her to be brave and yet cautious. He wanted to explain how much he respected her for this daring act of selfless courage, but words seemed inadequate. Instead, he stepped forward and kissed her lightly on the cheek.

Sofi had never been kissed before, and she found herself touching her cheek with her fingertips, as though trying to feel the kiss that might be lingering there.

'Now,' Wakaa said, 'would you like us to come across Blackheath with you?'

She shook her head. 'It's safer for us to go alone.' She turned as if to leave, but immediately turned back and looked at Tid and his grandfather. 'I'll be Mindful of you.'

Old Father Tim smiled. 'And we shall be Mindful of you, Sofi.'

With a brave smile, Sofi turned and, together with the Bushytails, walked out of the gates. Cob and his friends were not scampering around as usual, they were too nervous about what lay ahead.

Old Father Tim felt terrible, allowing them to walk away. He wished that there was another way. Sending a child into such a dangerous situation went against all he believed about protecting and cherishing children. He could only imagine the dangers she would be facing below ground. If only he could think of another way. But he could not.

They all stood and watched until Sofi and the Bushytails were out of sight.

'Did I hear her say she would be Mindful?' Wakaa

asked Old Father Tim when they were out of sight.

'You did.'

'She is not one of the Guardian People,' Wakaa rebuked him. 'How can she be Mindful?'

'We can be Mindful of her.'

'But what good will it do?' asked the Greenwich Guardian. 'We Guardians are one body, that is how we can be Mindful. Sofi is not one of us.'

Much to his surprise, Tid found himself speaking. He raised his face to this noble Guardian and said, 'Sofi may not be one of us yet, but she wants to be. Surely that is enough.'

'I do not think it is that simple,' Wakaa said sternly but not unkindly.

'It may not be that simple,' said Tid, boldly standing his ground. 'But I shall be Mindful of Sofi. I shall be Mindful of her for as long as she needs me. She might be closer to being one of us than you think and, although I am young and not very good at it yet, I shall do the best I can all the time she needs me.'

Old Father Tim heard Tid's words with pride. Stepping towards him, he stood close at Tid's side so that he should know how much he supported him.

The Guardians looked in astonishment at the words of this courageous young boy. It was Wakaa who eventually spoke, not to Tid but to his grandfather. 'You have taught your grandson well.' Then he said to Tid, 'You shame us, young Tid Mossel. Come, let us make our way to your home, and together we shall be Mindful of Sofi until this matter is resolved, one way or the other.'

Tid nodded and together they turned and started walking back. He was glad they were going to help, but he was very aware that Wakaa had said that they would be Mindful 'until this matter is resolved, one way or the other'. He would have been happier if Wakaa had said 'until she returns'.

It was at that moment that a chilling thought occurred to him: he might never see Sofi again.

As Sofi walked, she tried to be Mindful. At first she found that she could easily hold Old Father Tim in her mind, but the further away she went, the more difficult it became. He was getting blurred in her memory already.

She looked around Blackheath. There were a few Humans about, but she took no notice of them. She kept walking. Confused thoughts whirled around her head. It was difficult to believe that, after so much effort to prevent Sheldon taking her to the Underneath, she was now voluntarily going back there.

The thought of the Underneath brought dark shadows to her mind. She slackened her pace. This was terrifying. Going back to the dreary misery of her former home was bad enough – but what if they knew she had been away? If they had noticed her absence, her homecoming might be very risky. She had made light of the possibility to Tid and the others, but it was a possibility which filled her with dread.

Her steps became more and more hesitant. Cob noticed that she was beginning to trail behind. He slowed his pace and looked back. Sofi had almost stopped.

'Are you all right, Miss Sofi?'

She looked up, not quite sure what he had said.

Cob repeated it.

'Yer,' she said quickly. Not feeling it to be at all true.

Cob waited for her to catch up with him. Instead, she stayed where she was.

'We do not have much time,' he said.

Sofi nodded but still did not move.

Cob gave a despairing look at his companions.

'Miss Sofi.' He spoke tentatively, walking back to her. 'I am fearful too.' Even in the gloom, he could see the anxiety in her eyes and added, 'We all are, but the price of not proceeding is too high.'

Cob tended to speak in a strange manner that was unnatural to Sofi, but she understood his meaning and she knew he was right. No matter how terrible the reception that awaited her, not to try would be worse. There could be nothing more dreadful than the end of everything.

She managed a weak smile. 'Sorry,' she mumbled.

'Nothing to be sorry about.'

They started walking again. Sofi kept the pace brisk. She swung her arms at her sides, feeling that if she walked in a confident manner she might actually feel some of that confidence.

Although her Guardian friends had tried to help her prepare for what was to come, there was very little they could actually do. The reality was that they did not understand Wreccas. Sofi understood them all too well. She knew, as the Guardians could not, how disorganized and haphazard they were. There was no point in making a plan and trying to stick to it. Situations could change fast below ground, with Old Killjoy wanting one thing, Scratch another, Sniff trying to look clever, and the rest of the Wreccas blundering around, not too aware of anything. Her plan had to be simple and adaptable.

To return unnoticed was her first task. It would be difficult enough to sneak in alone, but to try and smuggle in a Bushytail as well would be far more difficult. She told herself there would be no advantage in having them there initially. She could not use them until she had established where the Tick was and how it was guarded.

The best thing would be to hide them near the entrance. She would go in alone, assess the situation and find a way of tricking the Wreccas into abandoning their prize. If she could make them leave the Tick unguarded for just a short time, she would call upon Cob to help her carry it away. The Topside door was not far from the safe chamber. The other two Bushytails would stay outside and help them once they were above ground again.

It wasn't much of a plan, but it was all she had. She had always considered the Wreccas not very bright but, listening to Tid talking about them, she had begun to understand just how slow their mental processes were. She felt that if she was lucky, it should not be too hard to outwit them. Trying to outmanoeuvre them physically would be more difficult. Being so young, if it came to a chase they would catch her for sure.

Sofi's steps began to falter once more.

'Miss Sofi.' Cob was concerned. 'Are you not well?'

'I's fine,' she said, but he did not believe her. He could see she was trying to make light of the turmoil she was feeling. 'I was just getting nervous,' she said. 'I's never been a leader before.'

'I understand,' Cob said gently. 'Do not concern yourself, we shall succeed.'

'Yer,' she said, hoping that if she agreed out loud, then she would begin to believe it.

They were nearing the lower Topside door. Sofi took them into the shadows not far from it. They stood and awaited her instructions.

'I's going in alone.'

'No!' Cob said, more sharply than he intended.

'Yer, I has to be secret. I can't risk you being seed.'

Cob did not like this, but he saw the logic of her argument.

'You wait here,' she told them. 'The Topside door is over there, in that messy bit.' She pointed to a dirty puddle, beyond which was a pile of mud and rubble. Hidden within the pile was a heavy door. 'When I need you, I'll come out of that door and call. I ought to whistle,' she added apologetically, 'but I can't.' Then she added, remembering Tid's comment about whistling, 'Girls isn't too good at that sort of thing.'

'Nonsense!' Hazel said forcibly. The irritation in her voice surprised Sofi. 'Girls are just as good as boys.'

'Hazel!' Cob reproved her. He did not think she should argue, but Sofi laughed and it felt good.

'Ner, Cob, she's right. I just forgetted for a bit, that's

all. Thanks, Hazel. Girls is definitely as good as boys.'

'Better in some respects,' Hazel said with a wink.

Sofi beamed. 'Yer.' She felt much better.

'We shall post a guard, Miss Sofi,' Cob said, sounding very organized, 'and watch that door until you return.'

'How much time has us got?' Sofi asked.

Cob looked at the sky. He could only tell the time vaguely. 'The rest of this night, all the next day and into the following night. Is it time enough?'

'It has to be.' And then she drew in a deep breath and said, 'Good luck, everybody.'

They smiled encouragingly at each other, but Sofi did not move. There was something she needed to say. 'If I doesn't return, go back to the park before the ... you know, before the end. Tell Old Father Tim that I done my best.'

'Do not speak like this,' said Cob. 'We shall succeed.'

Sofi gave a small nod and hoped he was right.

15

At the Foot of the Throne

It was not exactly the grand entry into the Underneath that Sheldon had fantasized about for so long. In his imagination, Wreccas lined the tunnel and cheered as he strutted past with his head held high. Sofi was to have been tucked under his arm. He had imagined Old Killjoy waiting with a smile of respect on his face. Sheldon had planned to drop Sofi at his feet with a flourish, and then the crowd were to have cheered even louder. At length Old Killjoy was supposed to hold up a hand and silence them. He would then pin a medal on Sheldon's chest, before welcoming him into the Underneath and giving him a golden chair next to his own glittering throne.

Alas, the actual scene was altogether different. Scratch was dragging Sheldon by the ear and Sniff was following behind, kicking him viciously. A crowd of Wreccas had gathered, but they were jeering, not cheering. No Wrecca had ever before witnessed one of the Guardian People being dragged into the Underneath before. This was legendary and everyone had gathered to enjoy it.

Old Killjoy was sitting on his throne of smelly rags, scratching his bottom. He looked up as Sheldon was unceremoniously dumped at his feet. The chamber became ominously quiet as Wreccas shuffled about, each trying to get a good view of the proceedings. Everyone was waiting for Old Killjoy's reaction.

'Is this him?' he asked, knowing that it must be.

'Yer.'

'Well, where's her, then?' Old Killjoy demanded.

Sheldon tried to speak, but no words came. He looked about him. His breathing was shallow and fast. Wreccas were sneering at him and some were making rude signs with their hands. Sweat beaded Sheldon's forehead. He looked back at Old Killjoy and tried to moisten his lips with his dry tongue.

'I . . .' His voice came this time, but it was hoarse and croaking. '. . . I was foiled by a conspiracy.'

'A what?' Old Killjoy asked. He leant forward, not understanding.

Sheldon thought that Old Killjoy was showing a morsel of interest. If only he could keep his attention, it might buy him some time. 'They're planning something,' he said hurriedly. Then he added, for good measure, 'Something big.'

Old Killjoy cast a questioning look at Scratch.

'Him's making it up!' Sniff said derisively. 'Deliver him up to the Ruckus.'

Old Killjoy smiled at the thought of a Ruckus and as he did so a tremor of a thrill flickered through the assembled Wreccas.

'I'm not making it up!' Sheldon cried. 'And what is more, I can prove it!'

These were bold words. Sheldon was playing for time. He did not have a whisper of an idea how to continue.

Sniff suspected Sheldon was trying to postpone the inevitable Ruckus. 'Then prove it,' he said with a sneer.

'They're doing a house search,' Sheldon said, having no idea where he was going with this statement but knowing he had to keep talking. 'That's how they found the girl and rescued her.'

'Go on,' Scratch said suspiciously.

'It doesn't prove anything,' sneered Sniff.

'Yes it does,' Sheldon said, desperately trying to keep their attention. 'Guardians always do a house search to prepare the ground for a . . . a . . .' He had to say something! Panic was rising within him. Suddenly, he had an inspiration. 'An invasion!'

'A what?' Scratch demanded.

Sheldon's mind was working overtime. He had to come up with something good and he had to come up with it now.

'An army!'

Sniff burst out laughing. 'Guardians fighting? What a bin load of rubbish! Guardians can't fight.'

Amusement spread throughout the watching Wreccas, some even laughed out loud. Old Killjoy silenced them with a frosty look. He liked to dictate their reaction. Sniff was stealing the limelight and needed to be put in his place. He stole another look at Scratch, who appeared to believe this gangly youth.

'Where's they going to get an army from?' Scratch asked.

Sheldon was shaking almost uncontrollably now. He desperately searched his mind for a plausible explanation. Suddenly he remembered what he had been thinking about before Sniff and Scratch found him.

'My father left Greenwich ten years ago. His mission was to gather an army.' He could see that he had everyone's attention. 'People said that he had not been called for the Harvest, but they were wrong. His was a secret mission, the most important mission of all.' Sheldon warmed to his story. 'Instead of going with the Middlers to become wise, my father was going to train them to fight.' He watched Old Killjoy carefully, but he could not tell if what he was saying was being believed. 'He is going to return at the head of the fiercest army this land has ever seen. I came as soon as I heard, to warn you.'

Old Killjoy said nothing.

Sheldon stole a look towards Sniff. He was no longer sneering. This was Sheldon's moment. He took a deep breath and then dramatically he announced, 'They are going to attack the Underneath!'

Sofi cautiously peeped into the Underneath. The door had opened surprisingly easily; inside, Sick was lying on the steps, picking his nose. He was taking no notice of the door he was meant to be guarding. In reality, he resented having to do guard duty when important events were taking place in the main chamber.

With care, Sofi crept in and pushed the door shut behind her before tiptoeing down the steps.

'Here!' shouted Sick, as soon as he saw her. 'Where's you been?'

'Nowhere!' answered Sofi, with a pout.

'You's been Topside,' said Sick aggressively. 'You wait 'til I tell Scratch.' Then he added with a cruel laugh, 'You'll be for it!'

'You tell him whatever you want,' she said, trying to sound as if she really did not care one way or the other, 'and I'll tell him you's so busy picking your nose that you didn't even see the door open.'

Sick's face turned an even paler shade of green.

'And you know what happened the last time you failed on duty!'

'I knowed you comed in,' said Sick defensively. 'I seed you.'

'Fine,' said Sofi, looking unconcerned, 'then you'll be just fine . . . as long as Scratch believes you.'

Sick bit his lip nervously. He liked getting others into trouble but did not like being punished himself. He knew that if he was caught again it would be the Ruckus for sure.

'All right, snotty-Snot, I'll let you off, just this once. But if I catch you Topside again, then I'll tell Old Killjoy himself!'

'I didn't go Topside,' Sofi lied. 'I was just testing you.' And she walked away, trying to look more confident than she felt.

The smell of the Underneath did not seem as bad as Sofi had thought it was going to be and, although this was a relief, it also made her realize that she was still very much a Wrecca. She guessed that the smell would have been unbearable to Tid.

She was not worried about Sick. He had behaved as she might have predicted. It was reassuring that he did not appear to have noticed her prolonged absence. She hoped it would be the same with the others.

The Underneath seemed deserted, and for a moment she wondered where everyone was. Then she heard familiar noises. There was much shouting and debating from the main chamber. Hesitantly, she made her way towards it, drawn by the sounds from within. Would anyone realize that she had been missing? Her heart was thumping noisily. She desperately wanted to run away but she knew she could not. She had to behave normally. It was vital that no one noticed anything different about her. The trouble was, she did not know how to behave normally because when she was being normal she did not think about how she was behaving.

'Snot'll do it!' came a shout. Sofi was immediately startled back to reality. It did not look as though anything had changed. No one seemed to have noticed that she had been missing.

'Yer! Snot'll do it,' chorused the others.

Sofi had slipped into the main chamber unseen. Old Killjoy was sitting on his foul-smelling heap as usual. The other Wreccas lolled around, picking their noses and scratching. Sheldon had been taken to the dungeons.

'Do what?' asked Sofi.

'Doesn't you listen to nothing?' Old Killjoy asked.

The watching Wreccas sensed that Sofi might be in trouble. They all watched eagerly.

'Her don't pay attention to nothing,' said Slime, pinching Sofi spitefully on the arm. She knew better than to react.

Slime was a particularly repulsive Wrecca. Living up to his name, he had green slime oozing from his nose, mouth and ears. He had always frightened Sofi more than most of the others, but she had taken care not to show it.

'Don't pay attention to nothing!' echoed the others.

'I'll do it!' she cried out, anxious to obey. 'You know I'll do it, but there was so much din I didn't hear all you sayed . . .' She was trying to stay calm. '. . . but I'll do it, all right.'

'Snot's a good choice,' Old Killjoy confirmed, 'cos her's been Topside before.'

'That's just why her mustn't go,' said Scratch mysteriously.

Old Killjoy threw him a questioning look.

'I'll do it,' Sofi said quickly, hoping that no one would follow up on Scratch's reasoning.

'You's not frightened to go above ground?' Scratch asked, allowing a long, sharp nail to trace the line of his cheekbone. He thought there was something about her that was not quite right.

'Not scared of nothing,' she said with forced confidence.

'Like it up there, did you?' Scratch asked suspiciously. Was she up to something?

Sofi shook her head. 'Ner, it smells,' she said, wrinkling up her nose in pretend disgust. 'That horrid sun thing shines all the time. It made my eyes hurt.'

'Well, someone has to go,' said Slime, wiping his chin with a piece of rag that was caked with dried ooze. 'Us has got to find out what them Topsiders is doing.'

Reference to the Topsiders made Scratch remember something Old Father Tim had said. He thought back to their meeting. It was hard to remember exactly what had been said, but he remembered the gist. 'If you don't give her back, it'll be the end for you.' The end. It had not made any sense to him at the time, but it did now. Perhaps those Topsiders were up to something. Maybe Sheldon had been telling the truth. Scratch's nails traced his lower lip as he thought. It might be wise, for the moment, to go along with what was being suggested.

'If they's up to something,' Scratch said suddenly, looking at Old Killjoy, 'Old Father Tim and his lot'll be making plans. Sniff and I'll go and check it out. We'll need a little'un. Someone to wriggle into small places and listen.' He looked at Sofi, pushing his face right into hers. His breath was foul.

Sofi bit her lip, trying not to show her revulsion.

'That's where you come in.'

'Course,' she said, trying to sound enthusiastic. 'When does us go?'

'Not so fast,' said Old Killjoy. He was in a cantankerous mood. All the time Scratch was not so sure, Old Killjoy was keen on the plan. Now Scratch was enthusiastic, Old Killjoy changed his mind.

Sofi looked up nervously. She wondered if this change had anything to do with her. Was he suspicious?

'Us'll wait,' Old Killjoy continued. 'Us'll talk to the traitor first.'

'Ner.' Scratch spoke quickly. 'There's no time to lose. If there's an army gathering Topside, us needs to know about it now.'

This was too much for Old Killjoy; Scratch was getting above himself. It was not his job to tell the leader what to do, and definitely not in front of others. Scratch had been showing off too much recently. He needed putting in his place.

'Us'll wait,' Old Killjoy breathed towards Scratch, 'because *I* says so.'

'But ...' Scratch began, and stopped. Old Killjoy was looking thunderously at him. What was a Guardian army compared to Old Killjoy in a rage? Scratch was confident that if it came to a battle in the Underneath, the Wreccas could defend themselves admirably. There was no hurry. A Guardian army held few fears for him. No point in making Old Killjoy even angrier.

Scratch nodded. 'Good idea. Think about it. No need to do nothing hasty. Good idea. Us'll go and talk to the traitor again. Well done, Killjoy.'

Slightly soothed, Old Killjoy settled back on his throne. A bored silence fell upon them.

Scratch knew he needed to find some entertainment to please his leader. 'Dance for us, Snot,' and he pushed her into the centre of the chamber.

Sofi did not want to dance. She did not know how to,

which was why Scratch wanted her to do it. When she danced, they sneered and criticized her, laughing scornfully at her clumsy steps and kicking her whenever she was within reach. However, Sofi knew better than to refuse. She began to dance and tried not to listen to their cruel words or feel their vicious kicks.

There was no music, in fact Sofi had never heard any. She just moved around, skipping every now and then and occasionally clapping her hands. She had no idea if she was actually dancing, but then neither did anyone else. Eventually they grew weary of her and found a new amusement. They began tormenting Snivel.

Snivel was a boy, younger than Sofi, who was easily upset and was unable to hide it. They goaded and teased him until he started to cry, and then they ridiculed him in his misery. Sofi had never felt comfortable when they did this. In the past, she had not known why it troubled her because, to a Wrecca, this was normal behaviour. But now she understood that they were being unkind. Sofi silently rejoiced in her discovery. She really was *not* like them! She wondered if Snivel felt the same.

Under the cover of this diversion, Sofi slipped out of the chamber. She was hoping that she could get the Tick away before Scratch decided to take her Topside. For the moment, she believed she was relatively safe. She knew that the Wreccas would content themselves with Snivel for a while, and then Old Killjoy would probably start showing off. He liked to show off, and everyone was too scared to stop him. The other Wreccas would clap and laugh and praise him and he would go on for ages.

This would give Sofi a chance to locate the exact position of the Tick.

She headed towards the safe chamber. It was situated at the end of a long, dark tunnel, lit at intervals by burning torches. They made creepy shadows on the rough walls. She hoped the Tick would still be there.

Hundreds of years before, when the first Wrecca had arrived in Greenwich, he started burrowing under the ground. As the years progressed, more tunnels were dug, leading to new chambers. There was no planning, and thus these tunnels rambled under the ground in many directions. There were chambers at the end of most of them, but some of them led nowhere at all, as if the Wreccas who dug them had forgotten where they were going. The walls were rough. No one had taken any care with the digging and so the ceilings and floors were also uneven.

As Sofi progressed, the tunnel became narrower. Then, another tunnel broke away at right angles to the original. Sofi walked down this new and shallower tunnel.

It was less well lit and was seldom used. Flaming torches were intermittently thrust into the walls, but there were places where it was completely dark. Sofi stopped by one such dark spot and carefully peered over her shoulder to make sure that she was not being observed. She backed up several paces, stopped, checked once more that she was alone, and started running. Then, quite without warning, she disappeared.

Of course, Sofi had not disappeared into thin air.

Instead, she had sidestepped into a hole in the wall. It was so well camouflaged that if you did not know of its existence it would be very difficult to see. Sofi had stumbled upon it by chance one day and thereafter had hidden in it when keeping out of harm's way. It was her own safe place and, as she had never seen anyone else there, she assumed she was the only one who knew about it.

Immediately, she came out of hiding and backed up several paces once more. Again she ran, this time faster, and entered the secret hole at speed. She did this a couple of more times until she was satisfied that she could dart into it at top speed. Then she returned to the original tunnel and continued on her way.

After some more twisting and turning, she saw Spew and Spite at the end of the tunnel, lolling in front of a door. She sauntered up to them.

'What you want?' asked Spew.

'Nothing. I doesn't want nothing.'

'You want to see the Tick,' said Spite, delighted by his own cleverness at working out her intention.

'What if I does?' shrugged Sofi, relieved to have its location confirmed. 'Everyone wants to.'

'Well, you can't,' said Spew. 'Old Killjoy willn't let you. Not now, not with the army and all.'

This was the second time that someone had referred to an army. Although curious, Sofi was unwilling to make her ignorance obvious by asking.

'The Tick belongs to him, and only him sees it,' Spew finished.

'Since when?'

'Since now!' sneered Spew.

Spite looked at her, as if he was trying to read her mind, and then he slowly said, 'Ner, that's not right. Anyone can see it, anyone at all.'

'Ha!' she declared triumphantly to Spew. 'Anyone can see it, Spite says so.'

'Anyone . . .' sneered Spite, '. . . anyone 'cept snotty-Snot!'

Spew and Spite fell about laughing.

Sofi shrugged off their nastiness. 'I doesn't care about the silly old Tick anyway!' she said, kicking a loose stone. 'Can't be very important if Old Killjoy has a couple of stupid, silly, ugly old Wreccas like you guarding it.'

Scarcely had the words left Sofi's mouth before she took off, running as fast as she could. She knew that Spite and Spew would not leave her words unpunished.

She was right. As soon as her meaning had penetrated their slow brains, they took off after her, desperate to exact their revenge.

They were fast, much faster than her, and they caught up quickly. Spite immediately lunged for her. As he did so, she twisted her shoulder out of his reach, causing him to grab at thin air. Consequently, he lost his balance and fell over, tripping up Spew as he went. Together, they fell in a tangled heap. Kicking and swearing at each other, they tried to get up, only to fall over again. This was all the time Sofi needed.

Without hesitating for a second, she ran on. When she reached the side tunnel, she darted into it. Within seconds she had nipped into the hiding place, and there she crouched, breathing heavily and listening carefully.

Spew and Spite untangled themselves and pursued Sofi once more. They ran at top speed past the intersection with Sofi's tunnel but Spite, having slightly more brain than Spew, slowed down. Spew looked around at Spite and nearly tripped over himself as he came to a clumsy halt.

Spite was walking back towards the narrow tunnel as he gasped in mouthfuls of stale air. Putting his finger to his lips to signal to Spew to stay quiet, he took one of the lighted torches from the wall and started walking stealthily down the side tunnel towards Sofi in her hole. Spew was panting hard and stood with his hands on his knees, trying to regain his breath, wondering what Spite was doing.

Sofi's breathing was slower now. Sitting at the back of the hiding place, she winced as grit from the rough floor bit into the raw flesh on her injured heel.

The hiding place was just big enough for three or four people to squeeze into. No one could see it from the tunnel as the narrow entrance was well concealed. Sofi did not know why it had been built. Perhaps the Wrecca who had dug it had intended to start a new tunnel at this point, or perhaps it had been made as a hiding place. Whatever the reason for its existence, it had long since been forgotten. Sofi hugged her knees and waited, wondering when it would be safe to come out. That was always the dangerous part. It was impossible to see beyond the opening. Even if extreme caution was shown, exiting the hole always held the possibility of walking straight into a passing Wrecca.

Her breathing was regular now. If Spite or Spew had seen where she had gone, surely they would have already found her. She counted to eight, which was as far as she knew how to count. She waited and then counted again before deciding that the coast should be clear.

As she waited, Spite was walking along the tunnel. His breathing had also calmed down. He reasoned that Sofi knew she could never outrun them; her legs were too short. She would have to play a trick if she was going to get away from them, and nipping down the side tunnel would be perfect. It was a place of no importance. Wreccas seldom used it. It would be a good place to hide.

Sofi decided she had given them enough time. Raising herself up off her backside, she gingerly felt along the irregular wall with her fingers.

Unbeknown to her, Spite had come to a halt right by the opening, torch in hand. He squinted into the shadows.

If Sofi had known he was there, she would have shrunk back and waited in silence, but she had no way of knowing because he held the torch away from the hole's entrance. Cautiously, she stepped towards the opening. Her foot accidentally kicked a stone and it softly clunked on to the wall opposite.

It had not made much of a sound, but Spite heard it. Wheeling round, he thrust the torch into the tunnel.

The light flashed past the opening and as Sofi saw it, she dragged in her breath in horror. Then she froze. Had she been heard?

His eyes lit up. There was no mistaking the sound of someone's complete and utter surprise. He had caught her! Spinning round once more, he held the flaming torch high. Eerie shadows licked up the wall. To his amazement, there was no one there. But he *had* heard her. He knew he had. He took a few steps along the dark tunnel, but then thought better of it and crept back. She was there, he was certain of it.

Sofi pressed herself into the blackness. She guessed she had been discovered. Holding her breath, she waited, eyes glued on the gap that opened into the tunnel, her hands flat against the wall behind her. What should she do?

The light moved past the opening of her hiding place once more and in the half-light she spied a small rock on the ground. She waited until Spite had moved down the tunnel a few paces and then noiselessly bent down and picked it up. Her fingers closed around it. When Spite's ugly face appeared in the opening, she would fling it at him as hard as she could and then run for it. With him blocking the narrow entrance, she knew her chances of escape were slim, but it was all she could think of. Holding the stone tightly, Sofi resolved not to give up without a fight.

Spite retraced his steps once more and cocked his head to one side. He was standing facing the entrance to Sofi's hiding place. The opening was well concealed in the dark, but the light would make it obvious. Spite's mean little eyes carefully ran over the walls.

Sofi could see the light from his torch. He was right by the opening. The game was up. Perhaps she should surprise him now. Jump out and make a run for it before he blocked the opening.

The problem was, Sofi could not move. She was transfixed with terror. The light was becoming brighter. She stopped breathing altogether and remained motionless, eyes wide open in alarm.

Spite was sure there was someone there. He could sense it. He carefully surveyed every crag and crevice, slowly scrutinizing the wall. Soon he would see the opening. There was no avoiding it.

Sofi started wondering when Old Father Tim would learn of her failure. If he knew early enough, maybe there would be time for the Guardians to try something else. When Spite caught her, he would deliver her up to Old Killjoy, that was a certainty. It was a serious offence not to tell about a hiding place.

Drops of flame were now falling into the opening. Sofi gripped her stone, shut her eyes and waited for the moment of discovery. She would not be able to see Spite approaching through tightly closed eyes, but her mind had stopped functioning. In the blackness behind her eyes she listened and waited for his bony hand to grab her and drag her out.

'Is her there?'

Spite was so surprised by Spew's sudden words that he dropped the torch.

'What the hell!' Spew demanded, jumping out of the way as it clattered to the floor near his feet. 'You gived I the fright of my life!'

Even for a Wrecca, Spew was not very bright. He did not understand that planning and hiding could be a method of escape. 'Come on!' he said, anxious to be following Sofi. 'If us don't hurry, her'll make the main chamber before us does.'

Picking up the torch, Spite held it high once more. He was certain there was someone there. His vicious eyes scanned the wall again. No one could just disappear. Perhaps he had heard a stray rat. Long ago rats had learnt not to venture into the Underneath. What Wreccas do to rats is too gruesome to relate, and baby rats were always warned by their mothers to stay away from playing there. However, occasionally one did wander in.

Spite suddenly got the feeling that he was wasting his time. 'Come on,' he snapped at Spew, as if he had been the one to delay them.

Sofi's thumping heart did not calm down as she heard their footsteps die away. Nor did she immediately leave her hiding place. Knowing that Spite was not particularly clever was a small comfort, but he had worked out that she might have tried to trick them and perhaps he was now lying in wait for her.

She did not move a muscle. Hardly daring to breathe, she waited in the darkness of her hole.

16

The Light at the End of the Tunnel

In the main chamber Old Killjoy was talking about one of his more bloodthirsty murders. He enjoyed showing off and was really exaggerating the facts. The Wreccas had heard it many times before but, as usual, they reacted as though hearing it for the first time. They 'ooohed' and 'aaahed' in all the right places.

Old Killjoy came to his favourite part. He was describing what could be done with somebody's innards, and everyone was listening in respectful silence. It was at this moment that Spew and Spite exploded into the chamber. Their entrance was sudden and spectacular. It might have been considered very funny if it had not had such dire consequences.

In his attempt to be there first, Spew had overreached his long, bony legs. Spite wanted to get to the main chamber before his companion and had tried to dodge past him, but there was no dodging Spew's angular legs. With a chaotic collision that had arms and legs flying in all directions, they erupted into the midst of the assembled Wreccas. Together, they ploughed straight into a unsteady table and scattered the chipped tankards

184

that had been upon it. These flew through the air and hit surprised Wreccas, who flailed their arms around to protect themselves. In doing so, they hit others. The inevitable result was that a number of fights broke out.

Amid all this mayhem, Spew and Spite continued their forward motion and fell in a tangled heap at Old Killjoy's feet. He roared, a deep, animal-like roar that brought the fighting to an immediate halt. In fear, every Wrecca turned their frightened gaze upon their leader. Slowly he stood up, eyes blazing and a vein throbbing in his forehead.

It was with relief that the gathered Wreccas realized that his anger was directed not towards them but at the hapless pair lying at his feet.

There was a terrifying silence before Old Killjoy proclaimed, 'Ruckus!'

Young Snivel stepped backwards quickly and quietly. He had witnessed a Ruckus before and he had no wish to do so again, not yet. He pressed his back against the wall and moved silently away from the scene that was now developing before his eyes.

The rhythmic chant of, 'Ruckus ... Ruckus ... Ruckus ...' was taken up by the gathered throng. As it throbbed around the chamber, so Spew and Spite were enclosed in a circle of menacing Wreccas.

The chanting grew louder and louder. Spew and Spite clung to each other in disbelief, their eyes bulging in their heads. They looked around at the gleeful faces of their companions.

At a signal from Old Killjoy, two Wreccas stepped

into the circle. Spew and Spite knew that they were in for the biggest beating of their lives, but they also knew that a cowardly Wrecca could expect only one thing. Death. If they were brave and fought well, Old Killjoy might spare them.

With trembling knees, they stood back-to-back, each ready to take on their first Wrecca fighter. It was an orderly affair to begin with. The first fights were often fairly even, but as soon as the first fighters had had enough, the next ones stepped into the ring and continued. As they did so, the first fighters sought the safety of the crowd and the next waited his turn.

In this way, the victims would face challenger after challenger and, no matter how strong or good a fighter he might be, he would eventually be overcome. When at last he lay on the floor, broken and bleeding, Old Killjoy had the choice of life or death.

A brave victim would usually be allowed to crawl away and tend his wounds as best he could. A victim who had been considered cowardly would be sentenced to death. This meant that the remaining Wreccas, who had so far only acted as the noisy audience, were allowed to attack the unfortunate Wrecca. They would not stop until his limp and lifeless body was a mass of blood and broken limbs. No one survived this.

Snivel shut his eyes. He could not bring himself to watch the ferocious battle that was about to take place. He believed this to be a weakness, and it confirmed yet again how feeble and stupid he was. When he was older, he reasoned, he would be able to watch and even take part in the Ruckus, but for now he wanted to be as far away from it as possible. Unobserved, he slipped out of the main chamber.

Sofi had finally plucked up the courage to leave her hiding place and was now running towards the chamber Spite and Spew had been guarding. It was with relief that she arrived at the door and, without even casting a look over her shoulder, she grabbed the handle and started tugging at it.

Like most things in the Underneath, the door was damp and the hinges rusted. Putting a foot against the wall, Sofi tugged at the handle with all her might. Slowly the door began to move and, when the gap was wide enough, she slipped through.

Inside, on a pillar of dung, stood the Tick, covered by a grimy, heavy cloth which could not mask the Guardian goodness that shone out. It had a wonderful brightness that filled her with hope. No wonder Old Killjoy had prevented the Wreccas from seeing it.

'It's the loveliest thing I's ever seed,' she found herself saying in an awed whisper.

For a while she forgot that she was in a hurry. Standing still, she wallowed in the glow which contrasted so totally with the drab, chill misery of the Underneath.

Eventually, she dragged herself back to reality. What should she do now? She had found her way into the chamber and discovered the Tick, but she was now unsure how to proceed. Old Father Tim and Tid were relying on her. She did not want to let them down.

The thought of Old Father Tim made her wonder what he would he do if he were in her place right now. Be Mindful. Of course, that is what she should do.

Sitting in front of the Tick with her legs crossed, she let her mind clear before thinking of Old Father Tim and his loving eyes. Immediately, one word come into her mind.

'Help.'

Sofi thought about it. Was this what Tid's grandfather was trying to say to her?

'Help.'

'I know I need help,' she thought. 'But who?'

All at once, Sofi had the feeling that she was not alone. The hair stood up on the back of her neck and her stomach churned. There was someone standing in the chamber with her. She had been discovered!

Letting out a cry of fright, she scrambled away from the intruder and huddled against the wall. Thrusting up her arms to protect her head from the blows that she felt certain would soon rain down upon her, she cried, 'The door was open! I didn't touch nothing!'

Every muscle in her body was rigid with fear.

Nothing happened.

She waited, but no blow came. Very cautiously, she peeped out from under her arms. There was someone standing in front of the Tick. He was not big. Who was it?

It took no more than a moment for her to realize, with considerable relief, that it was Snivel. He was staring, opened-mouthed, at the glowing cube on the dung heap. Sofi glanced about her. They were alone.

When Snivel had left the main chamber some time before, desperate to be away from the hell that was developing there, he did not care where he was going. When he saw a gentle glow at the end of the tunnel, he approached with caution.

The door to the safe chamber was open. Snivel should have run away. He was not very brave and usually found it best not to investigate anything out of the ordinary. However, the light was just too beautiful. Without being able to help himself, Snivel found that he had been drawn by the warming glow emanating from the gap. It was different from any light he had ever seen before.

Attracted by its beauty, and without thinking, he had stepped through the door and into the chamber. Now he stood before it, eyes shining in the Tick's reflected light.

'Wow!' she heard him whisper.

Sofi rose to her feet and went over to him. Silently, she waited, allowing him to become gradually aware that she was there.

Slowly, Snivel realized that he was not alone. Gripped by fear, he peered up nervously. It was an enormous relief to discover that it was only Snot.

All of a sudden, he reverted to his old self. Thrusting his hands deep into his pockets, he allowed his shoulders to slouch in a casual manner.

'Don't know what the fuss is about,' he said, casually kicking the floor with his toe. 'Them Topsiders can't make nothing near so well as Old Killjoy. This Tick is horrid.'

Sofi looked down into his face and gratitude filled her

heart. Old Father Tim must have sent him and, even if he did not know it, Snivel must be there to help.

Wakka, the Greenwich Guardian and Old Father Tim were seated around the fire with their eyes closed, focusing on being Mindful. Tid sat on a stool at his grandfather's feet, his face screwed up in an agony of concentration. At length, Wakaa opened his eyes and looked about him.

Old Father Tim opened his at the same time. He needed to voice something he had been feeling for a while. 'It is no good.'

'I cannot bring her to mind either,' Wakaa agreed.

At this moment, the Greenwich Guardian also opened her eyes. 'Nor can I.'

'It would be difficult to penetrate into the depths of the Underneath,' Old Father Tim concluded.

'That is not the reason we cannot reach her,' Wakaa expanded. 'She is not yet one of the Guardian People. It cannot work until she is. I do not think it would be possible even if she was in the next room.'

Deeply absorbed in his effort to be Mindful, Tid heard their voices but had not absorbed what they had been saying. Opening his eyes, he looked up and asked, 'Is it working?'

Old Father Tim sadly shook his head. 'No, my boy. We are not reaching her.'

'How can you tell?'

'Experience,' the Greenwich Guardian explained.

'We must keep trying, though,' Tid said.

No one spoke.

He looked from face to face and found agreement in none. 'But we must!'

It was Old Father Tim who answered, and his tone was gentle. 'Sometimes we have to accept that there are things we cannot do.'

Wakaa and the Greenwich Guardian nodded their agreement.

'But what else is there?' Tid asked forlornly.

No one answered.

'Are the Middlers going to come back?' he asked. He had heard rumours and was wondering if he might have the opportunity to see his own parents.

'No,' Wakaa said. 'We have been persuaded that will be of no use.' He looked at Old Father Tim as he said this and Tid knew that his grandfather had been the one to change Wakaa's mind. 'Guardians know nothing of fighting. If we are to survive this, then perhaps we should learn, but for the present it is too late.'

'Guardians were never intended to fight,' Old Father Tim said resolutely.

'So Sofi is all we have,' Tid said, a feeling of alarm stirring in the pit of his stomach. 'We can't give up! We just can't! What could be worse than the end of every-thing? We can't stay here and do nothing. Being Mindful is all we can do!'

It was the Greenwich Guardian who tried to explain. 'But we are not reaching her.'

Tid had always known Guardians to be wise and noble, and so he found it impossible to understand why they were giving up on his friend with no hope of another course of action. It was insane!

'But if we keep on trying,' he persisted, 'we might get through.'

'No,' Wakaa said. 'Whatever Sofi is doing, she is doing without any help from us.'

'Perhaps she has lost heart,' the Greenwich Guardian suggested, 'and stopped being Mindful herself, in which case it will definitely not work.'

Tid appealed to his own grandfather for support. 'Grandfather . . .' he began, but the look in the old man's eyes silenced him.

'Sofi is newly out from the Underneath,' Old Father Tim explained. 'She is not very close to being one of the Guardian People, and so being Mindful is not going to work.'

'But we promised!' Tid exclaimed, his eyes alight with anger.

'We should not have done.'

The dancing flames of the fire reflected in Tid's eyes as he stared into them. He hated the thought of giving up. There was Sofi, braving the horrors of the Underneath, and up here the grown-ups were doing nothing to help. Well, he would not sit there doing nothing. Stubbornly he sought a reason to continue. 'Perhaps it isn't working because she's so deep in the ground?'

Old Father Tim nodded. 'That could be one reason.'

'So,' Tid continued, hoping he was making sense,

'when she gets nearer the surface we might get through to her?'

Old Father Tim saw where his grandson was going with this. He did not want to crush all hope. 'It is possible.'

'Possible?' Tid's eyes contained more than hopefulness, he was challenging his grandfather to support him.

'It *might* be,' Old Father Tim conceded.

'But . . .' Tid glanced at the Guardians and chose his words carefully, '. . . a possibility, no matter how slight, is better than nothing.'

Wakaa had had enough of this. He thought that Old Father Tim was being too soft with the boy. It was time he heard the honest truth. 'If she has tried being Mindful and failed, then she will have given up altogether and we shall never get through.'

'But if Tid does not know that being Mindful is not working,' Old Father Tim said, surprised to find himself thinking this way, 'then maybe Sofi does not know either.'

'Yes!' Tid cried out, clenching his fist in victory.

Wakaa cast a disapproving look. Tid was on the verge of behaving disrespectfully and Old Father Tim was being sentimental and foolish.

'So we should keep trying?' Tid asked, his eyes shining with hope.

Old Father Tim was aware of Wakaa's disapproval, but he had to be true to his own belief. 'Yes, Tid, I think perhaps we should.'

'Well,' Wakaa said, standing, 'if you will forgive us,

I think that the Greenwich Guardian and I should make our way to the Line. Seegan may have come up with something.'

'What?' Old Father Tim asked.

'As yet, I am not exactly sure, but I have been told that Seegan is interpreting some ancient scrolls. He believes there is a ritual that can suspend time. If we could buy ourselves a few precious days or even hours, it could make a difference.'

'Are these the fourth-century scrolls from Guangdong?' Old Father Tim asked.

'Yes, I think they are.'

'I know them. I worked on a translation in my youth. They are complicated and misleading. For a while I believed, like Seegan, that time could be suspended. But I was wrong. I stopped my work. You can read my findings in the library at the Hither House. It cannot be done.'

'Perhaps you stopped too soon. Seegan has been working on them for several years. He believes it may be possible. It has to be worth a try.'

'I think not.'

'Well,' Wakaa said, not wanting to hear any more negative thoughts, 'you put your trust in Sofi and I will put mine in Seegan. If he is right, then our place is at the Line, assisting with the ritual.'

Old Father Tim put his hands on the arms of his comfortable chair and slowly stood. Tid could see that it took more effort than he was prepared to show.

'And if *we* are right,' Old Father Tim said, drawing

himself up to his full height, and with such authority in his voice that it was hard to believe he was no longer the Old Father, 'then our place is here, being Mindful.'

For a moment Old Father Tim and Wakaa faced each other. Wakaa felt that as the new Guardian leader, he deserved the old man's support. In truth, Old Father Tim agreed with him, but he also felt that he should stay and be Mindful with his grandson. A look of steely determination came into his eye. It made Tid feel safe to know that, although his grandfather's body was growing old, his mind and spirit were as strong as ever. Old Father Tim lifted one eyebrow, almost questioning Wakaa's right to demand any more of him.

Wakaa involuntarily lowered his head. 'We must go.'

Old Father Tim allowed his eyes to linger on Wakaa for just a moment before turning his gaze to the Greenwich Guardian. The look of steel had gone and his eyes were soft and gentle once more. He had known her a long time, he was fond of her and wanted her to stand with him.

She noted his silent appeal. With all her heart she wanted to agree with him. She had known and respected him since she was a young girl and had never disagreed with his point of view. But this time she believed him to be wrong. 'I agree with Old Father Wakaa,' she said softly. The very act of using Wakaa's new title made her feel even more the betrayer.

Old Father Tim nodded. He did not feel the betrayal, he was just saddened that at the end of everything he and she were not of the same opinion.

'I shall remain here with my grandson until I am needed to attach the Tick.'

'Very well,' Wakaa said. 'Farewell.'

Solemnly they shook hands. Then Old Father Tim offered his hand to the Greenwich Guardian, but she ignored it. Instead, she stepped towards him and kissed him respectfully on the cheek.

It was a rare act of affection. Guardians are not known for such displays, and Old Father Tim was very much touched by it. For a brief moment they looked into one another's eyes, and each understood the respect and deep affection they shared. Then the Greenwich Guardian turned and left with Wakaa.

The Plan

Snivel stood with his hands in the pockets of his raggedy trousers. He felt very strange. There was a peculiar sensation spreading throughout his body; he had never felt anything like it before. He suspected the feeling came from the Tick.

He looked at it carefully but could not really see it, covered as it was by the thick, grimy cloth. It appeared to be a large box, with every side the same length. Snivel noticed the hard lines leading to pointed corners where the glow seemed to be stronger.

Used as he was to hiding his feelings, he was not going to show Snot that this Tick thing had affected him. Tilting his head to one side and hunching his shoulders in the casual manner of a Wrecca, he looked up at her.

She was staring at him.

'What's you looking at?' he asked belligerently.

She was wondering what Snivel would be like if he were Topside. She thought he was a nice-looking boy, with freckles scattered over his nose and mousy-coloured hair that looked almost tidy, even though it had never been combed, not even with Scratch's nails. She imagined him sitting at Old Father Tim's breakfast table, and she smiled to herself. She wondered how much he would enjoy pancakes and syrup.

'Cut it out, Snot, or I'll land one on you,' he said, intimidated by her silence and the expression on her face.

'I's sorry.'

Snivel could not have been more surprised if she had suddenly sprouted wings and flown. Never in all his life had anyone apologized to him.

'What's your game?' he asked, immediately suspecting a trick.

'No game.' She stood in silence once more, trying to work out the best way to persuade him to help. If she should secure Snivel's assistance, then they could carry the Tick Topside together. It would all be so much easier if she did not have to bring Cob or the others inside. The Bushytails could help her carry it to the Park, once they were through the door. Yes, this was the best plan.

Snivel continued to stare at her, unable to decide what trick she was planning.

'I need your help, Sniv,' she said simply.

'Sniv don't help no one.'

'I can't do it alone,' she continued, ignoring his reply. 'It's too bulky. I need you to help.' Then she added, 'I doesn't think it's heavy. Us can move it together to the Topside door and then the Bushytails'll help.'

'Bushytails? Topside door? What *is* you talking about?'

Sofi took a deep breath and tried to be patient. 'Us has to move the Tick.'

Snivel backed away. 'I's not touching that thing. Old Killjoy'll butcher us for sure. I doesn't know what you's up to, but you can leave I out of it.'

Sofi realized that the truth was not helping. 'Us is doing this for Old Killjoy,' she lied. 'Him thought of this plan cos him don't trust Spew and Spite. Him thinks they's working for them Topsiders.'

Snivel's eyes widened in disbelief. 'Spew and Spite?'

'Yer, and Old Killjoy don't know how many Wreccas is working with them. Him can't trust no one, and so him comed up with this plan. Him wants us to move the Tick somewhere safe. Then him'll torture Spew and Spite and find out who they's working with.'

Sofi thought this was a very good story, considering she had made it up on the spot. She watched Snivel carefully, anxious to know if he would believe her.

'You's telling lies, snotty-Snot,' he said, turning away. 'I's off.'

'Suit yourself!' Sofi snapped. 'I'll just tell Old Killjoy that you willn't help.'

This instantly stopped Snivel. He did not trust Sofi, but he was terrified of Old Killjoy. 'Don't you tell him that!' he said, starting to snivel.

'Don't cry,' said Sofi, putting her arm around his shoulders.

Snivel pushed her away and backed off, distrustfully.

Sofi realized that Topside manners did not work in the Underneath. She had to act as a Wrecca or Snivel would never do as she wanted. 'Hurry up, you snivelling little wretch!' she said unkindly.

Strange as it may sound, Snivel was comforted by this; it was what he was used to. Without any more argument, he crossed to the Tick and prepared to lift it, but then hesitated.

'Come on!' she said impatiently. 'It willn't bite!'

Cautiously, he slipped his hands beneath it and then immediately withdrew them.

'What's the matter?' she asked, irritated.

'It's all warm.' In the cold dampness of the Underneath, warmth was something Snivel seldom felt.

'Get on with it!'

Snivel reluctantly put his hands under it once more.

'Ready, steady, lift!' Sofi declared.

Together they straightened up, holding the Tick between them. It was not heavy, but Snivel had to stretch his arms wide to hold it securely.

'Where's us going?' he asked.

'Through the main chamber.'

Snivel put it straight back down again and Sofi almost lost her balance at the suddenness of his move.

'You's mad! Us can't take it that way with a Ruckus going on!'

'What Ruckus?' Sofi asked.

'Spew and Spite made a racket while Old Killjoy was speaking. You know how much him hates anyone making a noise when him's in full flow.'

Sofi knew only too well.

'They charged into a table and sent everything flying. It was horrible. Everyone started shouting and throwing punches. Old Killjoy was mad angry!' He paused for a moment, trying to hide his anxiety. 'And then him ordered a Ruckus.'

'That's it!' Sofi declared triumphantly. 'That's the plan! Old Killjoy'll keep everyone busy with a Ruckus and give us time to get the Tick out.' She felt a little glow of satisfaction at a lie well told and working. 'It'll give us time to get the Tick away in secret.'

'If it's supposed to be secret,' Snivel asked, brow furrowed as he thought carefully, 'then why's you taking it out through the main chamber where anyone can see us?'

'Us can't take it out the back way, it's too far,' she tried to explain. 'If us is lucky and keep to the shadows, us willn't be seed. They'll be too busy.'

'You's got to be joking! Everyone'll see us! Hasn't you noticed how bright that thing is?' He thrust out his hand towards the Tick. 'You's not planned this right, snotty-Snot.'

'Old Killjoy planned it,' said Sofi defensively. 'The Ruckus is gonna to keep their minds off us. Doesn't you see? It's a good idea!'

'They'll see us.'

It was probably true. The wonderful brightness glowed intensely in the gloom of the Underneath and the cloth did not do much to diminish it. It seemed as if the Tick was openly defying the Wreccas' attempts to cover its brilliance by shining more brightly than ever.

'There's nothing us can do about that,' said Sofi reluctantly. 'Us has our chance and us has to take it.'

Snivel did not move. He put his hands back into his

pockets as if to emphasize that he was not going to use them to lift the Tick. 'If us is seed, they'll tear us limb from limb,' he said. 'It don't matter if Old Killjoy's telled you to do this or not, him willn't think twice about giving us up to the Ruckus if it's a good laugh. You know him willn't.' He paused and was encouraged because Sofi said nothing. 'Let's leave it here,' he said hopefully.

'But him seed I go,' she continued her lie, 'and if him seed I go, then him seed you go too. Us has to take it, in case him comes and checks on us.'

'Him seed I go?' asked Snivel nervously.

'Yer. Him knowed you'd come. Him's terrible clever.' This was stretching a point but she did not think Snivel would dare disagree. 'Him choosed you and I cos us is at the bottom of the heap. Him knows him can trust us cos no one takes no notice of anything us does. You's got to do it, Sniv, or him'll punish us both.'

'Well, I's not taking it through the main chamber,' Snivel said, sticking out his chin, 'not with a Ruckus going on!'

Sofi stared at him. He was younger than her. In the Underneath, size was everything. Wreccas used power and fear to get what they wanted. All she had to do was get him in a headlock or something equally vicious, and he would have to give in – and yet here he was, openly defying her. She respected him for it.

'I tell you what,' she said. 'I know a place where us can hide it until it's safe to go Topside.'

Snivel eyed her suspiciously. 'I's not moving it nowhere.'

'You're gonna have to, Sniv, or Old Killjoy'll come down on us like a load of rocks. And don't think that him willn't!'

He knew she spoke the truth. The fact that they were children would not protect them from Old Killjoy's wrath.

'What good will it do putting it somewhere else?' he asked, pouting.

'It'll give us time. You know they always crash out after a Ruckus and when they's fast asleep us can take it Topside.'

Snivel thought about this.

Sofi waited for his agreement. If he still defied her, then she would have to turn nasty, but she would rather not. She had never been comfortable pushing the smaller ones around and tended to do it less than the others; but now, having witnessed a completely different way of life Topside, she dreaded behaving so harshly.

Grudgingly, Snivel agreed.

Sofi was relieved. However limited, it was good to have his cooperation, even though she knew she could not trust him. Snivel was quite likely to give her up to the others as soon as he had the chance, and she would not blame him if he did. But for the moment she could use him, and it would give her the chance to get the Tick clear of the safe chamber before Old Killjoy thought of putting the guards back. And anyway, had not Old Father Tim sent Snivel to her? Of course he had! That proved it. For the time being at least, he could be trusted.

She pushed at the door to open it wide, and carefully

they manoeuvred the Tick through. Then they put it down so that Sofi could push the heavy, old door shut. If guards were sent back, chances were they would not look inside if they found the door closed. That would buy her extra time.

'Hurry up!' Snivel spoke with urgency.

Putting her shoulder to the door, she strained to shut it. Her feet slipped and scuffed on the uneven floor. The rusty hinges creaked as it moved.

'Be quiet!' hissed Snivel. 'Does you want them to hear us?'

'Sorry.'

She was too occupied to see the look on Snivel's face. Her strange behaviour was making him feel uneasy. A sudden loud roar from the Ruckus made Snivel look anxiously over his shoulder.

'Hurry!'

Sheldon crouched in a dingy dungeon. The ceiling was so low it was impossible for him to stand. His muscles ached with being hunched up for ages. He longed to stretch out on the ground, just to ease the aching, but it was so filthy that Sheldon could not bring himself to lie down. Old bits of mouldy food, smelly pieces of rag that had been used as rough bandages, and other debris littered the floor.

He wondered why he had ever longed to come to the Underneath. It was not at all as he had expected. The foul stench revolted him. Somehow, honest dirt smeared on to clean clothes was not the same as ingrained filth.

Pretending to be tough and throwing his weight about was not the same as being bullied and mistreated. His body was bruised and sore.

He was hungry, it was a long time since he had eaten anything, and he was thirsty. That was the worst, his raging thirst. His throat was dry and getting sorer with each intake of breath. Miserably he wrapped his arms around himself, trying to derive some comfort where there was none. It was cold and damp and he longed for his own fireside. How often had he moaned at his grandmother for the meagre food she put before him? They had little money and she coped as best she could, but even a bowl of thin soup would have been a luxury for Sheldon right now.

He blamed Sofi for his present plight. If only she had done as she had been told, none of this would have happened. He failed to wonder if the Wreccas would have treated him honestly, had he done as they had wanted. He also did not reason that, however popular he might be with Old Killjoy, the Underneath would have been just as foul.

He pulled his knees up and rested his head upon them. He felt he was the most wretched creature in all the world.

Snivel was very surprised when Sofi directed him into the hole that was her hiding place. He had no idea such a hideout existed. Carefully they put the Tick down and then went out into the tunnel. Even with the Tick at the point furthest from the opening, they could still see its light. The darkness that had aided the concealment of the opening made the Tick's glow all the more visible.

'It's no good,' Snivel said. 'It's too bright. Anyone can see it.'

Sofi took a step further back, hoping that the glow would fade away in the dark. It did not.

'Oh no,' Snivel began to snivel. 'Us is going to get it for this, I know us is.'

'Us'll have to cover it up with something else,' Sofi said, trying not to wallow in the hopelessness of it all. She looked about her. There was absolutely nothing to use.

'Our coats!' Snivel almost shouted with relief as the thought came to him.

'Great idea,' Sofi said, and started pulling off her ragged apology for a coat.

Snivel found himself taking pleasure in her praise.

Sofi covered the Tick. 'Keep your coat, Sniv, you'll freeze without it.'

'But you need it.'

Sofi looked at the Tick in dismay. It was impossible to cut out its comforting light.

Snivel held his own ragged coat out to her. Sofi took it with a grateful smile and covered the Tick once more.

'It still glows,' Snivel said, totally discouraged.

Sofi held her hands to her head in despair but, as she looked, the Tick's glow slowly seemed to lessen, as though the Tick was trying to help. She stepped out of the hole and back into the tunnel.

'It's not too bad from here.'

Snivel joined her. Two paces away from the opening it

could not be seen at all. It was not perfect, but hopefully it was good enough.

'It'll have to do,' Sofi said. 'Let's just hope no one comes down here.' She looked around. 'What does us do now?'

'You tell I.'

Sofi nodded. How stupid of her. She was the one in charge. She should know what to do. Her eyes felt heavy. She was very tired.

'Us'll rest for a while. I'll think more clearly after a quick nap.'

18

The Map

As there was no night or day in the Underneath, people slept when they felt like it. Generally, those close to Old Killjoy were guided by him. Other Wreccas slept when and wherever they could. The galley chamber tunnel was a favourite location as it was the warmest place in the Underneath. Sofi did not go there now. It might be disastrous if she slept too long. It would be easier to doze if she remained cold. Her head ached and she was very tired. She was finding it difficult to think clearly.

Finding a relatively quiet spot outside the main chamber, Sofi lay down. The Ruckus was less noisy now. She knew it would not be long before it would be over and the Wreccas would all fall into a deep sleep. Such activity always had that effect on them.

'I'll just close my eyes until it goes quiet,' she said to herself as she shifted around on the hard, damp ground. One arm was her pillow and the other wrapped around her as her blanket. She drew up her knees in an attempt to maintain whatever warmth she had within her. She missed her jacket, although, being so thin and raggedy, it would not have made much difference. Sofi's mind flitted momentarily to the Tick. She hoped it was safe.

Snivel settled down beside her. He did not immediately snuggle up to her, but she knew that when she was asleep he would move closer for the warmth. That was the way it was in the Underneath. Everyone benefited from sleeping close to the others. Yet Sofi knew that when she awoke she would push him off roughly and pretend to complain that he had encroached on her sleeping patch.

Sofi closed her eyes and allowed her mind to drift to her one and only memory of comfort. It was from a long time before. Vaguely, she remembered there being someone comfortable. This someone had protective arms that held Sofi close and hands that gently rubbed her back. Sofi did not have a face for this comfort but she had given it a name. She called it 'mother'.

There were no mothers in the Underneath, nor were there any babies. Occasionally, a small child would turn up. No one knew who brought it, but there it would be, standing alone in the tunnel, usually crying in bewildered misery. Sofi did not remember this happening to her but she realized that it must have.

Other early memories were cold, fear and hunger. Crying did no good, it just brought jibes and sneers from the others, and so she quickly learnt to keep her tears in check. Such outward signs of emotion were only for private moments. Food was usually short. It did not seem to concern grown-up Wreccas that a child might be hungry.

Scaggy was the first person Sofi remembered. She was several years older than Sofi and, unusually for a Wrecca, had blonde hair. Unlike the others, she never hurt the smaller children. She seemed to ignore them, but would often leave scraps of food on the ground that she had stolen from the galley chamber or had scavenged from the refuse. When she turned her back, the small children would hurriedly eat them.

When it came to sleeping, Sofi noticed that Scaggy would go to good places, better than Sofi could find by herself. She was not the only one to notice this, and Scaggy was often surrounded by several of the smaller children who found it hard to fend for themselves. Together they would hang back until they saw her settle down. Then they would quietly creep up and lie near her.

They had to be careful. If they snuggled up too early, before Scaggy was asleep, she would push them aside, but never roughly. Sofi learnt to wait until Scaggy's rhythmic breathing indicated that she had dropped off. Then Sofi and the others would huddle together to derive what comfort and warmth they could from each other.

When they awoke, Scaggy would always be gone. She did not push them or complain at finding herself the centre of a huddle. Instead, she disentangled herself and moved on.

As Sofi grew, she became more independent and needed Scaggy less. There would be long periods of time when Sofi never saw her at all. Thinking about her now, she could not remember one kind word having passed between them, not even a look of understanding, but there was a bond. Something that meant they never told on one another. Once, when Sofi saw Scaggy secretly slip through a Topside door, she kept it to herself, and when Scaggy saw Sofi steal a polished stone from one of the boys, Sofi saw her turn away and say nothing. If she had a friend in the Underneath, Scaggy would have been it.

Then, one day Sofi realized that she had not seen her for a long time, and she knew that Scaggy had gone. All the girls went in the end, just as Sofi knew that one day she would go. The men did not like women in their Underneath.

The children whispered about mothers and the tunnels where they lived, but no one knew where these tunnels were. No one knew anything for sure. Sofi was convinced that many tales were made up and some were deliberately scary in order to frighten the little ones. But deep in her heart, she believed in mothers.

It was strange, children did not arrive any more. Snivel had been the last one she remembered. Sofi did not have time to wonder why because she was gently drifting into a deep sleep.

Sheldon would have said or done anything for a drink of water, anything at all. So when Spit opened his prison door and demanded, 'Get out here!' Sheldon readily scrambled out after him. Just to stand upright was a relief for his aching muscles. Spit walked ahead and Sheldon's guards followed close behind.

He was taken along what the Wreccas considered to be a well-lit corridor, although Sheldon thought it dark and scary, with flaming torches casting strange shadows on the wall. Eventually they arrived at one of the larger chambers along Old Killjoy's private tunnel. Enjoying the drama, Old Killjoy had renamed it the 'war chamber'. He saw current events as nothing less than outright war.

The door was dragged open and Sheldon was pushed roughly inside.

The chamber looked like the rest of the Underneath: rough walls, uneven floors and low ceilings, with flaming torches providing the light. However, because this was part of Old Killjoy's private quarters, it was smoother, cleaner and brighter than elsewhere.

Sheldon looked around in dismay. He had hoped they were taking him somewhere clean, where he could eat. Pushing thoughts of nourishment aside, he looked at the gathered Wreccas. There were several there, including Old Killjoy, Sniff and Scratch, who were standing over a large and grubby piece of paper that was lying on a wobbly table. They looked up as Sheldon entered. He licked his dry lips.

'Does you know about maps?' Scratch demanded.

Sheldon's heart sank. If only he had paid attention during geography lessons at school; but flicking elastic bands across the class and pulling Pippa Lom's hair had been far more interesting.

'Well?' Scratch snarled, impatient for his answer.

'Yes,' Sheldon said, hoping to sound as if it were

true. He wondered if he dared ask for a drink of water.

Scratch stood back and pointed towards the paper that was stretched across the table.

Sheldon looked at it. He blinked once and lifted his gaze to the gathered Wreccas, who were waiting for his reaction. Was this a joke? Was he supposed to burst out laughing and share in the fun? But there was something in their combined seriousness that told him they were in deadly earnest.

Sheldon swallowed and looked back at the parchment. Lying on top was a blunt stub of pencil which had clearly been used to draw the few thick lines that Sheldon assumed was the map. He stepped forward and studied it carefully, desperately trying to make out what it represented.

Excited by the possibility of a war, Old Killjoy could not keep silent. To hurry things along he told Sheldon exactly what he needed to know.

'It's the park.'

Scratch frowned irritably. He had wanted to see if Sheldon could read the map for himself. If he was to be of any help, he had to know about such things.

Sheldon was relieved. Now he understood what he was looking at, it started to make some sort of sense to him. 'Of course,' he said, trying to sound knowledgeable.

Bad at geography though Sheldon was, he could draw maps better than whoever had drawn this. No attention had been paid to scale. The road was narrow and the paths wide. There were random circles drawn by the side of one of the roadways that must have represented trees, and a wobbly house right in the corner. Most stupid of all, there was the occasional crude picture of what looked like a person. To put something that was mobile on a map was totally ridiculous and Sheldon would have laughed out loud if he had not been so terrified.

Scratch pointed to the house. 'D'you know what this is?' He was not convinced that Sheldon understood the map at all.

Sheldon's mind was racing. It could be any number of homes in that part of the park. Only one had been drawn and so it had to be the home of someone important. Who were they interested in? Then a wave of relief flooded him as he finally realized. 'That's Old Father Tim's house,' he said in an offhand manner, as though it was clearly obvious.

Suddenly, he was aware of general approval. He ran his dry tongue over his cracked lips and looked around. Could he ask for a drink now?

'All right,' Scratch said, 'so you understand maps.' He looked up with pride as he stabbed the parchment with a bony finger. 'I drawed this.'

'It's an excellent map,' Sheldon said, half expecting to be punished for such an outrageous lie, but Scratch oozed with smugness.

'I know.'

Old Killjoy was not best pleased. Scratch was taking all the credit. It was the leader who was supposed to be the centre of attention. His second-in-command was beginning to annoy him again.

'This is the old fool's workshop,' he snapped, pointing at a roughly drawn circle.

Sheldon looked carefully. If he understood the map correctly, there were only trees along that walkway. 'In a tree?' he asked tentatively.

'I know,' Old Killjoy said with a sneer, his good temper immediately restored by the opportunity of rubbishing Old Father Tim. 'The dung-head thinked of nothing better than hiding it in a tree. Don't have no brains at all!'

Sheldon did not have time to feel satisfied that he had learnt the location of the Old Father's famous workshop. He had only one thought in his mind and, as everything seemed to be going well, he would risk his question. 'Would I be able to have a drink?'

'Of course!' Old Killjoy exclaimed benevolently. With a wave of an arm towards Slime, he ordered, 'Food and drink!' Then he added, 'I need food for all this brainwork.' Old Killjoy tapped his head. 'Can't use this without feeding it!'

Slime grumpily left the chamber to arrange the refreshments. He did not want to miss out on anything and resented having to be the one to go.

'Put your house on the map,' Scratch said, ignoring his leader and holding out the pencil stub to Sheldon. 'Us might need it.'

Sheldon would have preferred not to have his house on the map, but he reasoned that it did not matter, none of the assembled Wreccas would understand this apology for a map. So, with care, he drew a neat house in approximately the right place and labelled it, 'Sheldon's house'.

'What's that?' Scratch demanded.

'I thought I'd label it,' he said, nervously swallowing.

'What did you write?'

Sheldon thought this was a strange question. 'Sheldon's house.'

There was a long pause. Scratch's lip curled cruelly.

'Does you think I's a fool?' he asked menacingly. 'It don't say that.'

Sheldon was dumbfounded. It clearly said, 'Sheldon's house'. He looked around at the other Wreccas, who were peering down at the map. Surely everyone could clearly see it.

Scratch explained. 'My name begins with one of them.' He poked the letter 'S' at the beginning of Sheldon's name. 'Sssssss!' he hissed like a snake. 'Your name don't begin with Sssssss!'

Sheldon looked at him in disbelief. He had never before encountered a grown-up who could not read. He waited, expecting the others to explain to Scratch his elementary mistake. No one said a word. They were looking intimidatingly towards Sheldon. How could he explain without giving offence?

'My . . . I mean, your . . . you see . . .' He was trying to work out a way of praising Scratch whilst pointing out the obvious. What could he say?

'You're absolutely right,' he eventually mumbled. 'Y . . . your name does begin with a Sss. My name begins with a Shh and when you put this,' he gingerly pointed towards the letter 'h', 'after the Sss, it changes the sound into Shh.'

He waited for the reaction, terrified what it might be. Eventually, Old Killjoy began nodding sagely. 'Just as I thinked,' he said, stroking his chin. The others nodded their agreement.

Scratch felt anger rising within him. He did not like being the only one in the room who appeared not to understand such things, and the humiliation of his recently injured nose was still embarrassing him.

'Put the Greenwich Guardian's house on the map,' he barked, trying to change the subject.

'The Greenwich Guardian doesn't live in the park,' Sheldon replied.

Relieved to be able to act the hero, Scratch lunged at Sheldon, pinning him against the wall. His forearm pressed hard on Sheldon's throat. Totally surprised at the rapidity of this violence, Sheldon gulped and spluttered as his eyes grew bigger.

'I doesn't think you heared properly,' Scratch snarled, thrusting his face into Sheldon's, and yelling, 'I sayed, put the Greenwich Guardian's house on the map!'

Sheldon tried to nod. If Scratch wanted a house on the map, then Scratch could have one! In fact he would put anything and everything on this ridiculous map.

Scratch slowly released him and, putting his hand on his shoulder, pushed the gasping youth down on to the stool, remaining threateningly close. Sheldon started drawing with thick strokes all over the map. He drew quickly and explained as he went. 'This is the Greenwich

Guardian's house.' Sheldon thought that, although Bryn actually lived there, no Wrecca would know the difference. He reasoned that the Greenwich Guardian was Bryn's sister and so it was close enough. 'This is the Line, where the Guardians meet . . .' and so he went on, filling in all sorts of details, mostly real, but some imaginary. In fact, Sheldon even began to enjoy himself. 'Shall I put all the trees in?' he asked, looking up.

Old Killjoy nodded.

'There are . . .' Sheldon thought for a moment. He had no idea how many trees there were; he wondered if the Wreccas knew. He doubted it. 'Down this walkway there are . . . um . . . fifteen.' He waited. No one corrected him. Thus emboldened, he continued drawing.

Old Killjoy hung over the map, not noticing that he occasionally dribbled on it. He was too interested in the things Sheldon was drawing.

Scratch noticed. Inwardly he mocked his slobbering leader. Scratch had been the one to draw the map and he had captured the prisoner, but he had received none of the credit. Killjoy knew nothing but pretended to know everything.

More than ever, Scratch wanted to seize power. He longed to demonstrate to Killjoy which of them was the clever one. Holding his hand to his still painful nose, Scratch silently vowed that he would take his revenge, and he would take it soon.

19

An Unexpected Meeting

Sofi was awoken with a rough kick in her back. It was very cold and she gave an involuntary shiver. She knew not to dawdle. Quickly rubbing her eyes, she was instantly awake. Slow reactions would only result in another blow. Looking up, she saw Slime leering down at her.

'Go to the galley chamber and get some food.'

Sofi nodded as she began to stand up.

'Food fit for Old Killjoy. Take it to the war chamber,' Slime added fast. He was eager to get back.

Sofi was already on her way.

'And Snivel can help you,' he said, kicking Snivel for good measure as he left. Snivel sprang up, instantaneously alert.

Sofi blinked her eyes. She felt as if she had been awoken from a heavy sleep, and yet she had intended nothing more than a quick doze. Peering into the main chamber, she saw that a few Wreccas were still asleep after the strenuous Ruckus, but most were up and about. With horror, it dawned on her that she and Snivel must have been asleep for quite a while. However, she did not have time to ponder the fact; she knew she had to comply with Slime's wishes quickly or face the consequences.

As the galley chamber was the only consistently warm place in the Underneath, many Wreccas chose to sleep in the tunnel that led to it. Sofi and Snivel picked their way through the sleeping bodies. If they had been bigger, they would not have minded whom they trod on, but being small they were careful not to disturb anyone. They did not want to risk being on the receiving end of a well-aimed blow.

The galley chamber was the kitchen and it was manned by four red-faced and sweating Wreccas. Squabble was arguing with Slop when the children arrived. They explained what they needed. At the mention of Old Killjoy, the galley Wreccas started rushing about. Their leader always had the best food available and they knew from bitter experience that he did not like to be kept waiting.

The only way Wreccas could obtain food was to scavenge for it. The most nutritious fare they found was under vegetable patches. If they were lucky enough to stumble across one, they tunnelled underneath and pulled out the root vegetables as they grew. But there was nothing methodical about their garden-robbing. They had no understanding of how things grew, and so, when a garden was stripped bare, it would be forgotten and they would randomly set about searching for another.

The galley Wreccas did not know how to cook. Nearly everything that was scavenged was thrown into an enormous, greasy pot that endlessly bubbled in the steaming kitchen. Thus the vegetables that could have been a pleasure to eat had all the flavour and goodness boiled out of them until they were limp and tasteless.

The Wreccas who found the food were called Scavengers. They were trusted to go Topside at night to search the dustbins for provisions. This was a good time of year. Humans threw out all sorts of delicacies after the Christmas celebrations. Discarded turkey carcasses gave the thin stew some flavour. If they had left it at this, then maybe it would have tasted reasonably good. But everything else was thrown into the pot too. There were Brussels sprouts, half-eaten mince pies, pieces of Christmas pudding and also the bits of holly that people put on top of their puddings. All these things and more were mixed together and allowed to bubble away for hours.

Old Killjoy had all the goodness from the stew. He had the lumps of roast potato and the puddings and pies all slopped together. The other Wreccas had the thin soup that remained. Eating was not a pleasurable activity in the Underneath.

However, today there was a treat: Spittle had found a handful of sweets in a dustbin. A Human who disliked nuts had thrown away all the sweets containing them. Each one was elegantly wrapped in brightly coloured crinkly paper.

Squabble placed them on a piece of wood that served as a plate and said, 'There's a handful of these, snotty-Snot.' To prove it, he moved them across the wood one at a time. Each time he moved a sweet, he held up one finger until by the time he had moved each sweet, all five fingers on one hand were held up. 'So you's not to try nicking any, cos I'll ask Old Killjoy and if he don't get a handful you'll be sorry!'

'Willn't take none,' said Sofi sulkily.

Many beer and wine bottles had also been scavenged, and the dregs were drained into one of the bottles. There was just enough for Old Killjoy and Scratch too, if he was lucky. Everyone else was to have the water that had been sitting in a large dirty sink at the far end of the galley. The slimy water was scooped up into some empty beer bottles.

While they were waiting for the food to be prepared, Sofi moved cautiously across to a newly arrived pile of food. It had not yet been thrown into the pot. Furtively, she stole a stale bread roll and two carrots and stuffed them into her pockets.

Snivel watched. As soon as she stood aside, he quickly grabbed a lump of Christmas pudding and a raw potato and safely stowed them in his pockets.

When Old Killjoy's food was ready, Sofi and Snivel carefully carried the trays of refreshments out of the galley chamber. Squabble helped by clearing a path through the sleeping Wreccas in the tunnel. He knew that if any of the food or drink was lost because a young'un had been tripped by a sleeping Wrecca, they would all be in trouble. The galley Wreccas had suffered the consequences of such a calamity in the past, and none of them relished the prospect of it happening again.

As soon as they were clear, Sofi started wondering

about where they had been told to take the food. 'I never knowed there was a war chamber,' she said.

'It's only one of Old Killjoy's rooms,' Snivel explained. 'Him called it that on account of the army.'

'What army?' Sofi felt it was safe now to show a little of her ignorance to Snivel.

'You know, what the traitor told us about.'

'What traitor?'

'Where has you been, snotty-Snot? Doesn't you listen to nothing?'

Sofi thought it best not to press the issue. She would rather Snivel did not have the opportunity to work out that she had not been around for a while. 'Oh, that traitor,' she said, pretending to understand.

Snivel led the way. When they reached the war chamber, they kicked at the door to announce their arrival.

'Who's there?' came a suspicious voice.

'Snot and Snivel with the food.'

The door was opened and the two of them staggered inside.

Sheldon was still drawing. He was bending low over the map, embellishing it, disregarding any thought of being accurate. Snot and Snivel were told to put the meal at the other end of the table. Under the watchful eyes of the most important Wreccas in the Underneath, they concentrated hard so as not to spill anything. Carefully, they put the provisions down.

Immediately, Sofi picked up the piece of wood and, turning away from the table, handed it to Old Killjoy. 'Squabble says these is for you,' she said, handing him the piece of wood with the precious sweets. 'There's a handful of them,' she confirmed. 'That's five and they's all there.' She was proud that she could count more than most Wreccas.

Old Killjoy snatched them greedily. Immediately, he started unwrapping one and popped it into his mouth. For a moment he was transfixed with pleasure. He seldom had the opportunity to taste anything delicious, and he savoured the moment. All the other Wreccas watched him jealously. Each of them would have done almost anything to taste one of the colourful-looking delicacies. The sight of them alone was tantalizing. There was no colour in the Underneath other than browns and darkness and misery.

All the Wreccas were staring at Old Killjoy, who was greedily unwrapping the next sweet. Sheldon knew the refreshments had arrived and wondered how long he would have to wait for his drink. His thirst was almost unbearable.

Sofi's attention was drawn to the map. It did not make a lot of sense to her, upside down as it was.

From one side of the table, Sheldon stopped drawing and looked up, wondering if the Wreccas who had brought the drinks would give him one. At the same moment, from the other side of the table, Sofi looked up to see who was responsible for the drawing. Their eyes opened wide in shocked amazement as each recognized the other.

'You!' Sheldon gasped, stumbling to his feet.

Sofi was too shocked to say anything.

'It's y-you!' he stammered, once more.

He could not believe it. Sofi, the cause of all his trouble, was standing, wide-eyed, at the other side of the table! He looked about him. No one was taking any notice. He had to get their attention.

Sofi was stunned. She stared at him, too horrified to think straight. All she could think of was the Ruckus. If he told them all he knew about her, she would be delivered up to it and no mistake. Desperately, she searched her mind for a way to stop him from telling about her Topside activities – or at least to stop the others from believing him. But her brain was frozen with fear. She said nothing but continued to stare at him with wide, frightened eyes.

Sheldon stared back.

Snivel was confused. Why was she behaving so oddly? 'Does you know each other?'

'Do I know her?' Sheldon exploded. 'Of course I know her!'

Scratch tore his eyes away from the sweets. 'What's up?'

'Her,' Sheldon said, waving his finger towards Sofi. 'She's Sofi!'

This was the moment Sofi wanted to die. She longed to be struck down on the spot and to know nothing more. Her eyes became misty as they clung to Sheldon's face.

'She was in the World, you know ... Topside.' He used the Wrecca word he had recently learnt. 'And she was all clean!'

Scratch waited for what, to Sofi, seemed an eternity before snapping, 'Of course her was Topside.' He was still irritated that Old Killjoy had not offered him a sweet. 'Her was on a mission.'

'She was all clean,' Sheldon persisted, 'and with Tid.'

'Who else would her be with?'

'You don't understand.' Sheldon was becoming more agitated. 'She and Tid were together, like they were friends, and she was dressed as one of the Guardian People.' Then he stopped and spoke very slowly. 'I thought she was one of us.'

Old Killjoy was unwrapping the last sweet.

'Us knows this,' Scratch snapped angrily. 'I stealed a blue tunic for her.'

Sheldon looked back at Sofi. When he had seen her, she was not wearing a blue tunic, she was dressed just like Tid. Sheldon looked towards Scratch. 'You don't understand,' he said. But Scratch's attention was back on Old Killjoy and the final sweet that was disappearing into his mouth.

Sheldon looked back at Sofi. Her eyes were bigger than any he had ever seen and they were filled with . . .

He shut his mouth. Sheldon was overcome by the look in those eyes. They were filled with fear. No, not just fear, absolute terror. Only yesterday he would not have recognized that look, but today, after the treatment he had received in the Underneath, he understood it only too well.

'What?' Scratch snapped. Having watched Old Killjoy

swallow the last of the sweets, he dragged his attention back to the traitor. 'What's you saying?'

Sheldon drew breath to speak. This was his moment. He would tell them everything. 'I . . .' he began, but did not continue.

Sofi's desperate eyes bore into him, silently pleading. But Sheldon had no intention of helping her. After all, she was the cause of all his misery. If she had not run off, then he would have delivered her as promised. Then Old Killjoy would have been impressed, instead of treating him like a criminal, throwing him into a prison, no food, no water, no . . .

Without intending it, Sheldon found himself speculating about the treatment Sofi might receive, once he had revealed her treachery. Then another thought flashed through his mind. If Scratch already knew that Sofi and Tid had been together, why was she so scared that he might find out? Scratch would never allow Sofi to be friends with Tid, and so she must have been acting on Scratch's orders.

Sheldon's brow furrowed as he tried to work this out. Perhaps Sofi's secret was that she and Tid really were friends. When he saw her, she had not been dressed in blue. It had looked as though she was wearing some of Tid's clothes. If this was so, then it was possible that Old Father Tim was also involved. If Sheldon gave Sofi up to Scratch now, what would the Old Father do if Sheldon should escape? He was already in enough trouble; he did not want even more problems if he ever got back into the World.

'Well?' Scratch barked at him.

'I ... I ...' he paused. 'I was wondering if I might trouble you for a drink?'

Scratch would have happily dumped the dirty old beer bottle full of water all over Sheldon's head, but Old Killjoy smiled benevolently. The sugary taste of the delicacies he had just finished still lingered and he was feeling strangely mellow.

'Give him a drink!'

Sofi did not move until she felt a blow on the back of the head from Scratch.

'Give him a drink!' he bellowed.

Blinking herself back to reality, Sofi picked up a grimy beaker and roughly cleaned it with her dirty cuff. Then she poured in some of the unpleasant-smelling water and handed it to Sheldon. Her hand shook just a little.

Slowly, he took it from her and said nothing.

'Get out,' Scratch said, pushing her hard.

Sofi did not wait to be told twice.

20

A Breath of Fresh Air

Sofi staggered along the corridor, neither knowing nor caring in which direction her shaking legs were taking her.

Snivel hurried to keep pace. He did not really understand why he felt the need to stay by her side. Her recent behaviour had been weird, to say the least, but he felt safer with her than on his own.

Eventually she stumbled on the uneven floor and fell to the ground. Once down, she did not have the energy to get up again. Suddenly, the enormity of all that had happened overwhelmed her. Sofi buried her face in her hands and began to cry.

In the Underneath, crying was considered a weakness that gave power to others. Snivel saw her tears and reacted like any Wrecca.

'Cry baby, snotty-Snot,' he taunted her in a sing-song voice.

Sofi did not hear his mean words. It was her fear that caused her tears. She sobbed with great shuddering breaths that shook her entire body.

Snivel continued, 'Snivelling little wretch!' It was something he had been called often enough.

Sofi took no notice but pulled her knees up and, clasping them with her arms, wept on to them.

Snivel looked about him. They were alone. No one could see that he was behaving as he should. There seemed little point in carrying on. Without saying another word, he sat down beside her, leant against the wall, took out his food and started eating the Christmas pudding.

After a while, Sofi gulped one long, shuddering breath and her tears subsided. She wiped her nose and eyes on her sleeve. It was no use crying. Her tears would not transport the Tick to the Topside. Realizing how hungry she was, she pulled the stale bread roll from her pocket and sank her teeth into it.

Now that the shock of meeting Sheldon was subsiding, she began to feel annoyed. She was angry with herself for sleeping through the general exhaustion that had followed the Ruckus. How stupid! With everyone awake, it would no longer be feasible to try and take the Tick through the main chamber. The back tunnels were the only way now. They were long and dark, and she knew it would be difficult with only Snivel for help. She wished she had left Cob and the others at the rear Topside door. They would have been easy to contact there, but they were waiting by the lower door. Everything was more difficult than it should have been. Perhaps, she could contact the Bushytails and take them to the appropriate door, but that would take ages. She had no idea how much time was left. Maybe she should risk bringing Cob inside right away.

Sighing deeply, she closed her eyes. Her injured heel was hurting and her head was still aching. This was all too much. She felt like crying again.

Sheldon swallowed the water so quickly that he did not notice how dirty it was. His only thought was to quench his raging thirst. Without asking, he refilled the beaker and gulped down the contents once more. While he drank, nothing else mattered, but once his thirst was satisfied his thoughts returned to Sofi.

Why was she in the Underneath? In the World he had thought her to be one of the Guardian People, but in the Underneath she appeared to be a Wrecca. Whose side was she on?

He looked at the others, who were greedily slurping their food. No one offered him any, but he did not mind. The smell was far from appetizing. He sat down and looked at the map. He was beginning to wonder whether he had done the right thing, keeping quiet about Sofi. Telling all he knew about her Topside activities might have pleased Old Killjoy. He might even have given Sheldon the medal he had dreamt of. Maybe even offered him a home in the Underneath.

A home in the Underneath! This was something he had long wanted. To live side by side with these creatures had been a thrilling fantasy. Sheldon looked up at the dirty Wreccas gobbling their food. Their teeth were bad and some of them had open sores on their faces. All of them smelt unpleasant. Old Killjoy dribbled and Sniff picked his nose and ate what he had retrieved from it.

It was then that Sheldon realized something. It did not matter how popular he was with Old Killjoy or how many medals he was given.

He wanted to go home.

Together, Sofi and Snivel made their way towards the lower Topside door. Sofi limped as she walked because her heel was very sore. All her courage and energy had drained away. She no longer believed she could rescue the Tick, and she had stopped caring that time would end for all time. All she wanted was to get warm. If she was lucky, she would find a spot near the galley chamber, go to sleep again and allow time to end forever without her knowing anything about it.

Stopping for a moment, she leant against the wall and lifted her heel to her hand. Snivel stopped too. He did not mind waiting. The longer they took, the happier he was. He did not want to go anywhere.

Sofi's mind drifted to Old Father Tim and his loving eyes. She thought of the way she felt when she was with him and Tid. Safe. She had never felt that before, but she always felt it when she was with them. She touched her cheek, remembering how Tid had kissed her. Then she pictured Old Father Tim asking her to be his grand-daughter. A thrill of pleasure stirred deep inside at the thought of belonging to them.

Then a feeling of wretchedness overcame her. What if she was never to be with them again? Never able to share a meal around the table or sit in front of the warm fire? Closing her eyes, she allowed her mind to drift back to their cosy kitchen. She wondered what Old Father Tim and Tid were doing right now. Perhaps they were eating pancakes and syrup. She pictured herself with them and she felt a longing so powerful than it twisted her stomach and made it hurt.

She yearned to go back. She ached to be one of them. To live, learn and laugh with Tid, to be a granddaughter and feel safe with an old grandfather to love and protect her. These were the things she wanted so strongly that she would risk everything to get them.

She had no choice. She could not abandon their cause. If she failed, it would not be for want of trying. She would not give up. Not now, not ever. If she died in the attempt, she would continue until the end. They were her family now. A family. Sofi had a family! A new vigour filled her as she thought about it. No, she would never let them down.

She started walking, but this time with a purposeful stride. Snivel raised his eyebrows in surprise at the suddenness of her movement but he silently fell in beside her.

Sofi made plans as she walked. She decided that she would bring Cob into the Underneath and he would help her carry the Tick. The safest route was now the longest one. In her heart she knew that two Bushytails would be more helpful, but hiding one would be hard enough.

'Wait here, Sniv.'

'Why?'

It was a good question and one she knew she should answer, but how? She could not tell him she was bringing a Bushytail into the Underneath.

'Cos I say so!'

Snivel shrugged his shoulders and leant back against the wall. He had given up trying to work out why she was behaving so strangely.

Glancing at him to make sure he was staying put, Sofi continued up the steep incline and out of sight.

Spittle was on guard. That was unusual, for he was a scavenger and did not expect to do guard duty. In fact, he had been scavenging all night and, like most Wreccas, did not have the discipline to stay awake when he wanted to sleep. Lying across the steps, he was snoring loudly.

Carefully stepping over him, Sofi pulled the door open and slipped outside into the sunshine. For a moment the sun blinded her and she had to raise a hand to shade her eyes. Even the low, crisp, winter sun felt warm compared to the damp darkness of the Underneath. She thought about calling Cob but did not have to.

He and the others were waiting where Sofi had left them. He had organized them so that one Bushytail was on guard duty whilst the other two rested. It was difficult to relax because every muscle in their bodies was ready for immediate action, but they tried. The moment he saw her, he alerted the others and they silently ran to her side.

'You are here!' cried Cob, very relieved. 'You took so long, we began to fear for your safety.'

'I's fine,' said Sofi, happy to see them. She moved into

the shadows and kept her voice low. 'How much time is there?'

The sun was low in the sky. Cob knew it would soon be gone. 'Until midnight when the new year starts.'

It didn't sound long.

'You's got to come now.'

'Yes,' replied Cob. 'Lead the way, Miss Sofi.'

Walnut and Hazel prepared to leave with them.

Sofi looked at the three of them. 'Only you, Cob.'

'Very well, miss.' Cob was ready to obey orders without question.

'No.' It was Hazel who spoke. She looked lovingly at Cob. 'If Cob goes, then so do I.'

'Do not question Miss Sofi,' Cob reproved her. 'This is a military operation.'

'But the plan was for us all to go,' Hazel obstinately persisted.

Cob frowned. She was not behaving as she had been trained to do.

'I's sorry, Hazel,' Sofi said. 'There's been a change of plan. I can only smuggle one of you inside.'

'Why?'

Cob was appalled at Hazel's lack of discipline. 'Enough!' he said. 'Miss Sofi is in command.'

Sofi realized that Cob was happy to leave them behind. He would prefer to keep them safe.

To settle the matter, Sofi gave them some orders. 'You two go and wait on the edge of . . . er . . . the grass,' she thought for a moment. She could not remember its name. 'What's it called?'

'Blackheath.'

'Yer, Blackheath. You stay there and wait.'

'Why cannot we wait here?'

'Cos if you does us'll probably miss you when us comes out. Us is having to use another door.'

'Which door?' Walnut asked. 'We will wait there.'

Sofi looked uncomfortable. She did not like displaying her poor leadership qualities. 'Thing is, it's a bit muddled down there. The plan might change and then us'll use yet another door and miss you. But if you wait on the edge of Blackheath, then you'll see us cos us'll cross it, whichever door us uses.'

Hazel looked nervously at Cob.

'And us'll need you to be fresh.' Sofi tried to sound encouraging. 'You'll both have to be strong enough to help carry the Tick back to the park. By the time us gets to you, us'll be pretty tired.'

'Why cannot one of us wait by the door you think you might use? If you are tired, then the nearer we are to you, the better.'

'Cos you doesn't know where it is and I doesn't have time to show you and . . .' She ran her hand over her brow. She did not have the energy to answer so many questions. Why did they not just do as they were told?

Hazel was not impressed. She did not trust Miss Sofi with Cob's life. She looked at Walnut, hoping that he would challenge this foolish plan.

'Perhaps we should get some of the Guardian People to come out and wait with us,' he suggested. 'Carrying the Tick would not be difficult for them.'

Sofi shook her head. 'I doesn't want people hanging around and warning Scavengers that something's up.'

'Scavengers?'

'Wreccas what come up at night.'

'What about more Bushytails? We could put one on each door, if you told us where they were.'

'I doesn't have time to show you,' Sofi snapped irritably. 'And anyway, there'll be more than Scavengers out tonight cos of the army. If they see loads of people or Bushytails, they'll know something's up.'

'What army?'

Sofi immediately regretted saying so much. It only gave them the opportunity to ask more questions.

'I doesn't have time for this,' she said abruptly. 'Just do as I tell you!'

Walnut stood to attention and spoke respectfully. 'Very well, miss. We shall be waiting.'

Sofi smiled her thanks.

Hazel knew she had to accept the situation and she turned to her sweetheart. 'Take care of yourself, Cob, dear.'

'Don't fuss,' Cob said, but in a way which showed that her fussing pleased him. 'I shall do my duty and come home safely to you.' They touched noses.

'And we shall do our duty.' Walnut spoke for himself and Hazel. 'We shall be waiting. We will not let you down.'

'This I know,' Cob said with pride.

Sofi was anxious to be off. 'I'll have to hide you inside my shirt,' she said to Cob. 'I hope you doesn't mind.'

'Not at all, but surely I shall be seen,' Cob replied. 'I will make too big a lump.'

'Not if I put my hands in front, like this.' Sofi folded her arms. 'What d'you think?'

Cob nodded and Sofi lifted him up and slipped him inside her shirt. He wrapped himself around her body and tried to make himself as flat as possible.

Sofi folded her arms in front. 'Does him show?'

'Well, yes,' Walnut and Hazel said honestly.

'But it's dark in the Underneath,' Sofi said, hoping to convince them that it would be all right.

'It might not be so bad in the dark,' Walnut agreed dubiously.

'Well, it's the best us can do.'

'All will be well,' Cob said in a muffled voice from under her arm. 'We must proceed.'

'You's better go,' Sofi said to the Bushytails.

Hazel was clearly unwilling to leave, but Walnut touched her with his paw and she reluctantly followed him.

Cob was soft and warm against her skin, and Sofi realized once more how very cold she was without her jacket, even in the winter sunshine. Carefully, she kept her arms folded in front of her, trying to conceal the giveaway bulge.

'There's a Wrecca on the other side of the door,' she whispered as they approached it.

'I am not afraid of a Wrecca,' Cob boldly replied in a stifled whisper.

'Him's asleep,' Sofi continued. 'All Wreccas sleep like

the dead, and so us'll be fine, but stay quiet and out of sight.'

'I am ready.'

Sofi took a deep breath to fill her lungs with the delicious air of the Topside. Then she opened the door and carefully retraced her steps back inside.

It was not difficult. Spittle continued to snore loudly. Sofi crept past him and back to Snivel, who was sitting where she had left him, chewing the last of his raw potato. Not being able to see the door, he had no idea that she had been Topside. His arms were wrapped around himself and Sofi realized that he was cold too. She was conscious that it was her fault he did not have his jacket but she said nothing, feeling all the more guilty for the little warmth that Cob gave her.

Sheldon followed his guards down the tunnel. They were obviously very proud of their enhanced status. Neither had guarded so important a prisoner before; but, as the more able Wreccas were on the newly formed War Council, the lesser Wreccas were taking on more significant jobs.

Sheldon was dreading the return to his dungeon with the low ceiling. He wondered if he should have asked Old Killjoy for better accommodation. Now he was helping with the map, maybe they would treat him better.

'Where are you taking me?' he asked, knowing the answer.

'To the dungeon,' Stupid replied.

'Don't tell him!' snarled Scrag, clouting Stupid across the back of his head.

'What you do that for?' Stupid asked angrily, rubbing it.

'You's not to talk to the prisoner!'

'I'll talk to him if I want!'

'Oh yer?'

'Oh yer!'

'Say another word to him and I'll belt you proper!'

'Yer? You and whose army?'

'Army? I doesn't need an army to keep a stupid old Wrecca like you in order.'

'Who's you calling old?'

'I's calling you old! Old as the tunnels!' He thrust his face into Stupid's. 'Old, worn-out and very stupid!'

'Stupid!' Stupid fairly exploded.

'It's your name.'

'It don't make I stupid. Unlike you, you brainless dung beetle! You're so thick, it's hard to tell the difference between you and that wall.' He jerked his thumb behind him.

'Thick?' Scrag was deeply insulted. 'You old skeleton!' and he pushed Stupid hard in the chest.

'Don't push I!' Stupid squared up to Scrag.

Both Wreccas pulled back their shoulders in order to make their chests look bigger, and they breathed heavily. Each wanted to look brave and reckless, but in reality neither wanted a fight.

For a moment they stood motionless, glaring at one another. Scrag snarled and Stupid tried to look fierce.

'As soon as us get the prisoner safe, I'll sort you out!' Scrag grunted, playing for time.

'I'll sort *you* out, more like,' Stupid countered.

Scrag glanced at Sheldon. Or at least he glanced where Sheldon should have been standing. Quickly he looked one way and then the other. Stupid did the same.

Sheldon had gone.

21

Miss Sofi of the Topside Guard

Sheldon gasped for breath. Leaning his hands on his bony knees, he dropped his head and dragged in a lungful of foul air. However deeply he breathed, he was still short of breath. 'There's no blasted air down here!' he muttered bad-temperedly.

He looked about him. Which way to go? The tunnel branched into two. He had no notion where he was or how far he had come. He could not believe that no one had stopped him. With a nervous glance over his shoulder, he took off down one of the darker tunnels.

Sofi and Snivel went straight to the hidden hole in the wall. The warmth from Cob hiding in her shirt had given her renewed energy and Sofi felt more optimistic. They squeezed into the hiding place, gazing in awe at the wonderful brightness that oozed from the covered Tick.

From his hiding place inside Sofi's thin shirt, Cob saw the light. He poked his head out. 'Is the coast clear?'

Never having been Topside, Snivel had never seen a Bushytail before and he fixed a horrified stare on Cob.

Sofi helped him out from her shirt and Cob settled himself at her feet and started to groom his rumpled fur.

'You doesn't need to be scared, Sniv,' Sofi said, remembering her own worries the first time she had seen a Bushtyail. 'This is Cob. Him's gonna help us.'

'Happy to make your acquaintance,' Cob said, bowing politely.

Snivel's eyes grew even wider with fright and he stepped back into the wall with a gentle thud.

'Stop behaving like a wimp and pull yourself together,' Sofi snapped, remembering that kindness did not work with Snivel.

Cob was taken aback by her harsh words.

'Come on,' she barked in an angry whisper. 'Us can't do this alone.'

Snivel did not move. His eyes were still firmly fixed on Cob. He was transfixed with terror. To snap him out of it, Sofi kicked him on the shin.

'Miss Sofi!' exclaimed Cob, truly horrified. 'I never would have expected to see you behave in so spiteful a manner.'

Sofi threw Cob an exasperated look. More explanations! She marched out of the hole, beckoning him to follow.

'Him thinks I's still a Wrecca,' she whispered as soon as they were in the tunnel and safely out of earshot. 'Him willn't help if I told him the truth.'

'He does not know the truth?' Cob asked, once again shocked. 'You mean you are deceiving him?'

Sofi sighed deeply. Behaving like this was disagreeable

enough, without a horrified Cob watching and judging. Constantly explaining her actions only added to her burden. 'Wreccas is cruel and spiteful,' she elucidated. 'When I's kind, him gets even more scared.'

Cob said nothing. Sofi could see that her words were not convincing him.

'I doesn't have a choice,' she said bluntly. 'There's ner time to do this the nice way. I has to be nasty.'

'I do not like to see you shame yourself in this manner.'

Suddenly, all of Sofi's frustrations and feelings of inadequacy burst out of her as she yelled, 'I doesn't like it either!'

Cob rapidly looked about him, fearful lest they had been heard.

Sofi took a deep breath to calm herself. 'What choice has I got?' she asked more quietly.

Cob had no answer. All his life he had practised goodness and honesty. Now he was being asked to go along with something deceitful and spiteful. It made him feel uncomfortable.

'The tunnels is long and dark,' Sofi continued. 'It'll be hard even with Sniv. Us doesn't stand a chance without him, and so I do what I has to.'

Cob said nothing.

'I'll make it up to him when I can,' Sofi said more gently. 'Maybe him can stay Topside with us.'

'Stay where?'

'The World.' She tried not to sound irritated by his ignorance. 'Us calls it Topside.'

All at once her heart stopped. She had referred to

the Wreccas as 'us'. Miserably, she realized that it was hopeless to imagine she could ever be anything else.

'Oh, and by the way,' she added, 'you can't call I Miss Sofi. My name's Snot.'

Cob drew his head back in surprise. He repeated the name to himself in a way that made it look as if the word had left a nasty taste in his mouth.

'I know it's a horrid name,' Sofi said, ashamed of herself and her origin.

It was now Cob's turn to feel guilty. 'Forgive me. That was rude. You cannot help the name you are called down here. In the World you have a lovely name.'

Sofi appreciated his attempt to be kind, but it did not make her feel any better.

Now, she turned her attention to Snivel. It was unfortunate that Cob had spoken before she had had the chance to explain who he was.

'Right, Sniv,' she said after re-entering the hole. He was sitting, white-faced, against the wall. 'Listen. I didn't tell you about Cob cos I . . .' Her reason was going to sound lame, but she could think of nothing else. '. . . Cos I wasn't sure about trusting you.'

Snivel looked at her suspiciously. 'Why did that thing call you "Miss Sofi"?' he asked, motioning towards Cob. 'What's a "Miss Sofi"?'

Sofi furrowed her brow. There was not a thought in her head that could explain this. Cob came to her rescue. 'It means "leader" on the . . . the . . .' He had forgotten the word.

'Topside,' Sofi helped, grateful for his support.

'Topside,' continued Cob as though he had known all the time.

'It's ... it's a scary-looking furry thing,' Snivel whimpered.

'I am the leader ...' Cob paused to correct himself, '... I mean the "Miss Sofi" of the Topside Guard.' Cob noticed that this did nothing to calm the frightened young Wrecca. 'How do you think the door to the Topside is kept secure?' Snivel did not respond and Cob continued, 'That idiot lounging on the steps could not prevent an outright attack from the ... the ...'

'Topsiders,' helped Sofi.

'Topsiders,' repeated Cob. 'No indeed,' he continued with a flourish. 'It is we in the Topside Guard who protect you.'

'Yes, Sniv,' Sofi continued, thinking fast, 'and ... and Old Killjoy wants us to take the Tick to the Topside Guard to keep safe 'til him's sorted out who's the traitors.' She watched him carefully, hopeful that he believed her.

Snivel's eyes wandered from Sofi to Cob. 'Why d'you need I when you's got him?'

This question made Sofi quite hopeful. Snivel might have continued questioning her about the Tick and Old Killjoy's involvement in the plan, but he had not. He seemed to have accepted her story. With renewed confidence she continued, 'You know how long the back tunnels is. Us needs help.'

Snivel shook his head. 'I's not doing it.'

'You has ner choice,' Sofi said harshly, nervously

glancing at Cob, who did not react to her sharpness this time. 'You know you has to help or take the punishment.'

Snivel said nothing, but he looked very sulky.

'Punishment from Old Killjoy himself,' Sofi added menacingly, leaning over Snivel threateningly.

Snivel knew he was beaten.

Sheldon was desperately searching for a Topside door, but there seemed to be no logic to these tunnels. They twisted this way and that for no apparent reason. If only he could find a door! He longed to be above ground. Breathing was becoming more and more difficult. There was no air! He kept to the shadows, freezing in panic every time he heard someone approaching. When a Wrecca passed, he discovered that if he stood with his face towards the wall, they went by without looking at him. He wondered how long it would be before the news of his escape was generally made known.

Scrag and Stupid were in desperate discussions. They were nervously standing before the closed door of the empty dungeon. So far, no one had noticed that the prisoner had escaped. They had told no one.

'What'll us do?' Stupid asked.

'You tell Old Killjoy.'

'Why I?'

'Because *you*'s clever,' Scrag said, trying to sound as if he meant it. 'Old Killjoy'll understand if *you* tell him.'

Stupid looked dubious. Despite all his arguments to the contrary, he knew that he was not as clever as some of the others, and he was finding it difficult to understand why Scrag had said that he was.

'Maybe us should wait,' he suggested. 'Take time to think about it.'

'That's not a bad idea,' Scrag agreed.

The notion that he could come up with an idea that was not bad genuinely surprised Stupid, and he could not resist puffing out his chest just a little.

'Old Killjoy'll send another guard sooner or later,' Scrag went on. 'And when him does, us doesn't need to say nothing about the empty dungeon.'

'And when Old Killjoy finds out,' Stupid said, delighted to have understood, 'they'll be in trouble, not us.' And then he added hopefully, 'Think it'll work?'

'Maybe,' Scrag said doubtfully.

'I's good at thinking,' Stupid boasted.

'It's not your idea.'

'I sayed it's best to wait.'

'But I thinked of the blaming the other guards.'

'You only did that cos I sayed us can wait.'

'You only sayed to wait cos you's too scared to tell Old Killjoy.'

They were so engrossed in their argument that neither of them noticed that someone had joined them.

'Too scared to tell Old Killjoy what?' came a suspicious voice from behind.

Immediately, Stupid and Scrag fell silent, their eyes widening in fear. Slowly, they turned in unison to discover Spit standing behind them.

'Nothing,' said Scrag, trying to look innocent.

'Nothing at all,' Stupid agreed.

Both stared at Spit, wondering if they had got away with it.

'It didn't sound like nothing,' Spit said suspiciously. 'What's you hiding?'

'Nothing,' said Scrag once more, backing slowly towards the door of the dungeon as if to protect it.

'Nothing at all,' Stupid agreed, moving back too.

Spit ran his tongue around his thin lips. He was sure they were up to something. At another time it would have been an entertaining diversion to discover what, but right now he was too busy. War was coming and Spit was determined to play a major part in it.

'Just do as you's told and stop messing about!'

'Yes, Spit!' Scrag said, stamping to attention.

'Yes, Spit,' echoed Stupid, doing the same.

Unfortunately for Scrag, it was his foot that Stupid stamped on.

Frightened that Snivel might run away if he was given the opportunity, Sofi made him hold the other side of the Tick while Cob scampered down the tunnel a little way ahead to see if all was clear. They had no one to guard them from behind; Sofi and Snivel just had to listen out carefully.

Even covered by the cloth and both jackets, the Tick still glowed. They had chosen the dark tunnels that were not used as much as regular ones, but the very darkness that had made her feel more secure made the brightness more noticeable.

Cob regularly returned to ask directions. 'Which way? The tunnel breaks into two up there.'

'Take the one on this side,' Sofi said, nodding her head to the left.

'That's the left,' Cob explained.

'What's this side?' Sofi asked, nodding her head the other way.

'The right.'

As Cob scampered off again, Sofi nodded her head one way and mumbled, 'Left,' and then, nodding in the other direction, repeated, 'Right.'

The thought of war had brought much excitement in the Underneath and everyone wanted to voice their opinions on exactly how to beat the enemy. In practical terms this kept them out of the tunnels. Most Wreccas were in various chambers, discussing tactics.

After what seemed like ages, Snivel snivelled, 'I's tired.'

So was Sofi, and he was smaller than she. 'Put it down,' she said kindly.

Gratefully, Snivel did so and sank to the floor. Sofi stood up stiffly and looked ahead, rubbing the base of her spine with her fingers.

Cob scampered back. 'Is there a problem?'

'Sniv's tired.'

'I shall take over,' Cob said, preparing to slip his tail under the Tick.

Sofi looked at Snivel and wondered if she could trust him. 'You'll have to be lookout,' she said, not too happy at the thought of sending him on alone.

'I's not moving.'

Sofi gave him a sharp kick and he quickly stood up.

'Keep going 'til you come to the next tunnel split,' she ordered. 'Check out the one on the left.' She held out her left hand. 'If you see anyone, come back and tell us.' She felt uneasy. Could he be trusted? 'You's better not forget,' she warned.

Snivel nodded and jogged off down the passage. He had never liked the dark tunnels, they were scary, but today he was glad of them because it did not take long for him to be out of sight. He wanted to put as much distance as possible between him and them. He had already decided to run away and hide. Although terrified at the thought of angering Old Killjoy, he was more scared of the Tick, the furry creature and the risk of being seen in the presence of both. He reasoned that the war would be occupying Old Killjoy, and he hoped that all this nonsense with the Tick would soon be forgotten. He would lie low and leave Snot to sort this one out by herself. When he approached the split in the tunnels, he ignored what Sofi had told him and ran down the right-hand one instead.

Sofi and Cob were unaware of his defection. When they reached the side tunnel, they hesitated.

'I only told him to come back if he seed anyone,' she said.

They took the left-hand tunnel, but Sofi was on edge and listened carefully, straining her eyes to see if she could detect movement ahead. When she saw some-one approaching, she gave a sigh of relief and reproved herself for not trusting Snivel. But suddenly the 'some-one' stopped, as if surprised to see them.

Sofi watched the figure. Slowly, it began to dawn on her that this was not Snivel.

She stopped walking, frozen in terror. Where was Snivel? This was what she had dreaded. There was no escape, nowhere to hide. The Tick glowed brightly. In the darkness it now seemed to Sofi to be as dazzling a light as any she had ever seen. No wonder they had been discovered. It was all over.

'You's better run!' she whispered urgently.

Cob peered into the gloom but could not see why Sofi sounded so frightened.

'What is the matter?' he asked.

Sofi put the Tick down and moved to the front so she could stand protectively in front of it. She stretched out her arms, as if to shield it from whoever was approaching. 'Run!' she said, more agitated than before. If she was going to get caught, she had no wish for Cob to suffer too.

Cob stood by her side and stared at the approaching figure. 'We shall face this together,' he said quietly.

22

The Nasty Brute

Sheldon's breathing was becoming shallow and his head was beginning to feel light. Some of this was undoubtedly due to lack of oxygen, but he had also not eaten for a considerable time. The tunnels seemed to dance before his eyes and he had to blink several times to restore normal vision.

Then he saw a light. It appeared to be propelling itself along the tunnel. He blinked his eyes once more. Surely they were playing tricks on him again, but this time blinking did not help. The distant light continued to advance with a strange bobbing motion. He rubbed his eyes and looked again. The light had stopped still.

It was then he realized that there was someone silhouetted by the light, and it did not take long for him to recognize who that 'someone' was.

'You!' he roared as he rushed towards her. All his hatred and anger surged out of him as he grabbed hold of Sofi and slammed her against the wall. Her body slumped as her head snapped backwards. She exhaled with a groan as the impact forced all the air from her lungs.

'Get off her, you nasty brute!' Cob shouted. With all the ferocity stored within his courageous little heart, he jumped up and clawed at Sheldon's face.

Blinded by the violence of this sudden assault, Sheldon dropped Sofi and began to swipe at the unseen monster that was attacking him.

Agilely, Cob avoided Sheldon's wildly flailing arms. 'Run!' he commanded Sofi, taking off at great speed.

Stunned though she was, Sofi scrambled to her feet and started running. She could not move fast, being too confused by the force of Sheldon's onslaught.

Sheldon began whimpering. Whatever had attacked him in the dark had hurt his face. There was blood dribbling down his cheek.

Sofi ran as best she could, but she had still not recovered from the force of Sheldon's strike. Cob encouraged her to hurry, but she stumbled and fell to the floor, gasping for breath. Cob ran a few paces back to check that they were not being followed, giving her a few moments.

Sofi lay with her hand to her chest, as if the very act of holding it there would help it to expand and drag in the air she so desperately needed. As she lay gasping, she put the facts together. Sheldon was in the tunnel by himself. Old Killjoy would never trust him without a guard. He must have escaped!

'Come, Miss Sofi, we must go.'

'Ner.' Sofi's voice rasped from her throat.

'I will not leave you,' Cob said, believing that Sofi was suggesting that he should run on alone.

Sofi staggered to her feet and started back towards the Tick and Sheldon.

'This way!' Cob said, thinking she was disorientated and going in the wrong direction by mistake.

'Ner,' Sofi said again, in a voice that sounded a little more like her own.

'But that is the wrong way.'

'Cob, you go. But I can't leave the Tick.'

Cob was suddenly ashamed. How could he, in a moment of panic, forget the one thing that was so vital to them? He ran to her side.

Sheldon was sitting on the floor, trying to wipe his bleeding face with his tunic cuff. It took him a while to realize that he was not alone. At first he jumped in fright, but he quickly relaxed when he saw it was only Sofi. 'What did you have to go and do that for?' he whined, pulling a handkerchief from his pocket and pathetically trying to tend his face.

It was only now that Cob recognized the victim he had so bravely attacked. He remembered him from the park as the boy who found it amusing to hunt and hurt Bushytails.

'I was protecting Miss Sofi!' Cob said, hatred blazing in his eyes.

'Good grief!' Sheldon exclaimed, as he saw Cob properly for the first time. 'A Bushytail in the Underneath?'

Cob drew himself up to his full height and stared angrily at his enemy; but Sheldon was not intimidated now he knew who Cob was, and he continued to dab his bleeding face with his handkerchief. Sitting forlornly on the floor, he did not seem the fearsome person Sofi had once thought him to be. Below ground, he was helpless. She realized her advantage.

'Here,' she said, 'I'll do that.' Bending down, she took the handkerchief from him and started cleaning his face.

'I wouldn't have hurt you,' he lied, trying to justify himself.

'You did,' Sofi scolded.

He accepted the reproof in silence.

'How did you get away from them?' she asked.

'It wasn't difficult,' Sheldon said. Then he added confidentially, 'They're a bit thick, these Wreccas, aren't they?'

Sofi nodded, gently dabbing at his face.

'Who *are* you?' It was a question that had been puzzling him for some time.

'Sofi.'

'I know your name,' he said, somewhat irritated by her obvious answer. In the war chamber he had wondered whether she was a Wrecca or one of the Guardian People; but now he saw her with Cob, he was convinced that she was the latter. 'What is one of the Guardian People doing down here?'

Sofi hung her head in shame. ''S a Wrecca.'

Now Sheldon was very confused. 'Then what were you doing in the World with Tid?'

Sofi sat down next to him. Tid. She had not thought of him in quite a while. 'It's a long story.'

Sheldon thought for a moment and suddenly realized that he did not care who she was. He was not going to stay in the Underneath a moment longer than he had to. 'Well, I don't have the time to listen to it,' he said, getting to his feet. 'I'm off.'

'Where's you going?'

'Out of here.'

'How?'

Sheldon scratched his head. He had no idea. His eyes rested on the Tick. 'What's that?'

'That's a long story too,' Sofi said somewhat absent-mindedly. An idea was forming in her head. 'D'you know how to get out?'

Sheldon looked along the tunnel. A scheme was taking shape in his brain too. It occurred to him that if Sofi was a Wrecca, then she would know the way out. If he could make her show him, he could escape to freedom.

Knowing only one way of asking, Sheldon grabbed hold of Sofi's arm and cruelly twisted it behind her back.

'Leave Miss Sofi alone!' Cob shouted, jumping up at Sheldon.

In Cob's initial attack, Sheldon had been surprised. This time, knowing it was only a Bushytail, Sheldon swatted him away with ease. Cob was knocked to the floor but immediately sprang up and turned around, ready to attack once more.

'Ner, Cob, stop!' Sofi shouted.

'Show me how to get out of here,' Sheldon snarled, 'and I'll not turn you over to Old Killjoy.' He tried to look fearsome.

Although her arm was causing her considerable pain, Sofi thought it was strange that she no longer found

Sheldon frightening. 'I'll show you how to get out of here,' she said calmly, wincing as he jerked her arm. She was certain that Sheldon would not give her up to Old Killjoy. He would be as frightened of the Wrecca leader as everyone else. 'But you has to help us,' she added.

'I'm not helping anyone.' Sheldon tightened his grip.

Sofi cried out in pain but obstinately said, 'Then I willn't show you nothing.'

Sheldon enjoyed bullying people smaller than himself. It gave him the feeling of superiority that he so craved. With his other hand he grabbed her by the neck and squeezed.

She found it hard to breathe.

Cob watched in dismay. He was too small to force Sheldon to leave her alone. He had to out-think him.

'What good will it do you if you kill Miss Sofi, you foul brute? She is the only one who knows the way out of here.'

There was logic in this. Sheldon reluctantly released his grip. Sofi doubled over, coughing.

'Just find me a door,' he growled.

'Yer,' she said, clambering to her feet and holding her bruised throat. 'I'll show you the way,' it was hard to talk, 'if you carry that.' She was pointing at the Tick.

'No,' Sheldon said defiantly. Then curiosity got the better of him. 'What is it? It doesn't look as though it belongs down here.'

'It don't.' Sofi was still finding it difficult to speak. 'It's Old Father Tim's,' and she doubled up as a racking cough seized her.

Sheldon stared at it in surprise.

'The Wreccas stole it,' Cob explained. 'Miss Sofi and I are taking it back. We have to return it before midnight.'

'Is you going to help?' Sofi asked, clearing her throat. There was no point in telling him what would happen if they were late. She doubted it would make him any keener to leave the Underneath, and she reasoned that knowing the truth might make him even more jumpy.

'And why should I do that?' Sheldon asked with a sneer.

'Cos if you doesn't, you willn't find a door and you'll be lost down here forever.' Sofi's voice was thin and strained. 'And if you does,' her voice changed, becoming persuasively sweet, 'Old Father Tim will be dead happy with you.'

Sheldon's expression changed. He repeated these words softly to himself. The gratitude of such a person could make all the difference. Such appreciation could give him some standing in the Guardian community. He might even be Harvested!

Sofi noticed the effect her words were having on him. 'In fact,' she continued, pushing home her advantage, 'all the Guardians will be very, very happy. The Tick is ever so important.'

She knew she was winning, but a little flattery could speed things up and so, in order to clinch the deal, she added, 'Cob and I is too small and weak to do it alone, but you's big and strong.'

Cob did not like being called 'small and weak' but said nothing.

Sheldon's chest swelled at the flattery.

'And if you do it, then . . .' she tried to think of a reward that would be of interest to Sheldon.

'Would they give me a medal?' Sheldon asked.

Sofi inwardly smiled. 'I think so.'

Sheldon nodded and a smug grin crossed his lips.

Sofi knew that she had won.

A dense mist hung over the park, making it difficult for Tid and his grandfather to see any distance. They were walking towards the gates.

'How long do we have?' Tid asked.

Old Father Tim paused and looked up at the sky. Although the mist was heavy, it did not seem to impair Old Father Tim's ability to calculate time. This was a gift given to few. 'Less than three hours,' he said.

'Is it long enough?'

His grandfather leant heavily upon Tid's shoulder. 'It will take time to re-fit the Tick.'

'How long?'

'It is difficult to say. It depends how much damage there is.'

This was a complication that had not occurred to Tid. 'Why should it be damaged?'

Old Father Tim vaguely shook his head. He did not know.

'Do you think she'll be here in time?' Tid was hoping for reassurance, but his grandfather had none to give.

'I am going to talk with Bryn.'

'Why?' Tid asked.

'I want him to send some people on to Blackheath. If Sofi gets out, they will be well placed to help her.'

Tid did not move to follow his grandfather.

'Are you not coming with me?' the old man asked.

'I think someone should stay and be Mindful. It might work better from here.'

Old Father Tim nodded. 'Of course. I will be back as soon as possible. Keep moving. It's too cold to stand still for long.'

In the Underneath, Sheldon was getting weaker. The combination of lack of nourishment and breathing foul air was taking its toll. 'I'm hungry,' he whined. 'I need food.'

Sofi searched her pockets. She thought she had a carrot left, but it must have fallen out. 'There's plenty Topside,' she said, trying to encourage him to put in extra effort to get there quickly.

Perspiration dripped down Sheldon's face and he could no longer make his eyes focus properly. It did not bother Sofi that he was having difficulties; her priority was to keep him moving. Progress was easier, now she was no longer burdened with the Tick.

Suddenly, Sofi heard the scuffed footsteps of approaching Wreccas.

'Quick!' she whispered and, grabbing Sheldon by his shirt, she propelled him back the way they had come. Sofi had been careful to note each abandoned tunnel they passed and, signalling to Cob to follow, they now darted down one in order to hide.

Sheldon asked no questions, he followed without thinking, and when they came to a halt he gratefully accepted the rest. Slowly he closed his eyes, slid down the wall to the ground and waited, with the Tick balanced precariously on his lap.

Sofi and Cob listened carefully. They heard footsteps approach and then die away.

'We can go now,' Cob said, as soon as he felt it was safe.

'Us had best wait a bit to be sure,' Sofi replied.

'We don't have time to be sure.'

It was true. Sofi had no idea how long they had, but she knew time was running out. She shook Sheldon until he was awake then pulled him to his feet. They retraced their steps and continued their journey.

Old Killjoy awoke from his alcohol-induced slumber. There was an unpleasant taste in his mouth and a dull ache in his head.

'I want a drink!' he yelled at Scratch, who was still asleep. 'Get I a flaming drink!' he roared once more, lashing out with his foot but not connecting with anything.

Scratch blearily opened his eyes and stumbled to the door. He waylaid the first Wrecca he could find. 'Fetch some refreshments!' he demanded and sent him off with a smack on the back of his head.

Old Killjoy was in a foul mood. He moaned and grumbled at Scratch while he waited. As soon as water arrived, he swallowed it fast, dribbling it down his chin.

Then he grabbed the food and stuffed it into his mouth, spitting out fragments as he demanded to know how the war preparations were going.

Scratch kept his distance.

After eating, Old Killjoy felt a little better. The refreshments had restored his health, if not his temper. He stomped around the table where the map lay, trying to understand it. The diagrams and pictures that had made so much sense before were no longer comprehensible. Unwilling to show his ignorance, Old Killjoy angrily blamed everyone else and demanded that the traitor be fetched to explain it once again.

'And who is guarding the Tick?' he roared.

No one spoke.

'THEN FIND OUT!'

Scratch set out for the safe chamber, and Spit was dispatched to the dungeons to collect the traitor. Noting Old Killjoy's foul temper, he thought it wise to hurry.

'Open up!' he pompously demanded as soon as he arrived.

Scrag and Stupid looked nervously at one another. No one had come to replace them as they had hoped.

'Open up!' He shouted louder this time.

They dared not open the door, but nor could they ignore him. Instead, they stepped aside to allow Spit to pass between them. Annoyed by their laziness and anxious to be quick, he marched to the dungeon door and dragged it open. 'Get out here!' he demanded.

There was no movement from within.

Spit looked questioningly at the guards, who shrugged

their shoulders, pretending to be ignorant of the problem. Irritated beyond belief, Spit shouted, 'Prisoner! Get out here!'

No one came. Angrily, he bent low and scrambled inside. For a moment he was unable to see much in the poorly lit dungeon and it took a while for his eyes to adjust to the dimness. Crouching in silence, it slowly dawned on him that the cell was empty.

'Scrag!' he shouted.

No one answered.

'Stupid!' he roared louder.

No one came.

In fury, Spit stamped out of the dungeon, ready to berate the guards who had so clearly failed in their duty. But there was no one there.

Scrag and Stupid had fled.

23

An Act of Courage

The rear Topside door was guarded by two Wreccas who had never guarded a door before. Because of this, one might have expected Slob and Smell to do a bad job, but they did not. They were extremely pleased with themselves, having been given such a high-status job, and they were determined to impress. Slob stood in front of the door whilst Smell marched (as smartly as a Wrecca can march) down the steps and back up again. Then he stood by the door while Slob marched. This was a pattern they had worked out for themselves, and they were immensely proud of it. Their hope was that some-one would come and see them performing their duties so well.

Sofi watched in dismay from a safe distance. Then she returned to the waiting Sheldon. He was squatting on the floor, having dumped the Tick roughly on the ground.

'I need a drink,' he moaned hoarsely.

Sofi did not answer. Her mind was on the guards.

Cob arrived. 'Have we reached the door, Miss Sofi?'

'Yer.'

'Thank goodness,' Sheldon mumbled, staggering to his feet and preparing to leave.

'Not so fast,' Sofi said, in a hushed voice. 'There's two guards.'

Sheldon sat down with a bump. His eyes may not have been focusing properly, but his mind was still functioning well enough to realize that two guards were more than he could handle.

'What do we do?' Cob asked Sofi.

'Let I think.'

She remembered the time when she had pestered Spew and Spite. Cautiously, she crept back and peered at Slob and Smell. Slob was marching down the steps whilst Smell was alert and looking about. These two would not be so easy to pester. They were organized and doing their job properly. She peered at them again, and then a warm feeling of certainty welled up within her. They could never keep up this level of concentration. She knew it would not be long before one of them would annoy the other, and then the squabbling would begin. That was the way it was with Wreccas. Then they would be easy to pester. Feeling a little better, she returned to the others.

'Us'll wait.'

Sheldon and Cob looked at her in disbelief.

'We'll what?' Sheldon asked. Being so close made him all the more eager to get out.

'Us'll wait.'

'But we have so little time,' Cob said, deeply concerned.

Sofi bit her lip. She knew they should hurry, but she could think of no other plan. 'It's our best chance.'

Spit had to report back about the traitor. This would now be difficult because Old Killjoy was bound to blame him for the empty dungeon. However, if he said nothing at all, Old Killjoy's wrath would eventually be much worse. With fear clenching at his stomach, he decided what to do. Wording his announcement carefully, he summoned up his courage and burst into the war chamber declaring, 'Those boneheads, Stupid and Scrag, has let the prisoner escape!'

Old Killjoy's reaction was swift and violent. He launched a well-aimed blow into Spit's face. Then he picked him up, smashed him against the wall and asked, 'What is you talking about?'

Nose bleeding, Spit spluttered how he had discovered that the dungeon was empty and the guards had run away. Old Killjoy dropped the unfortunate Wrecca and stormed out of the war chamber with Scratch at his heels.

Sofi's mouth was dry and her heel was hurting. Sheldon's eyes were closed and he seemed to be asleep. Cob prowled up and down. Yet again, she crept back to spy on the guards. Time was passing, and yet these two Wreccas were as diligent as ever. It felt as if she had been watching them for ages. Leaning back against the wall, she thought the problem through yet again. She had to get the Tick out. She regretted Snivel's defection. How much easier it would have been if he had still been with them.

Thinking of Snivel saddened her. It was obvious to her that he had run away. She did not blame him, neither did she fear that he would go to Old Killjoy and inform. No, Sniv was too terrified of their leader to do that, but she had hoped to take him Topside and let him see how much better life could be up there.

With a deep sigh, she pushed Snivel from her thoughts and tiptoed back to the others. 'It's no good,' she whispered, 'us'll have to risk it.'

'Risk what?' Sheldon asked, instantly awake. He did not want to risk anything.

'I'll pester them.'

'How?' Sheldon and Cob asked together.

Sofi sighed. More explanations!

'You two guard the Tick. I'll annoy the guards. I's good at it. I's been doing it all my life. I'll call them "stupid" and "ugly" or something. That'll work. They'll give chase and I'll lead them down there.' She jerked her thumb to the side.

Cob understood where she meant. He had been checking their position. They were standing in the smaller of the two tunnels that opened into a confined hall where the Topside door was situated. Sofi was saying that she would make sure that the guards chased her down the other tunnel. 'If only one of them follows,' she continued, 'you, Sheldon, will need to attack the other. Take him by surprise. You's bigger than him and if you hit him hard you'll knock him down. Then grab the Tick and run for it.'

Sheldon nodded. He was certain he could beat one

of these stupid creatures if he had the benefit of surprise.

She turned to Cob. 'You know what to do once you's Topside?'

'I do, but I do not like the sound of this plan.' He feared that, once Sheldon had knocked the guard down, he would put his own freedom before the Tick and take off without it.

'Neither does I,' admitted Sofi. She found it very hard to be so close to the Topside and not escape. 'I's sorry I willn't come with you.'

'You will be joining us later?' Cob asked, suddenly concerned.

Sofi tried to sound confident. 'Yer. I'll outrun them and double back.'

'Can you outrun them?' Cob asked, doubting it. They were much bigger than she.

'Yer,' she lied.

Sheldon had had enough of delay. He wanted to get out and he did not care whether Sofi could run faster than the guards or not. If she could distract them for just a couple of moments, then he could be out and away.

'Let me do it,' said Cob. 'I am quicker than you. You must allow me the honour.'

Sofi shook her head. 'You doesn't know the way. It's easy to get lost down here.'

'But, miss . . .'

'Look, Cob, this is my fault. I *has* to be the one to do it.'

'But I am fast.'

'It don't matter.'

Sheldon was becoming impatient. The thought of escape had brought with it a new burst of energy. He wanted to get going.

'One of you do it and let me get out of here,' he grumbled.

'Miss Sofi,' Cob spoke formally, 'it has been a privilege working with you.'

Sofi smiled. It made her very proud to be respected by someone like Cob.

'You must always remember,' he continued, 'that whatever happens in the future, you have more than repaid any debt you may once have owed. Everything you do now is because you have a courageous and generous heart.'

Sofi knelt down and placed her cheek next to Cob's soft, furry face. She doubted she would ever be able to outrun Slob and Smell, but somehow it did not matter any more. All she hoped was that she could run quickly and keep them out of the way long enough for Sheldon and Cob to escape. Once Topside, she hoped that the thought of his reward would spur Sheldon on to get the Tick to Old Father Tim without delay.

She stood up and took a deep breath. This was it! 'Oh, Grandfather!' she muttered.

All at once, Cob was running. She stared in astonishment as she saw the brave little Bushytail taking on the responsibility that was rightfully hers.

'Cob!' she exclaimed in a hoarse whisper.

'Shut up!' Sheldon hissed in her ear. He did not mind which of them sacrificed themselves as long as he got out.

The guards were still alert, neither showing any sign of flagging.

Cob had dashed to the end of the tunnel and now came to a halt in the hallway. He stood up on his hind legs and stared at the guards. Sofi and Sheldon followed at a distance and remained hidden from view.

'Cob!' she wanted to shout, but all she dared do was whisper his name.

He must have heard her, for he turned and winked before turning back and clearing his throat loudly.

'What's that?' asked Slob, eyes alert.

'Over there!' said Smell. 'I seed something move.'

Cob was working out the abuse he was about to hurl at these two ragged creatures.

Sofi watched, her heart beating fast. Cob stepped out of the shadows and revealed himself to the guards. She gripped her hands so tightly that her nails bit into the palms.

'Run!' she said under her breath.

Cob stood in full view.

'Run!' she screamed in her head.

Still Cob did not move.

Sofi's eyes went from Cob to the guards. They were standing like statues. Sofi looked back at Cob. Why did he not run? They had seen him. He could not wait. He had to run!

But Cob knew what he was doing. He was near enough to see something in their eyes. Something Sofi could not see.

Slob and Smell were mesmerized with fear. Never

before had they witnessed anything like Cob. Their terror seemed way beyond that which Sofi or Snivel had felt on first seeing a Bushytail.

As he stood watching them, Cob fully understood this effect. Stepping grandly forward, he swished his tail dramatically and said, 'Oh my! You two are in trouble!'

Slob stepped back in alarm and bumped into Smell.

Cobb held his position. He could see how petrified they were. It would not be a case of him running off to draw them away from Sofi and the Tick. Instead, he would be doing the chasing! These Wreccas were terrified of him, and it made him laugh. All thought of danger left him as he threw back his head and guffawed loudly. In the World it was the Bushytails who were supposed to be afraid of everyone. Here, in the Underneath, it was a small Bushytail who petrified creatures several times his size. Cob maintained his position between the guards and his friends. If Slob and Smell were going to run, then it would not be towards the Tick.

The laugh was the masterstroke, although Cob had not intended it as such. The terrified guards mistook it for the laugh of the victor just before he overwhelmed the enemy. They were not brave. They would not wait to be vanquished. After the initial shock, their only thought was flight.

It was Slob who took off first. Smell waited no more than a moment before darting after him.

Cob turned and gave a triumphant wave to Sofi. 'Go!' he shouted as he gave chase.

Sofi took a couple of steps towards him. Her instinct was to follow and make sure that he was safe.

'Come on,' Sheldon said urgently.

She did not respond.

'Get on with it!' he shouted as he grabbed the Tick, ran towards the steps and struggled up them.

Sofi did not move.

'Open this flaming door!' Sheldon screamed.

Reluctantly, Sofi threw one last look down the tunnel before dashing to the door. Sheldon stood back as she dragged it open. Without waiting for her, he was through it and gone.

Sofi stood in the doorway. 'Us is out now, Cob,' she was saying to the empty tunnel. 'You can come back.'

But Cob did not return.

Out in the night, Sheldon was relishing the deep breaths that filled his lungs with crisp, fresh air. He would have been happy to run on and leave her, but he did not know the way. Normally, he would have done, but his eyes were still playing tricks on him. The merry holiday lights that had been strung up in the distance by the Humans were making strange patterns in the mist.

'Sofi!' he shouted.

She still had important work to do and, reluctantly, ran to Sheldon, leaving the door just far enough ajar so that Cob could get out if he returned. She was deeply concerned about him. She knew that Slob and Smell would run blindly on, darting left and right down tunnel after tunnel. If Cob chased them for too long, she did not believe he would ever be able to find his way back.

Old Father Tim had returned from talking to Bryn. He now stood at the gates with his grandson.

Wakaa arrived. 'Is there no sign of them?'

Old Father Tim shook his head. 'Bryn is out there with some of the others. As soon as they see Sofi crossing Blackheath, they will be able to help.'

'Will they be able to see in this mist?'

'It is probably not so bad out in the open.'

Wakaa nodded.

'What of Seegan and his ancient manuscripts?' Old Father Tim asked.

'That has come to nothing. You were right. There is no way to suspend time. Sofi and the Bushytails are our only hope now.' He looked at the sky. 'Time flies. I fear they will come too late.'

'We shall move the new Timepiece to the Line,' said Old Father Tim. I will restore the Tick there.'

Wakaa was shocked. 'We cannot present the new Timepiece incomplete.'

'Do we have a choice?'

Wakaa reluctantly acknowledged that they did not. Together they looked towards Tid. Old Father Tim was going to suggest that he should accompany them to the Line. He did not want to leave his grandson alone at a time like this.

'I will stay here,' Tid said, before his grandfather could voice his concerns, 'and wait for Sofi.'

Old Father Tim's gaze lingered on his grandson, standing there, so small and yet so determined. He was very proud of the boy.

As the new Timepiece was brought before the Gathering of Guardians, there was a gasp of awe. Unfinished though it was, it was still a miracle of workmanship. When it had been carefully put in its proper place next to the old Timepiece, everyone waited for the ceremony to begin.

'It is time for the Mashias,' Wakaa said, lifting his staff high in the air.

Tid continued to wait by the gates. He rubbed his hands together and blew on his chilled fingers as he looked out into the misty darkness that shrouded Blackheath. His ears strained for sounds, any sounds that would warn of Sofi's approach. He walked out of the gates a few paces but then returned because he thought he might miss her should he venture out too far.

'This is not doing any good,' he thought to himself. So, closing his eyes, he concentrated on being Mindful once more.

Sheldon stumbled on. The Tick was getting heavier with every step. He followed Sofi as best he could, but his eyes were now barely focusing. He squinted into the distance. He had lost her.

'Sheldon?' Sofi called, turning back. 'Where are you?'

On hearing her voice, he realized that he was going in the wrong direction and abruptly twisted round. He still couldn't see her. He thought his ears must have been deceiving him. Twisting again, he turned once more.

It was one turn too many. His legs were slow to respond. One foot became entangled behind the other leg, and he tripped. Clumsily, he lost his balance. Without a thought for the Tick, he threw his hands up to try and protect himself from the inevitable fall, and he flung the Tick high into the air.

It soared above Sofi's head.

Its ragged coverings lifted and gracefully floated away.

Sofi watched in horror.

The Tick appeared to fly. Then it started to fall. At first it descended slowly but then it gathered speed and, with a sickening clatter, crashed to the ground.

24

Searching

Cob allowed the guards to outrun him. He believed he had given Sofi enough time to get Sheldon and the Tick away. He had carefully noted his route, but when he tried to retrace his steps he became thoroughly confused. For a long time he wandered about before he finally accepted that he was completely lost.

Aimlessly, he walked down dark and deserted tunnels. Sometimes they were dead ends. Normally good at working out which direction to take, he was at a total loss below ground. Then he heard a sound. He stood and listened, his head cocked to one side. The noise became louder. With dismay, he realized that a group of Wreccas was heading straight towards him. He turned and ran swiftly in the other direction, only to come to a sudden halt. This way was also barred by another group of Wreccas, all approaching in a noisy huddle. By the light of the torch they carried, he could see that they looked mean and determined.

Cob looked behind him, then he looked in front.

He was trapped.

*

With her heart beating fast, Sofi stared at the Tick as it lay on the soft grass where it had landed. Without its coverings, its light shone more brightly than ever and reflected off the heavy mist that hung all around.

After a moment, she apprehensively approached it. The Tick's outer covering was gossamer thin. It looked so fragile that she dared not touch it, fearing that even the lightest contact might break the delicate membrane. And yet, had they not been carrying it for a long time now, giving no regard for how flimsy it might be? Maybe it was stronger than it looked. She could now understand just why it shone so brightly. Such a delicate skin was not up to the task of concealing a light that burned like a furnace deep within.

She could see no markings or patterns. It was completely plain and yet beautiful. There was one tiny silver screw in each of the four corners of the top panel and nothing more. She knelt down and peered at it from this way and that but could not see a single scratch or dent. Carefully, she brushed some soil from one corner. There was no damage. Had it not been for the sickening clatter as it crashed to the ground, Sofi would have thought it unharmed.

Sitting back, she assessed the situation. She could not bear to imagine that it had been damaged. With trembling hands, she tentatively laid her fingers upon it. As usual, it felt warm. Then she put her ear to it, but she could hear no sound. Never having listened closely before, she did not know if this was a good or a bad thing.

She rubbed her forehead with a slightly shaking hand. If it was broken, all her efforts would have been for nothing. Dark shadows clouded her mind. All for nothing? That would be too cruel. No, it could not be so. She would not believe that.

'It don't look breaked,' she said, and felt better for having spoken these words out loud.

Sofi now turned her attention to Sheldon, who was lying, face down, on the grass.

'Get up!'

He did not stir.

She went over to him. 'You dropped it!' she said, accusingly.

He did not respond.

'But I think it's all right.'

She waited for him to say something. He did not.

'You has to get up.'

Sheldon groaned. He did not want to move. Now he was out from the Underneath, he felt safe. 'Leavemealone,' he mumbled.

Sofi pulled at his arm. 'You has to get up.'

'Go away.'

Sofi was beginning to despair. He had to move. How could she make him? What could she say to revive him?

'You has to take the Tick to Old Father Tim or you willn't get your medal.'

Sheldon's only reply was to roll on to his side and curl up in a ball.

'Old Killjoy'll find you if you stay here. Him'll come looking, for sure.'

These words had no effect on Sheldon, but they did on Sofi. It suddenly occurred to her how vulnerable they were, out in the open. Grabbing at his shirt, she shook him roughly.

No reaction.

She pulled his hair and kicked him in the ribs.

Still he did not move. Lack of food and sleep had finally got the better of him. Sheldon was unconscious.

Sofi looked about her in anguish. She glanced backwards, hoping to see Cob running up behind her, and for the first time she understood the extent of the fog. It was so thick she could not see much more than three paces in front of her.

'Is anybody there?' she called, but not too loudly. She knew that she could have been followed from the Underneath. The mist that frustratingly hid them from anyone who might help also hid them from anyone who might be giving chase. She could not risk shouting.

She went back to the Tick, with her hands shaking and heart pounding. She could not carry it alone and yet there was no one to help. Her breath began to come in short, shuddering gasps. She was losing control.

Walking back and forth, she looked up into the sky, but she could see no further upwards than she could see in front of her. It was like being back in the Underneath, enclosed all around, except out here the air was fresh and the dampness hung in the mist rather than rising up from the ground and oozing from the walls.

She stopped with a short gasp. She had nearly walked into the Tick! Supposing she had stumbled into it and damaged it? Her heart thumped. Her breath was coming in short, sharp bursts. She was trembling all over. Her mind was clouded. She was unable to move or think.

Sofi was panicking. But then the light from the Tick flooded over her. She felt its warmth. No, it was more than warmth. What was it? It was hope.

Kneeling down, she put out her hand and touched it. She felt something she had never felt before. There was a throbbing from deep inside the Tick that timed with the pounding of her heart. It was beating fast.

Sofi put both hands flat on its surface. The throbbing was stronger now. It echoed in her head. She closed her eyes and welcomed the beat that gently pulsated through her hands, along her arms and through her entire body. Gradually it became slower and, as it did, so her heartbeat kept the rhythm and slowed down too. Gently, the wild thumping of her heart subsided. As the pulse became regular, so Sofi became calmer.

After some moments, she opened her eyes. Her breath was coming normally and her panic had subsided. She felt so at peace, for a moment she wanted to do nothing at all, just stay with the Tick and wallow in its glory.

Her mind was clear.

Then, quite suddenly, she remembered that Hazel and Walnut were waiting close by. Of course! She had forgotten all about them. They would help.

She looked about her, trying to get her bearings, but all she saw was great clouds of grey mist. Which direction would the Bushytails be? She looked back at the Tick.

'I wonder,' she muttered. Purposefully, she placed her hands upon it and asked, 'Which way?'

The throbbing had subsided. Sofi waited. Sofi listened. She was certain that the Tick could show her the way, but she felt and heard nothing. The Tick was silent. Reluctantly, she realized that she would have to work this one out by herself.

Standing up, she looked towards Sheldon. She could only see part of him; the rest was blanketed by mist. 'If he fell with his head towards the Tick,' she said, working logically, 'we must have come from over there, and so the Bushytails must be somewhere . . .' she spun around, '. . . in that direction.' She hoped she was right.

Sofi ran. It did not matter that she could not see far in front of her. It was all or nothing now. She could have run straight into a brick wall and she would not have cared. It might almost be a relief to pass out and know nothing about the end.

As she ran, she noticed that the mist was patchy, sometimes so thick that she could not see the hand in front of her face and sometimes so thin that she could see some distance.

'I think I can see her.' The voice was muffled by the fog. 'I *can* see her!' It was Hazel.

'Miss Sofi!' Walnut called.

Sofi did not slacken her pace for a moment. Still running, she shouted before reaching them, 'Come with I!' Without pausing, she turned around and started back.

Happy to be of use at last, Hazel and Walnut followed at her heels, without asking any questions.

As they had waited throughout the long night, every minute had seemed like an hour. They had whispered their fears and tried to console each other. They reasoned that rescuing the Tick would take a long time. Then Walnut had suggested that Hazel should sleep whilst he stood guard. But every few minutes she had been alert, thinking she heard someone approaching. Walnut had not been much better when it was his turn to rest. Endlessly they had stared into the night sky, trying to judge how much time remained. When a big black dog had arrived and started barking at them, his intrusion was almost welcome. Avoiding him and trying to stay out of sight until he and his owner had gone made the time pass more quickly. Then the mist started descending. They wondered if they should go to the only door into the Underneath they knew of and wait there. But that was risky. It could be disastrous if they missed her. And so the two of them had kept vigil, both straining their eyes and ears for any sign of Sofi. It was now a relief to actually be doing something.

Old Killjoy stomped through the tunnels, rallying support. When finally he burst into the main chamber, it was full of curious Wreccas who had picked up the feeling that something was wrong. Old Killjoy stood on his throne and declared dramatically, 'I has been betrayed!'

Everyone booed.

'The traitor is free!'

They booed some more.

'Stupid and Scrag has let us all down!'

There was plenty of jeering and hissing.

'When they's catched they'll be punished. I'll deliver them up to the Ruckus!'

Everybody cheered.

Suddenly, everyone turned their attention away from their leader. Scratch had theatrically marched into the assembly. He had been biding his time. Conscious of the fact that his news had to be delivered at precisely the correct time, he stopped in the middle of the proceedings and stood still, breathing heavily. He looked as if he had something important to say, but remained silent.

'Well?' Old Killjoy snapped, irritated because he was no longer the centre of attention. 'What is it?'

Scratch drew breath very slowly and quietly said, 'The Tick is missing.'

Realization dawned slowly on the gathered Wreccas.

'What?' Old Killjoy asked, turning purple with rage.

'Someone has stealed it.'

'Stealed it?' Old Killjoy roared. 'Stealed it?' he repeated, as if he was having difficulty in accepting the fact. 'Who stealed it?'

'I doesn't know.'

'Ask Spew and Spite.'

Scratch ran his nails over his lips, a little nervous of how Old Killjoy might react to his next few words. 'Them's still out cold. They can't tell no one nothing.'

It looked as if Old Killjoy were about to explode with rage. 'Find the stealers and bring them to I!' he roared.

At once, everyone became exhilarated at the thought of a chase.

'I'll give a fat reward to the Wrecca that captures the scum!'

At this, the gathered throng became wildly enthusiastic. Seeing an opportunity for advancement was always popular and each was determined to be the one to succeed. Restlessly, they waited until Old Killjoy sat down. That was their signal. Desperate to be first, there was a rush for the exits as they kicked and pushed their way out.

The search was on.

Sofi took the Bushytails back to the Tick. She tried to slow her breathing, anxious that too much oxygen might make her ill, as it had in the past. 'Quick,' she said, 'us has to take it to the park.'

Hazel looked about her. 'Where's Cob?' she asked, quietly.

Sofi paused as she bent to pick up the Tick. Breathing heavily, she looked across at the worried Bushytails, wondering how much she should say. 'Him's coming later.'

'What's happened?'

Sofi swallowed, not knowing what to say.

Walnut was preparing to lift the Tick on his strong tail. He had seen Sheldon lying on the ground and had guessed that he was injured. Noticing Sofi's reluctance to speak of Cob, he thought he understood why.

'Hazel,' he spoke firmly. 'Cob said that he knew we would do our duty. Are you about to let him down?'

'No,' Hazel instantly replied, pushing to the back of her mind all unpleasant thoughts. She stood next to Walnut and they prepared to take a corner each. With Sofi ready at the other side, the three of them lifted the Tick. It wobbled a bit and made Sofi appreciate the strength and cleverness of Cob, who had managed the other side so easily by himself.

Cob stood alone in the Underneath. He had looked fearfully from one end of the tunnel to the other. Wreccas were closing in on him from both directions. He knew there was no escape.

Suddenly, from nowhere, he felt a hand grab his tail. Cob was too stunned to react.

This was the end.

He thought of Hazel. He would never see her again.

With a sharp tug, Cob was pulled into a dingy hole in the wall.

'What the . . . ?' he stammered.

'Sssh,' was the only reply.

Cob held his breath and kept still. Whoever had pulled him into the hole in the wall was sitting by his side, equally silent. Both listened to the noises that came from the tunnel.

'Halt! Who's there?'

There was the sound of a brawl. Clearly, the two groups of Wreccas had reached one another, and both were aggressively standing their ground.

'What the flaming Nora is you doing?' someone said. 'Let go of I!'

'Squabble? Is that you?'

'Of course it's I! Who the hell does you think you is? Let go!'

'Stop sneaking up on people!'

'Us isn't sneaking. Us is on a mission!'

'Us too!'

This information was well received, and the Wreccas started talking in hushed whispers. Cob listened very carefully. He caught only the occasional word.

'. . . Topside . . . traitor . . . Killjoy . . . reward . . .'

Suddenly, the whispering stopped. Someone further down the tunnel was shouting.

'Over here!'

'Where?'

'Quick!'

In a scuffle of feet and a howl of excitement, they were gone.

Cob sat in the blackness, not sure what to do. The Wrecca who had grabbed him was by his side. Neither of them moved. Cob could sense that his companion was edgy.

'Is you all right?' the Wrecca whispered.

Cob recognized the voice.

'Snivel, is that you?'

Tid opened his eyes. Being Mindful took all his concentration. He had no idea how long he had been standing by the gates. The mist was clearing from the park and he was relieved that he could see for some distance. He looked up into the sky as his grandfather would have done and tried to calculate the time. But he could not read the signs.

He rubbed his hands together to warm his chilled fingers. Tid thought of Sofi and wondered where she was. He walked up and down, stamping his cold feet. His mind drifted to thoughts of time ending for all time and he wondered what would happen, how it would feel. Would it hurt?

Realizing that such thoughts were not helping, he settled himself again. He had no idea if being Mindful was working, but it was comforting to try. Closing his eyes, he focused his mind on Sofi once more.

Sofi's heel had been so numbed by running, she no longer felt it, but her back hurt. Because Hazel was not as strong as Walnut, her corner continually dipped, and Sofi had to twist to compensate.

Hazel was puffing hard, finding it difficult to keep up. Walnut thought that he could manage better by himself and suggested that Hazel should take a rest.

'I am all right,' she puffed, reluctant to stop, although the strain of carrying the Tick was immense.

Sofi understood her reluctance, but she was hindering more than helping. 'Go and take a look up ahead,' Sofi said. 'The park gates'll be there somewhere.' She waved her arm in the direction that she thought was right.

Grateful to be relieved of the heavy work, but happy to still be useful, Hazel relinquished her share of the load and scampered off.

Walnut carefully manoeuvred himself so as to balance the Tick alone, and prepared to move off.

'I am ready,' he said.

Sofi did not move.

'We should keep going.'

'I need to catch my breath.' And, without giving Walnut a chance to argue, Sofi put the Tick down.

In part, this was true. She was beginning to feel the familiar feeling she associated with running too much on the Topside. But it was not the whole truth. For some minutes now, she had had a growing fear that they were completely lost. The mist was confusing. Whenever she came to a clearer patch, she looked around for a familiar landmark to guide her. Her knowledge of Blackheath was, at best, sketchy.

Hazel came back, as fast as her weary little legs could carry her.

'Did you see the gates?' Sofi asked hopefully.

Hazel's reply was not encouraging. 'They are not there. At least, I could not see them.'

'Maybe it's that way,' Sofi said, looking in a totally different direction.

'Do you not know?' Walnut had not meant to accuse.

'How can I?' Tears filled her eyes. 'I's lived all my life underground. I hasn't a clue. Doesn't you know?'

'No.' Hazel and Walnut lived in the park. They knew little of what lay beyond the gates.

'Us ought to be there by now,' Sofi sniffed, brushing her tears away, but new ones immediately defied her. 'Us has been carrying this thing for ages!' She spoke resentfully, plonking herself down on the damp grass and burying her head in her hands. To be so near! Failure would not have been so bad to endure if it had happened in the Underneath, but to have come so close was cruel and Sofi felt the failure keenly.

Hazel and Walnut looked on helplessly.

'Cob would have known the way,' Hazel said quietly.

25

Lost and Found

Bryn thought he saw someone. 'Sofi?' he called, peering through the white mist that wafted, thick and thin.

'It's me,' came the answer. Joss appeared.

'Have you seen anyone?'

'Well, yes.' Joss sounded baffled. 'It's a bit odd.'

'What is? Who have you seen?'

'Sheldon Croe.'

'What on earth is he doing?'

'Nothing good, I'd be certain of that.'

'What did he say?'

'Well, that's the really strange part.' Joss scratched his head. 'He was asleep on the ground, all curled up as if he was in bed.'

'Out here, on a night like this?'

'He was absolutely dead to the World.'

'He's a strange boy and no mistake. What have you done with him?'

'Nothing. I could not wake him and so I left him.'

'Quite right.' Bryn was anxious to continue his search. 'We cannot waste time on the likes of him. Right now, it is more important to find Sofi and the Bushytails.'

'That's what I thought. How much time do we have?'

Bryn looked up at the sky but could not see it for mist.

'Not enough,' he said ruefully. 'Keep looking.'

Sofi rubbed her eyes. The fog was thick. They were lost. Each was exhausted. There was no hope.

It was the end.

'Oh, Grandfather,' she mumbled to herself, 'I's let you down.'

In her mind she saw Old Father Tim's loving eyes. How she longed to be with him again. Her thoughts turned to Tid, and she imagined his face. 'Tid, I's sorry.'

There was a feeling in her head that Sofi did not understand. It was not the woozy feeling she had had before. She sat motionless for a while as the strange sensation grew stronger. Slowly, she rose to her feet, keeping her eyes set on the fog, just a few paces in front of her. Leaning down, she picked up the Tick.

Walnut was watching her closely. In the gloom he could see there was something unusual in her expression. It was as though she was hearing something. He cocked his head to one side, but there was no sound. He did not question her. Instead, he struggled to pick up the other side of the Tick.

Exhausted though she was, Hazel also tried to help. She placed her tail under the Tick, but it was Walnut who was doing most of the work.

Sofi stayed silent, fearing that speech might break the spell. Incredibly, although she did not know how, she felt herself being drawn. She did not fight it. By some miracle, she knew which way to go.

Through the haze of this peculiar sensation she heard someone calling.

'Sofi!'

At first she thought it was just in her head, but then there was no mistaking it.

'Sofi!' It was louder this time.

Gradually, the mist cleared enough for her to see someone. Her heart leapt as she heard her name once more.

'Sofi!'

Overwhelming relief drenched her. At the same time she felt her legs beginning to give way.

'Tid!' she shouted back.

They ran towards each other. Sofi was elated at the sight of her friend. Tid was relieved, not only at the sight of the Tick, but that she was safe. He wanted to hug her. He wanted to cry for joy. He wanted to sink to his knees with thankfulness.

'Help us,' Sofi cried.

Tid pulled himself together. He looked at the exhausted trio and took in the situation. Sofi was clearly worn out, but the Bushytails were in a worse condition. Knowing there was no time to pause, he quickly asked Sofi, 'Are you all right?'

'Yer,' she gasped. 'Take the other side!'

At once, he grabbed the Tick from the stumbling Bushytails. Gratefully, they relinquished their load and crumpled to the ground, totally drained.

With renewed strength drawn from the sight of her friend and the knowledge that her task was almost completed, Sofi quickened her pace.

'How much time?' she puffed.

Tid did not know, nor did he waste breath saying as much. Together, they ran towards the park gates.

The tunnels were being searched by bands of Wreccas. None of them was organized and so they criss-crossed each other in a haphazard manner. Snivel kept alert, and with Cob's help they managed to avoid discovery by darting down dark side tunnels at the appropriate moment.

Snivel was leading Cob to a secret exit he had once heard some Wreccas whispering about, although he had no idea if it was really there. He was not entirely sure why he had saved the furry creature. Perhaps he felt sorry for him, or maybe it was because he had no wish to witness another Ruckus-like massacre. Whatever the reason, he felt no loyalty to Cob. In fact, his plan was to dump him at the first opportunity; but, as the furry creature was a fast runner, this had to be carefully timed.

Suddenly, Cob put his head to one side. He could hear something.

It was a while before Snivel picked up the sound. 'What's that?' he asked, instantly suspicious. He had never heard anything like it before.

'Keep moving,' Cob said.

'Does you know what that noise is?' Snivel asked him.

'Ssh! There is someone coming!'

Snivel had only been listening to the roaring sound, so this announcement came as something of a shock. He did not know whether to be relieved or scared.

'Quick!' Cob commanded, scampering off.

Snivel made as if to follow but stopped, instinct telling him to stay. If Wreccas were chasing them, then he would wait for them. He felt he would be safer with his own kind.

'Come on!' Cob said, anxious to be gone.

Snivel did not know what to do; he was too frightened of the furry creature to openly defy him. Cob brandished his tail aggressively, and that settled the matter. Snivel followed him.

The tunnel was going deeper and deeper. The rushing noise was becoming louder and louder.

When Cob suddenly stopped, it was so unexpected that Snivel nearly ran into him. He skidded to a halt just in time. By now, the noise was thunderous. Snivel was confused. Why had the furry creature stopped so suddenly? Then confusion turned to understanding as he looked down. There was nothing in front of them. Completely without warning, the ground had stopped. A deep chasm sprawled open at their feet and from it came a deafening sound.

They both leant over to see what lay beneath, carefully keeping back from the crumbling edge. A wave of icy air hit their faces. It was as Cob had suspected. There was an underground river far below.

'What's that?' Snivel shouted, raising his voice over the din.

'It is a river,' Cob replied very loudly. 'Can you swim?'

'What's that?' Snivel asked. No one in the Underneath had ever had the opportunity to swim.

'Oh my!' Cob exclaimed to himself. How could he be expected to help such an ignorant little boy? He ran a short way back up the tunnel and peeped around a large boulder. To his horror, there was a band of Wreccas approaching. He hurried back to Snivel, suppressing the fear that was welling up inside. Anxiously, he scanned the area for another exit. There was none. They were trapped.

'We don't have any choice!' he yelled.

Snivel could not hear him. He bent down and Cob shouted into his ear.

'We will have to jump!'

Snivel was certain he had not heard Cob properly. 'Jump?'

'Yes.' Cob stood at the edge. 'Together, one . . . two . . . three . . .'

Snivel did not move. He watched Cob without the slightest intention of following.

Cob threw a look over his shoulder, expecting to see the approaching Wreccas, but they were not yet in sight. He knew he would not hear them coming; the roaring of the water was too loud.

'You have to jump!' Cob bellowed, agitated by the delay.

'Not on your life!'

Cob turned once more and this time he saw the

Wreccas rounding the boulder. They were moving quickly. Each wore a menacing expression on his face. Cob's alarm rose to the level of panic.

As the Wreccas spied him, they stopped dead in their tracks. The expressions on their faces turned to terror, just like the guards on the Topside.

Cob knew this was his chance. He could not hope that their fear would keep them away indefinitely, but a delay might be crucial.

'Come on!' he shouted to Snivel, and prepared to jump. Snivel did not move.

The band of Wreccas was being led by Sniff, who was only momentarily halted by the sight of the furry monster. He had been Topside and knew something of Bushytails. He was wary of Cob, but not as terrified as the others, and anyway, lust for reward propelled him forward.

Cob peered down into the icy torrent. The river was violent and angry. He did not like the idea of jumping, but what else could they do? He grabbed at Snivel's hand and tried to encourage him, but Snivel pulled away.

Looking at the options that lay before him, Snivel's stomach felt some of the icy chill that rose from the savage water. Both options terrified him, but if it were a choice between the Wreccas and the gushing water beneath, he would take his chance with the Wreccas.

The Wreccas did not want to approach such a frightening monster, but Sniff urged them on with a mixture of cussing, fury and bribery. Fear of Old Killjoy's thunderous rage at their failure, combined with promises of his generous behaviour to those who succeeded, emboldened them. Clustering close together, they felt a bravery that was new and exhilarating. They edged forward, a grunt rising up from deep within their throats. It was slow and rhythmic, and it renewed their courage. With each step the chanting grew louder until the noise they made rivalled the roaring water.

As their chant rose, so it drifted to Cob's acute ears and mingled with the sound of the thundering water. The Wreccas' eyes were wild and their fists were clenched. He did not doubt for a moment that, if caught, he would be torn limb from limb. His courageous little heart was beating wildly. He was beginning to doubt that he could survive such a jump, but Snivel might. He was bigger and stronger and might have a chance.

Cob's eyes were now drawn to Sniff, whose expression was contorted with hostile, violent hatred. And he was getting closer . . . closer . . .

It was now or never. He tore his eyes from Sniff and glanced towards Snivel, who appeared to be as frightened of the approaching band as Cob himself. Snivel's terror galvanized Cob into action.

Quickly leaping up on to the still crouching Snivel, Cob grabbed his hair. Startled by the suddenness of the attack, Snivel started flailing his arms, trying to knock Cob off, but the Bushytail clung on tightly. Snivel shook his head, desperate to be free of the furry monster, but Cob did not loosen his grip. As Snivel wildly thrashed the air, he lost his balance.

Then it all happened at alarming speed. With a cry of

terror, the two of them toppled over and started falling down . . . down . . . down . . .

The icy water struck them hard as they crashed into it. The force caused Cob to let go of Snivel's hair and pushed the air out of his lungs.

The water enveloped them.

They sank deep.

Cob found himself moving in slow motion through the icy water. He opened his eyes and was alarmed to discover that he could see nothing. He felt about him, hoping to grab on to Snivel, but he was not there. Using his tail as a rudder and his paws to feel his way, Cob tried to navigate the freezing water. He had to make it to the surface. He had to get some air.

Suddenly an undercurrent took him. He was thrown this way and that. His body thumped against rocks on the riverbed. By now, his lungs were empty. He thought they would burst.

Then he remembered no more.

26

Tide healdath, ealle brucath

Tide healdath, ealle brucath

At the Line, the ceremony was under way. Each Guardian was playing his or her part.

> *'In the long, long ago when time stood still,*
> *Nothingness became the universe.*
> *From the brightness of his eye and the strength of his will,*
> *Energy exploded and made earth.'*

The Guardian chant developed into melodious singing that wafted around the Gathering and rose, sweetly enchanted, into the air.

There was no need for Enderell to be at the ceremony. Only Guardians were needed for the ritual. As Bryn and the others were on Blackheath looking for Sofi and the Tick, she had been asked to position herself inside the park to keep watch. She stood vigil where the roads crossed, while listening to fragments of the ceremony as it floated through the night air.

Every now and then she glanced at the little gold

timepiece that hung from her waist. Sometimes she gave a barely perceptible shake of the head. Surely, by now it was too late.

Her mind drifted to her family and friends, and she wondered how they were feeling. Families all over Greenwich had gathered in their own homes, waiting for the moment when they would know whether time had been saved or lost. Most of them did not understand the details of what had happened. They had heard that the Wreccas had stolen time and that the Guardians were doing all they could to find it. Grandparents sat by their fires with their arms around their little ones. Each would have felt more confident if Pa Mossel had been the Old Father. This was probably not entirely fair, but they knew him better than they knew Wakaa and so they trusted him more.

Enderell wanted to be with her family too, but when the Greenwich Guardian had asked for her help she did not hesitate. Now she looked about her at the park that she loved. It was her home. She sighed, not sad for herself but for the park.

As she stood alone in the misty dark, trying to comprehend what would happen to the World once it was frozen in time, she saw a movement up ahead. Wondering if the thin, wafting mist was deceiving her, she craned her neck so as to see better. There was movement.

She took one step towards it. Someone was coming. No, not someone, two children and they were carrying . . .

The moment she identified the glow, Enderell's one thought was to reach the children as quickly as possible. Her usual grace was just a little less elegant as she rushed to them. As soon as she was close enough, one glance told her how tired Sofi was. With a brief smile of thanks, she took the Tick from their arms, turned and hurried away towards the Line. She had no idea whether they were in time, but she was not going to waste a moment thinking about it.

As soon as her burden had been taken from her, Sofi sank to the ground.

Tid hesitated. He wanted to follow Enderell. How much time was left? Could his grandfather attach the Tick before it was too late? He desperately wanted to know what was happening, but loyalty kept him with his friend. Kneeling beside her, he saw that her eyes were closed. She had momentarily lost consciousness. He put a comforting hand on her shoulder.

No longer a Guardian, Old Father Tim was not required at the Mashias, and so he was standing outside the Guardian Circle where he had a good view of the Wide Way. To look at him, no one would have suspected the turmoil in his heart. The end of everything was imminent and he firmly believed it to be his fault. He absolved Tid and Sofi of all blame. They were children. Tid had done no more than betray a confidence to someone he had thought was a friend, and Sofi had done nothing more than conform to the rules of those with whom she lived. There was no way she could have known the wrong she was doing. No, it was his fault. He had given too much knowledge to a young boy. Old Father Tim accepted the responsibility, although he found it a heavy burden.

The relief that flooded through him when he recognized the source of the glow clutched in the approaching Enderell's arms was almost overwhelming. For a moment he hesitated, unable to move. The joy that had burst within him was immediately quenched by concern. Was there time?

With a glance at the sky to estimate the minutes that remained, he turned and walked through the ceremony and towards the two Timepieces. He caught the Greenwich Guardian's eye. She immediately understood that the Tick was on its way and quietly touched Zeit on the arm. Together they moved to the outer edge of the Guardian circle, ready to receive the Tick.

Enderell was very out of breath when she arrived. The Greenwich Guardian had never before seen her in such disarray. Her usual sleek hair was awry and perspiration glistened on her forehead. Without comment, the Tick was taken from her arms. Enderell stood back, breathing quickly. Instinctively, she ran her hand over her hair.

It was tempting to grab the Tick and run as fast as they could with it, but the two Guardians maintained the dignity that befitted the occasion and respectfully carried the Tick as quickly as they dared to Old Father Tim. He was now standing on the second rung of a ladder that leant up against the new Timepiece.

Each Guardian cast his or her eyes towards the stars

in order to estimate the amount of time that remained. Everyone was relieved that it was Old Father Tim who stood, ready to reattach the Tick. He was the one man, above all others, whom they trusted at a time like this. And yet, even with him there to restore the Tick, they were deeply troubled. Was there enough time?

No one faltered. No one destroyed the harmony. They knew the importance of the Mashias. What good would it do to restore the Tick in time, but fail because the ceremony was interrupted?

Wakaa looked at Old Father Tim, who nodded to confirm that he was ready. Wakaa had to remain in the centre of the Guardian Circle. It was his duty to continue leading the Mashias to its climax, but his eyes darted anxiously towards the old Timepiece. How fast could the old man work?

Old Father Tim knew that the responsibility was his alone. His aged fingers had to work as nimbly as they had ever done. He flexed and wriggled them, trying to loosen his aching joints.

The Greenwich Guardian and Zeit passed the Tick up to Old Father Tim, who stooped down in order to take it. He then turned and climbed one more step, before carefully slipping it into position.

Some distance from the Line, Sofi's eyes flicked open. She lay on the ground, trying to fight off a feeling of nausea and a lightness in her head. Although weak, she had a weird feeling of elation. Even if they were too late, it no longer seemed to matter. She had completed what she had set out to do. She had not failed them. She was content.

Tid was impatient to get to the Line. He saw that Sofi's breath was coming with less effort now. 'Shall we go?' he asked hopefully.

In reality, Sofi did not want to move, but from Tid's expression she could see that he was eager to be off. She nodded her reply.

Tid helped her stand. With his arm firmly around her waist for support, they limped to the Line.

Old Father Tim was methodically connecting the Tick.

> '*Tide healdath, ealle brucath*
> *Time is guarded to serve all.*
> *Tide healdath, ealle brucath*
> *All the World echoes our call.*'

Tid and Sofi drew close. The air was full of sweet harmony. It made Sofi feel deeply happy. She was listening to music for the first time in her life. Never had she heard anything so wonderful.

Tid did not concentrate on the music. He was watching every move of Old Father Tim's fingers until the connection was finally completed. Only then did Old Father Tim withdraw his hands and step down.

Tid's heart was wildly beating, triumph bursting in his head. 'We've done it!' he whispered jubilantly.

Sofi's eyes shone.

Old Father Tim was standing before the new

Timepiece, studying it carefully. Something was not right. Concern was clearly visible on his face.

Tid and Sofi both saw it and looked nervously at each other. Had something gone wrong?

Old Father Tim was climbing back up to the Tick.

He was disconnecting it!

'What's him doing?' Sofi asked.

'I don't know,' Tid replied. 'Maybe it's damaged.'

Sofi remembered Sheldon falling and the Tick soaring through the air and crashing to the ground. 'Us dropped it,' she confessed mournfully.

Tid's eyes widened in horror but he said nothing. Instead, he watched his grandfather, who had removed the Tick and was unscrewing the top panel. The light clearly illuminated his worried face. He shook his head hopelessly as he surveyed the mechanism. The jolt of the fall had broken a link between two tiny fastenings. They hung untidily among a myriad of interconnecting wheels.

Old Father Tim had brought his tools with him. Reaching across for his cavernous bag, he dipped his head deep into it and rummaged around. Once or twice he pulled something out and looked at it, before dropping it back inside and resuming his search.

Everyone watched him closely. Each could see the concern that was clearly visible on his face.

Old Father Tim needed some thread to mend the Tick, but it was not in his bag. There was plenty of twine, but either it was not slender enough to fit the tiny fastenings or it was not strong enough to endure for a thousand years. He knew the exact cord that would work, but it was sitting on a shelf in his workshop.

Old Father Tim's instinct told him to send someone to collect it, but he knew, even without checking the sky, that it was too late for that. No one could run there, find the cord and bring it back with enough time left for the Tick to be fixed and connected.

Swallowing the fear that was beginning to rise within him, he thought carefully.

Sofi took hold of Tid's hand.

Old Father Tim was working through the options that now lay open to him. Perhaps it was worth risking a flimsy cord that might last only a few weeks. In that time he could try to develop a way of replacing it without stopping the Timepiece from working. However, he did not believe it to be possible. Or perhaps he could deactivate the whirring mechanism and divert the work-ings along a different route. But that would take too much time.

All eyes were upon the old man, but he did not feel them. He was concentrating too deeply to be aware of anything else.

The Mashias continued, but the Guardians were distracted. The song wavered just a little as each lost con-centration while they judged how much time remained.

Old Father Tim rubbed his bristly chin. He was used to solving problems. Quickly, another idea came to him. His beard was too short to be of any use but his shoulder-length hair was not. Putting his hand to his head, he plucked out one silvery hair. Then he plucked another and another, until there were several hanging from his hand.

Rapidly he began twisting and tying them. The Tick's light illuminated his hands as he deftly caught the hairs into the finest of braids. As he worked, he muttered darkly to himself, conjuring up powerful magic that bound itself into every twist and knot.

Finally, when he had finished, he turned back to the Tick and carefully started to thread the glistening cord through the broken link.

The ceremony was slowly drawing to its climax. Everyone was looking at the old man as he bent over the brightly shining Tick.

Old Father Tim continued working methodically. His hands were steady. He had cast off all thought of time.

The chanting came to an end. The singing floated away. A deathly hush fell on the Guardian Circle.

Tid could hear the Humans merrymaking in the distance. Then came the countdown, hundreds of Human voices coming together.

'Ten . . .'

The fastening was secure and Old Father Tim was screwing the lid back on.

'nine . . .'

'eight . . .'

Tid watched the hand on the old Timepiece making its weary journey to the top for the very last time. Carefully, Old Father Tim climbed the ladder.

'seven . . .'

'six . . .'

The Greenwich Guardian and Zeit lifted the Tick up to him and he slotted it back into place and started connecting it.

'five . . .'

'four . . .'

'three . . .'

Tid looked at his grandfather.

'. . . two . . .'

Old Father Tim was still working.

'. . . one . . .'

Silence.

Nothing moved.

The World waited for the first tick of the New Era.

Tid and Sofi held their breath.

The Guardians were openly staring at the new Timepiece.

Even Wakaa failed to hold up his staff. His dark eyes were fixed on the dextrous hands that were connecting the Tick.

Then, Old Father Tim dropped his hands.

Tid started to wonder if this was what the end of time felt like.

Nothing.

Peace.

Emptiness.

'Tick.'

It was very faint, but all the World heard it.

A tremendous roar went up from the Humans.

Sofi felt large tears of relief pricking her eyes.

Tid put his arms around her and they hugged.

Home

It is not the Guardian People's way to make a lot of noise at New Year. Their celebrations are quiet and respectful, but there was a hint of elation in the air as the Guardians resumed the Mashias.

Old Father Tim walked around the edge of the Guardian Circle to join Tid and Sofi. He put his arms around both of them and they all hugged each other.

'Hazel and Walnut is on . . .' Sofi hurriedly said as they broke apart, but Old Father Tim put his finger to his lips. The ceremony could not be disturbed.

Quietly they walked away from the Line. As soon as they had enough distance between themselves and the Guardians, Sofi started gabbling her worries. She still had responsibilities.

Old Father Tim listened patiently to her request that Hazel and Walnut should be given aid. When she mentioned Sheldon, both Tid and his grandfather's jaws dropped in surprise. Neither of them had expected him to help.

It was not long before Bryn, realizing that the new era had begun, triumphantly returned. 'Congratulations!' he cried to Sofi as he approached; however, as soon as he saw the expression on her face, all thought of celebration disappeared. Patiently, he listened to her, and then he and Enderell set off to search for the Bushytails and Sheldon. They would collect Joss on the way.

It was a weary trio who walked back to Old Father Tim's house. The mist lingered thinly in the park, forming ghost-like shadows that paid homage to the saviours of time. The dark and majestic trees stooped protectively over them as they passed, as if in grateful thanks. Tid and Sofi did not notice. They were feeling more tired with every weary step. However, Old Father Tim heard the deep whisperings of the ancient park echoing its respect.

All Tid and Sofi longed for now were the comforts that only a dearly loved home could provide. Sofi sat in the cosy kitchen, soaking her injured heel in a bowl of antiseptic water and gratefully swallowing a drink of the sweetest water she had ever tasted. Tid ran a warm bath for her while Old Father Tim prepared hot soup and spicy bread and Sofi explained about Cob.

'I doesn't know how it happened,' she said. 'I didn't mean him to pester the guards, really I didn't. But he runned past and there was no stopping him.'

'Cob chose the path of honour, as always,' Old Father Tim comforted her. 'He was a noble and brave Bushytail. His sacrifice saved us all.'

The children were too tired to eat much, and soon they were in bed. Sofi tried to lie awake and enjoy the feel of the clean sheets against her skin, but her eyelids drooped and she was quickly asleep.

Tid lay in his bed and talked with his grandfather, who sat heavily on the edge. 'I felt her,' he whispered excitedly. 'I was being Mindful of Sofi, and then I knew. I just knew where she was. I knew it as clearly as I know that you are sitting on my bed now. I concentrated harder than ever, Grandfather, and I guided her in. It was easy!'

Old Father Tim kissed Tid on his forehead. 'You have taken an important step into the grown-up world of the Guardian People,' he said with pride.

'And so has Sofi?'

'Yes, so has Sofi.'

Tid was elated, but his happiness was tinged with sadness. 'What do you think happened to Cob?'

A cloud passed behind his grandfather's eyes. He liked and respected the Bushytail leader and did not want to think how he might have suffered.

'We shall probably never know,' he said softly.

Snivel remembered nothing of his ordeal in the freezing water. As he opened his eyes, the first thing he knew was that he was lying on the ground, shivering. There was no way for him to know that he was on the bank of the River Thames. Unused to the brightness of the Topside, he squinted through half-closed eyes, looking apprehensively about him. He was colder than he had ever been in his short life, and Snivel was used to being cold. His clothes were almost dry. He must have been lying in this strange world for some time. Everything smelt and sounded alien to him. It was terrifying.

In the Underneath, the Wreccas would tell horrifying tales of the Topside to the young ones in order to discourage them from running away. Now, Snivel scanned the scenery, searching out the terrors that he had always believed inhabited this place. It did not look threatening or frightening, but he knew that it must be. His one desperate hope was to find a door that would take him home as quickly as possible.

Painfully, he stood up. His head throbbed, his muscles ached and his body was bruised from his rough journey in the icy water. He had no way of estimating how much time had passed, but it seemed like forever. When he heard his name called, his heart leapt. Somebody in this place knew him. He was not alone! He looked in the direction of the voice and was very much disheartened to discover a dishevelled Cob limping painfully towards him.

'I thought you had drowned!' Cob exclaimed in a hoarse voice. 'Thank goodness you are safe. Are you feeling all right?'

Disappointment and fear turned to anger. 'Ner I's not!' Snivel shouted, forgetting to be scared. 'You nearly killed I!' and he lashed out with his foot, but Cob was standing at too great a distance for him to reach. 'I's frozen and everything hurts and it's all your fault! Why did you go and pull I in? I wanted to stay where I was.'

Cob closed his eyes as a bout of nausea overtook him. 'You are much safer here,' he said quietly, holding on to the overhang to steady himself.

He wiped his brow with a bruised paw and tried to

understand the situation. When he had regained consciousness, his first thoughts had been of Sofi. Clearly, she had returned the Tick in time for, although he did not know the hour, it was definitely the next day. Time had not stopped. If he had not been in so much pain, he would have felt elated. He winced as another bout of nausea rose up within him and he paused until it had passed. Then he thought carefully. He reasoned that if the Tick was safe then so was Miss Sofi. If he took Snivel to her, then he would be safe too and Cob would be free to go home. Longingly, he thought of Hazel.

Cob had no notion where they had been washed up. His body was cut and battered from the pounding the water had given him, and his fur, usually soft and gleaming, was matted with dried blood. He shivered, for he was exceptionally cold, but his head was burning. He knew it was likely that he was running a temperature. His instinct was to rest before finding his way home, but he was unsure what Snivel would do whilst he slept. He doubted that the boy would wait, and Cob did not want him to wander off. He would not leave Snivel unprotected.

'I want to go home!' Snivel wailed.

'And so you shall,' Cob said, giving an involuntary shiver. Deep inside, the cold was gnawing at his bones. How could he feel hot and yet so cold at the same time?

'Come on, then.' He tried to sound confident. 'If we are lucky, we will find the park before it gets dark.'

Cob knew enough about the river to understand that they must have been washed downstream. Thus, if he wanted to get back, they would have to travel upstream. Unfortunately, he had seriously underestimated how far the river had carried them. He also did not understand how desperately ill he was. The battering he had taken in the river had severely weakened him and he could move only with difficulty.

Snivel did not seem to notice their slow pace. Topside life was too overwhelming for him to do anything other than fearfully follow Cob. He quickly learnt that Humans could not see him, but he still took care to keep out of their way. There were so many amazing sights, every one of them scary.

Humans walked at various speeds. Some Humans were silent as they walked but others chatted with their companions. Snivel had never seen such cheerful faces, nor had he ever heard laughter that bubbled forth from sheer happiness. In the Underneath, laughter was always intimidating or cruel.

And everything was so clean! Humans were tidy and their faces were not covered in grime. There was some litter on the streets but not nearly as much as there was in the Underneath. The houses had gardens and front doors and windows – and oh, the colours! There were so many colours!

As the light began to fade, so Christmas illuminations were lit. Snivel found it hard to tear his eyes away from the twinkling lights. His astonished eyes took in every detail, but he was always careful to keep pace with Cob. He did not want to be left alone in this big, bustling world.

Cob's mind was completely focused on finding his way home. He did not really notice anything of his surroundings. Most of the objects he passed wafted in and out of focus, but he doggedly followed the river.

When they finally arrived at the Great Ship, Cob was too exhausted to comment. Snivel looked up in awe at the tall masts which cast strange shadows in the half-light of the street lamps. Wearily, Cob passed it by without comment and shuffled along the pavement towards the gates of the park. It was only his strength of will that kept him going.

Painfully, he stumbled through the gates. A feeling of joy overwhelmed him. How he had longed to be home. He breathed deep, for even the air seemed to be tinged with love and happiness. He closed his eyes and very gently the last ripple of energy ebbed away. Gratefully, he sank on to the grass of his much-loved home.

Snivel watched him. 'What's you doing?'

Cob tried to speak, but his voice was faint and rasping.

'What you saying?' Snivel asked.

Cob spoke once more, and still Snivel could not hear him. Kneeling down, he peered into Cob's exhausted face. His words were very faint and Snivel had to put his ear close to Cob's lips so that he could hear him.

'Up the hill . . . this way.' Cob lifted a trembling paw and indicated right. 'Miss Sofi . . .' Slowly, Cob's eyes opened, 'Miss Sofi . . .' he whispered, '. . . up there . . .'

Cob did not understand why Snivel's face was not in focus. He looked beyond the young Wrecca to the trees of his home. He could not see them clearly, but to know they were there was enough. With a weak smile of pleasure, he lay his head down on the sweet grass of his beloved home and died.

The following evening, Sofi and Tid were sitting on the low wall that surrounded Old Father Tim's neat garden. She was dressed in some of Tid's clothes and her hair was clean and shiny. As the winter sun sank slowly behind the trees, they talked happily together.

Old Father Tim came out of his front door and quietly shut it. Sofi noticed how easily doors closed in the World. There were so many differences that she had to get used to.

'Are you two ready?'

The children nodded. Neither was enthusiastic. They had been summoned to appear before the Gathering. Tid remembered with shame the last time he had stood before them. He would never forget his feeling of humiliation as he had explained how he had told Sofi the location of the workshop. This time, he comforted himself, would not be so bad because he was not in trouble and Sofi would be by his side.

Sofi was also nervous at the thought of facing so many important Guardians. They still scared her, although Tid had assured her that there was no reason to be afraid.

Old Father Tim had told them that Zeit had taken Sheldon to Reform School in Germany. Sofi was certain he had not gone willingly but she understood that he had been given no choice. Zeit was used to dealing with youths who had forgotten where their loyalties lay. Old

Father Tim had told her that when he had learnt to respect himself, he would soon learn to respect others. Sofi had no idea if this was true, but she believed that Old Father Tim knew best.

When they arrived at the Line, all the Guardians were sitting in a circle, several deep. The Greenwich Guardian smiled and showed them where to sit.

Wakaa took his place in the centre. He had been waiting for the children to arrive.

'Young Sofi,' he began.

She sat up straight, feeling very self-conscious. She had done far worse than Sheldon. If she had not stolen the Tick in the first place, none of this would have happened. She wondered if she would have to go to Reform School too.

'In the last two days you have displayed qualities beyond your years,' Wakaa said. 'To be honest, you have astounded us all. No one could have done more. You are resourceful, courageous, determined and, I understand, you have succeeded in being Mindful. This is surprising in one so young, not born to our ways. In short, you completed a task that would have daunted most adults. I think it is safe to say that you have a great future ahead of you.'

Sofi blushed the deepest pink and wondered when he was going to get to the bad bit.

'You have travelled a long way towards becoming one of the Guardian People. In fact, if you are willing, it has been agreed that you are to be accepted as one of us this very night.'

Sofi looked up at Old Father Tim, astonished by this tremendous news. Her eager eyes told him how much she wanted it to be true. He smiled gently and nodded, and she knew that it was. A delicious feeling of happiness spread throughout her body.

'If you wish it,' Wakaa continued, 'Pa Mossel has said that he will receive you into his family as his own granddaughter.'

Tears of joy welled up in her eyes. She had no words to speak. Gently, Old Father Tim put his arm around her, understanding something of what she was feeling. Overcome with emotion, she buried her face in the folds of his garments.

Everyone applauded.

'I will take it that you have agreed,' Wakaa smiled.

'You should say, "thank you",' Old Father Tim gently prompted her.

Sofi looked up and wiped the tears from her face. Shyly she mouthed the words 'thank you' and Wakaa smiled once more. She needed to do no more and he prepared to move on to the next subject, but Sofi had not finished.

'I ... I ... has to say ...' she mumbled. She was nervous of speaking, but it did not feel right to take all the credit. She looked earnestly at Old Father Tim. 'Sheldon helped and Cob was great, but us willn't have getted the Tick away without Snivel. Him's a boy Wrecca, who is a sort of a friend, 'cept us doesn't have friends down there.' She looked towards Wakaa. 'I think him's choosed to stay in the Underneath. Him's too scared to come with us, but I has to tell you ...' Suddenly she realized that she was saying too much and finished at a rush. '... that him helped, and us only getted the Tick out cos of him.' She stopped abruptly and waited, hoping that she had not done wrong in talking to such important people.

'Thank you, young Sofi,' Wakaa said warmly. 'We acknowledge the assistance of this young Wrecca.' He could not bring himself to mention his unpleasant-sounding name. 'If we ever have the opportunity to thank him personally, we shall welcome it.'

No one seemed cross with her for speaking, and Sofi snuggled up to Old Father Tim, glowing with the happy thought that she now belonged to his family.

'Now,' Wakaa said. He knew the Guardians were anxious to begin their homeward journeys. Not wanting to delay them longer than necessary, he turned towards Tid, who realized that it was his turn. Suddenly he felt his face becoming hot. He very much wished that Wakaa would not say anything about him, but he knew he must endure what was to come. He waited with a pounding heart, but Wakaa did not speak.

Tid apprehensively looked up and saw that the noble Guardian's eyes were not upon him. He was looking towards the edge of the circle. He was not alone in this. Everyone was looking to one side.

Thankful for the interruption, Tid turned and knelt on his seat to get a better view. In the dimness of the night he saw a bedraggled young boy timidly approaching. Everyone saw him, but it was Sofi who spoke.

'Sniv? Is that you?'

The Guardians moved aside. Snivel had no notion who they were. His heart was beating fast. They were strange-looking people. Someone was walking towards him. She seemed familiar but he did not recognize her.

'It *is* you,' she said as she drew near. 'But you's all clean!'

The involuntary bath in the river had considerably altered his dirty appearance.

He stared at her. 'Snot?'

She giggled. 'Yer, it's I!'

Then she did a strange thing. She put out her arms as if to hug him, but he stepped back abruptly.

'Is you all right?' she asked, letting her arms fall. 'How did you get here?'

He did not want to answer questions. He wanted to go home.

There was a movement behind her and an old man with a silvery beard drew near. He spoke quietly to Snot. Snivel could not hear his question, but he heard her answer.

'It's Snivel!' she exclaimed in delight. 'The Wrecca I told you about. The one that helped us!'

A boy, dressed like Snot, also approached. Snot turned excitedly towards him.

'It's Snivel,' she repeated excitedly. 'Him's finded us!' Then she turned back to Snivel. 'I can't believe you's here! What happened?'

Snivel was still not inclined to answer. He did not trust her.

'What's all this?' he asked, looking warily at the Gathering.

'These are Guardians.'

Snivel's eyes grew big and he stepped back fearfully.

'My boy,' the old man said in a low, velvety voice. 'Are you hungry?'

Hungry? Oh yes, Snivel was very hungry. He gave a slight nod, not trusting the man at all, but his empty stomach hurt.

'Grandfather,' Snot was addressing the man. 'Can us take him home?' Her eyes were alight with happiness. 'And give him pancakes and syrup?'

28

The End of the Beginning

Living in the Underneath all his life, Old Killjoy thought he knew every bit of it, but this was a tunnel he had never explored.

Sniff was looking nervously at him. 'Then the monster jumped over the edge,' he yelled, trying to make himself heard over the din, 'and pulled Snivel with him.'

Old Killjoy flung a menacing looked towards Sniff, who fearfully edged away.

'Why was I not telled about this place?'

Sniff backed off and cowered behind Scratch, who was looking at Old Killjoy with contempt. He was wondering how his leader could not have known about the roaring tunnel? In his position, Scratch would have known. If fact, Scratch had known.

Old Killjoy was furiously storming up and down, grinding his teeth, his anger all the more intense because he felt stupid. Lashing out, he kicked at a boulder that stood, heavy and unmovable. 'Aaagghh!' he screamed in pain, grabbing his damaged foot and jumping about in agony.

Scratch turned away. The humour of the situation had

not escaped him, but his hatred of Old Killjoy suppressed it. This was not the time to openly ridicule the leader. The time for that would come soon enough. Right now, he felt that he was being presented with the opportunity he had long waited for and he was not going to ruin it by laughing out loud. To be so ignorant of the layout of the Underneath could raise questions about Old Killjoy's suitability as leader. This was Scratch's chance.

A group of Wreccas were gathered some way up the tunnel. Leaving Sniff with the injured Killjoy, Scratch marched towards them.

'The roaring hole in the ground is a danger,' he shouted as soon as he was near enough to be heard. 'This tunnel needs to be blocked.' He paused dramatically. 'It's time to build for the safety of us all!'

The Wreccas stood in silence, staring at him.

'Do you want to be slaughtered as you sleep?' Scratch taunted them.

Each shook his head fearfully.

'This hole,' Scratch waved his hand towards the end of the tunnel where the river was, 'is an opening to the Topside!'

They drew in their breath in horror. An opening to the Topside!

'A gaping hole,' Scratch embellished, 'that the Guardians has used to spy on us.'

The Wreccas looked at each other in fear. The Guardians?

'If us doesn't block this tunnel, then it will be the end of us all.'

There was a collective gasp.

'Block the tunnel!' Scratch shouted.

There was a moment of stillness before the Wreccas exploded into action. Turning, they scrambled down the tunnel, elbowing each other and stumbling over outstretched legs that had been extended, intending to trip a rival. Each one was trying to impede the others in order to get a head start, for they all wanted to be first, believing this would impress Scratch.

With a contemptuous sneer, Scratch watched them go. They were so easy to manipulate. Now they had gone, his actions could not be witnessed. Turning, he walked back up the tunnel, knowing exactly what he was going to do.

The pain in Old Killjoy's toe was subsiding but his anger was not. He needed to take it out on someone.

'You bringed the monster in!' he yelled at the trembling Sniff.

'Ner!' Sniff shouted, wildly shaking his head.

'It was you!' Old Killjoy thundered as he advanced, fury directing his actions. 'You's a traitor!' he screamed as he lunged at the hapless Wrecca, grabbing him by the throat.

Sniff tried to break free, desperately clawing at the hands which enclosed his neck. He started to see coloured blotches in front of his eyes as all the breath was being squeezed out of him.

Scratch calmly observed the scene. He had always known that if he waited long enough his chance would come. He watched Old Killjoy slowly throttling the life out of Sniff, who was now sinking to his knees. The only question in Scratch's mind was: one or both?

Having made his decision, Scratch knew what to do. He strode towards the struggling pair and, reaching out, grabbed Old Killjoy by the roots of his hair and yanked him backwards.

The pain was swift and violent and it caused Old Killjoy to loosen his hold.

Spluttering, Sniff fell backwards.

Old Killjoy now grasped at Scratch's hands. Desperately, Old Killjoy tried to wrench the fingers apart but Scratch's grip was firm.

Spinning Old Killjoy around, Scratch leant into his face and breathed, 'It's the end for you, you useless dung-head!' and, using all his might, he heaved Old Killjoy towards the chasm.

The sudden movement took Old Killjoy unawares and he totally lost his balance. With a cruel sneer, Scratch loosened his grip so that the Wrecca leader would stumble backwards towards the gaping hole. Amazed to be free of the brutal grip, Old Killjoy tried to steady himself. He waved his arms around wildly and, with relief, he felt his balance returning. Staggering on tiptoe, he regained his stability.

Old Killjoy understood exactly what Scratch had attempted to do, and it was with a fleeting triumphant yelp that he celebrated Scratch's failure. With arms outstretched his balance finally returned and he came to a halt. Slowly, he straightened up. He now set his heels down so that he could stand tall and begin the cruel revenge that was already forming in his mind.

His heels went down, but they did not settle on firm ground as he had expected. A moment of doubt crossed his mind as he understood that something was wrong. His heels were hanging over the edge of the chasm. Small pieces of earth crumbled away beneath him. The triumphant glint in his eye changed to one of panic as he desperately clutched at the air, in an attempt to stay upright. Wheeling his arms around, he made one last, desperate effort to remain standing. 'Help!' he gasped.

Scratch stood and watched as the ground slowly gave way.

With a blood-chilling cry, Old Killjoy toppled backwards over the edge and down into the deep river below.

Scratch leant forward to witness his leader plummeting ever downwards, eyes wide with fear and hands outstretched in the forlorn hope that there would be someone or something to grab hold of him and thus arrest his descent. There was nothing. Finally, Old Killjoy crashed into the icy water far below.

Sniff, still clutching at his throat, crawled to the edge and peered over, not sure whether he believed what his eyes had seen.

Both stayed for some time, watching and waiting to see if Old Killjoy would re-emerge, but he did not. Eventually, Scratch straightened up and walked away. Sniff scrambled to his feet and, giving a final glance over his shoulder, followed, unable to comprehend what he had just witnessed.

When they were far enough down the tunnel so they could hear themselves speak, Scratch coldly said, 'I did what I had to do. It was the only way. Him tried to kill you.'

Sniff stood breathing heavily, totally bewildered by what he had witnessed.

Scratch thought he had better say it again, just to make sure that Sniff fully understood who had rescued him. 'I did it to save your life.'

Sniff nodded his gratitude, unable to speak.

'Old Killjoy had lost control. Him was a danger to us all.'

Sniff made silent agreement.

'Us must block up this tunnel.' Scratch weighed him up through narrowed eyes. 'Can I trust you?'

Sniff was still stunned and stood there, blinking.

'If I can't, I'll find someone I *can* trust.'

Sniff was not so dazed that he misunderstood. He knew that he was being offered second-in-command. Not trusting his voice, he frantically nodded. Then he turned and ran away as fast as his shaking legs would allow. He was going to organize the blocking of the tunnel and he was going to make it look good.

Scratch watched him disappear. 'That was well done,' he congratulated himself. A shallow smile played on his lips. 'Very well done indeed.'

Snivel stayed with Snot in something they called a cottage. There was a room downstairs with a warm fire and comfortable chairs and a rug on the floor. Snivel surveyed everything with large eyes.

Sofi understood how he was feeling and left him alone.

This house belonged to the man she called 'Grandfather'. He seemed to be the leader of this household, but he did not shout or bully. Instead, he smiled at the children and asked them to do things in a gentle, warm voice. They always did as they were asked. Snivel wondered why.

The food was delicious, but it made him so nervous that he ate little. Clean clothes felt peculiar against his skin. A bed was made for Tid on the floor of Grandfather's room, and Snivel found himself sleeping in Tid's bed. It was the most luxurious thing he had ever experienced and it scared him so much that he found he could not sleep. He listened to Snot as she excitedly talked about the new bedroom that was going to be built for her. He found himself feeling jealous but did not know why; after all, he had no intention of staying Topside.

He did not tell anyone about Cob, thinking it dangerous to admit that he had been with him when he had died. He trembled as he wondered what Guardians might do to someone they thought was a murderer. When eventually the news came that the Bushytail's body had been found, he witnessed the outpouring of genuine grief. People openly wept and took care of one another.

But it was Snot who surprised him the most. He

realized that Guardian People were strange, but Snot was born a Wrecca, like him, and yet she behaved just like the others. She cried when news of Cob arrived. When his body was buried, he watched her tenderly comfort other furry creatures, putting her arms around them and hugging them. Everyone said how brave and noble Cob had been and how much they would miss him.

Back in the cottage, he watched Snot help with the washing-up and put things tidily away. There were so many things. There were dishes, cups, knives, books, toys, pillows, chairs and so much more. Everything amazed him, but he said nothing and bided his time, waiting for the chance of escape.

In the evenings, Snot played with Tid. Although obviously still sad about Cob, she smiled a great deal and sometimes laughed, especially when Tid tried to teach her how to whistle. She was kind, thoughtful, clean and happy. Snivel was very confused.

All he wanted was to get back to the life he was used to, but he never asked to be taken to one of the Topside doors. He convinced himself that no one would tell him, and it would only cause trouble. One day he would run away and find it for himself, but not now.

Grandfather asked many questions. At first Snivel answered none of them. He just sat on the stool and sullenly pouted, waiting for Grandfather to become angry and violent. But he never did. Instead, he patiently waited, and eventually Snivel found himself talking. Before he knew it, he was explaining how he had rescued Cob, and how they had discovered the underground river. Later, Snivel worried that he had said too much. He hoped that Old Killjoy and Scratch would never find out.

'Please don't call I Snot no more,' Sofi said to him one day, when she had finished sweeping the floor. 'I's Sofi now.' Then she thought for a moment and said, 'And I think we should change your name. Snivel isn't very nice, is it?' She had been careful to use 'we' instead of 'us' because she was trying to talk like Tid.

Snivel said nothing. Sofi furrowed her brow, trying to think of something suitable. She asked Tid for his opinion.

'How about . . .' Tid said, putting his hand to his chin and thinking carefully, 'How about . . . Saxton or Seth or Sol or Sasha? Vremya says Sasha's a boy's name where he comes from.'

'Who's Vremya?' Sofi asked.

'He's the very old Guardian with the funny accent and the quiet voice who sits at the front. The one who often looks as if he's smiling when he isn't. He comes from somewhere in Russia.'

Sofi did not know where Russia was. There was so much she did not know.

'What do you think?' she asked Snivel, 'Do you want to be called Sasha?'

'I doesn't care,' said Snivel, shrugging his shoulders and trying to look as if he really did not.

'I like Seth,' said Tid. 'It's a good, strong name.'

Sofi smiled to herself because Tid sounded very much like his grandfather sometimes.

Snivel liked the idea of having a good, strong name. He nodded in an offhand way.

The following week they were summoned to attend the Gathering. The Guardians had decided not to leave Greenwich until they had heard all that the Wrecca boy had to say. Old Father Tim faithfully reported to the Greenwich Guardian the conversations he had had with Snivel. In turn, she passed everything on to Wakaa, who shared the information with other Guardians. Soon they all knew what had happened.

Once more, the children set out to walk to the Line with their grandfather. This time they had a worried Snivel, now called Seth, with them.

He hung back when they arrived. The Guardians were sitting around the circle and he felt they were all looking at him. As was the custom, Wakaa was standing in the centre. The Guardians were finishing a lively debate, but all fell silent when Old Father Tim arrived with the children. They took their seats.

'Welcome, young Seth,' Wakaa said. 'I understand this is the name you have chosen.'

Snivel said nothing but sat as far back in his seat as possible and put his chin on his chest.

Wakaa ignored his silence and said, 'We, the Guardian People, thank you for the assistance you gave to Sofi in our hour of need. Because of that help, we have decided that you should be offered the chance to live in the World with the Guardian People.'

Sofi smiled broadly.

Snivel said nothing.

'Is this what you would like?' Wakaa asked.

Snivel set his lips tightly together, determined to say nothing.

Sofi nudged him. 'Go on, Seth,' she said encouragingly. 'Say, "Yes please".'

But Snivel remained silent.

'He wants to,' Sofi said to Wakaa. She so much wanted Snivel to stay that she forgot to feel afraid. 'He's just a bit scared.'

'You must overcome your fear, young Seth,' Wakaa said. He was not sure how this boy felt. He was anxious not to make a mistake and allow the boy to stay when it would be wrong for him. 'Whether the answer be yes or no, you must tell us.'

Snivel was in turmoil. He still thought he should go back to the Underneath. That was his home, but what would this stern Guardian do to him if he said so? He wondered if they were laying some sort of trap for him, trying to trick him into saying something he would regret.

'Go on,' Sofi encouraged him. 'Stay here with us. You'll have clean clothes and a warm bed and you can go to school. I's going to learn how to read. Doesn't you want to read?'

Snivel was not sure if he did.

'If you stay, you doesn't ever have to be frightened again.'

Not be frightened? Snivel was always frightened! That was all he had ever known. It was a habit that was not easy to shake off. The sight of the Guardians sitting in their circle was enough to scare him to death!

'Say yes,' she urged.

'Well?' Wakaa waited patiently.

'Maybe,' Snivel murmured.

Sofi looked up at Wakaa, hoping that this was enough.

This answer did not satisfy Wakaa. He glanced at Old Father Tim, who nodded, as if to confirm that it was acceptable. Having lived with the boy for a few days, he thought he understood him a little. He knew Snivel to be anxious about everything. Old Father Tim had watched him sitting in the kitchen, silently trying to be aloof but finding it very difficult when Tid and Sofi were having such fun. The old man guessed that he was longing to join in. It would take time. He had seen fear and loneliness in Snivel's heart, but alongside it there was goodness. The old man was certain that, once he was confident of his surroundings, Snivel would want to stay. What was more, Old Father Tim felt that he deserved the chance of a new life.

Wakaa turned to the Greenwich Guardian. 'May we leave this with you? Perhaps we should give this young boy a little time to see if he settles.'

She readily agreed. For some years now she had wished for a grandchild of her own and had already decided that she would talk to Pa Mossel about taking Seth into her own home.

'And now, to Tid,' Wakaa said.

Tid felt his muscles tense. He had hoped that with all

the talk of Seth he would be forgotten. He might have known that a Guardian would not forget.

'It was your foolishness that began this.'

Tid hung his head. All the shame he had felt before came flooding back.

'A young one must learn not to be tricked by anyone,' and he smiled at Sofi, 'no matter how pretty she may be.'

A chuckle rippled around the Gathering.

Tid felt his face colour.

'You gave an outsider details of the Guardian People that should never be revealed. That was a dishonourable thing to do, but it has to be remembered that you stood before us and had the courage to tell us of your wrong-doing. This courage was demonstrated again when you made the journey to the Hither House and talked to the Greenwich Guardian for, without that interview, none of us would be here now.'

Tid kept his eyes downcast.

'But I think your greatest act of courage was to tell the Greenwich Guardian and myself that you would continue to be Mindful of Sofi when we had given up hope. It is never easy to challenge a Guardian, but you, young Tid, did so with wisdom and determination.'

Tid still stared at his knees.

'Lift your head.'

Reluctantly, he looked up.

'Normally, young Tid, you would not be considered old enough to be Mindful, but you guided Sofi home alone. It has been recorded in our histories that your grandfather showed much wisdom when he was young.

It is with confidence that I stand here, in this most special of all places in our World, and declare that when you have grown in experience that only years can bring, it is expected that you will become the Old Father Guardian of Time.'

Sofi gasped in awe. Had she heard correctly? Was Wakaa saying that one day Tid would be the Old Father? She looked at Tid and saw that his amazement surpassed her own. Sofi's heart was full to bursting and she found her eyes brimming over with tears of happiness.

Tid's eyes grew very big as he understood the enormity of what Wakaa was saying. This was the greatest honour that could befall anyone, but this could not happen. Tid had not intended to speak, but he could not help himself. 'That can never be . . .' he began falteringly. 'The new Old Father has to follow the old Old Father. Grandson must follow Grandfather. It is written . . .' and then he added, not quite so sure, '. . . isn't it?'

Wakaa shook his head. 'No, Tid, it is not written, but it is usual practice.'

Then Wakaa spoke to all the Guardians. 'This brings me to the final act of this Gathering. It has been my honour to be its custodian, but now it is appropriate to stand aside and allow the true Old Father to retake his place.'

The Greenwich Guardian moved into the centre, carrying an old staff that was very familiar to Tid and his grandfather. She handed it to Wakaa.

Wakaa took it and, holding it horizontal, lifted it high above his head. He muttered a few words before lowering it.

'Pa Mossel, you served us with distinction for many years. You have conducted yourself throughout this time of difficulty with honour, dignity and wisdom. It is the request of the Gathering that you should retake your old position of leadership and, once again, be the Old Father Guardian to us all.'

Bryn, standing apart from the Gathering, caught these words. With a nod of satisfaction, he left. He had heard all he wanted to hear. The Old Father was back.

Tid thought his heart would burst. Knowing that he had been the reason for his grandfather's disgrace had been a heavy burden. Now everything would be all right again. He looked at his grandfather, who sat totally still. For one alarming moment Tid thought he was going to refuse, but then he felt the weight of his grandfather's hand as he leant heavily upon Tid's shoulder. Slowly, he stood up and walked to the centre of the circle.

There, Old Father Tim bowed to Wakaa before receiving his staff in both hands. Then he closed his eyes and lifted his face to the sky. Tid knew he was offering up a few words of thanks. Opening his eyes once more, Old Father Tim turned to the Guardians and held the staff high above his head.

'*Tide healdath, ealle brucath.*'

If any Humans had been walking through Greenwich Park at that moment, they might, if they had been listening very carefully, have heard the thunderous applause that welcomed Old Father Tim as he retook his rightful place as the Old Father of Time. And no one clapped louder than Tid and Sofi.